The Pitcher Shower

Books by Donald Harington

The Cherry Pit (1965)

Lightning Bug (1970)

Some Other Place. The Right Place. (1972)

The Architecture of the Arkansas Ozarks (1975)

Let Us Build Us a City (1986)

The Cockroaches of Stay More (1989)

The Choiring of the Trees (1991)

Ekaterina (1993)

Butterfly Weed (1996)

When Angels Rest (1998)

Thirteen Albatrosses (or, Falling off the Mountain) (2002)

With (2004)

The Pitcher Shower (2005)

Donald Harington

The Pitcher Shower

The Toby Press

First Edition 2005

The Toby Press LLC
POB 8531, New Milford, CT 06776-8531, USA
& POB 2455, London WIA 5WY, England
www.tobypress.com

ISBN 1 59264 123 7

A CIP catalogue record for this title
is available from the British Library

Typeset in Garamond by Jerusalem Typesetting

Printed and bound in the United States by
Thomson-Shore Inc., Michigan

For Matthew Miller
המוציא אותי לאור

Chapter One

Coming into a town, he would blow his bugle. Although he knew only the one tune, or melody, it was another of his several talents, another thing he could do, as protection against feeling that he wasn't worth nothing. He could have just honked his horn, but the horn was a common thing that said, "Cow, get out of the road," and his bugle, a different sort of dented horn, said, "From far yonder down the road, here he comes again, folks, Hoppy Boyd, the happy moving showman of moving pitchers to show you another good'un." That's more or less what that tune or melody was trying to say, although it sounded to him less like a reveille than a taps and seemed to speak of the nameless wistful nightfall reaches beyond these hills.

He drove the truck easy with one hand so's he could stick that bugle out the window and give it all those toots that let everybody know he was back again. And as usual they came a-running, even the grown-ups and womenfolk. This was his favorite part of the whole six days he would play this town, the jubilation that grabbed everybody when they first learned he was here. Yonder was Billy Millwee jumping up and down beside his little wagon, which he'd somehow painted white just so's it would look like Hoppy's truck, the only white truck in the Ozarks, an ordinary old ton-and-a-half flatbed Chevy whose back end he'd carpentered himself to make a little house, a combination projection booth and traveling home, with his bed and kerosene stove and all. And Billy had done more or less the same to his little wagon, and even rigged up a play-like projector out of tin cans and spools and junk. Hoppy had named his truck "Topper" after the real Hoppy's fine big white horse, and little Billy Millwee called his wagon "Topper-Too," and Hoppy was so pleased with him he'd offered to let him in free to the shows, but Billy was a proud little cuss who had him a rat terror named Jack and went around to henhouses catching rats for five cents per, the price of a kid's ticket to the pitcher show. Now here was Billy acting like it was Christmas and his birthday and the Fourth of July all rolled together, and Hoppy stopped blowing his bugle long enough to wave at him. Billy was even wearing a cowboy hat, a black one like Hoppy's, not a ten-gallon of course because his head was so small but leastways five gallons.

"Hi yoop!" Billy hollered.

"Hi yoop yoreself," Hoppy hollered back at him.

And over yonder shading her eyes from the evening sun even though she had on a big sunbonnet was Birdie Woodrum, Leaster's woman, who was yelling her head off. Hoppy couldn't make out the words because she talked so fast but not faster than the noise his truck motor made. He knew what she was saying: she was inviting him to stay to supper, so he hollered "Much obliged, ma'am" back at her. He could count on a handsome table at the Woodrums. Leaster was a tie hacker, that is to say, he'd made a fair living hewing oak logs into railroad ties with a broadax, but the last train to Pettigrew down the road had stopped hauling out the ties the year before and Hoppy had tried to persuade Leaster to try his hand at making chairs, which Leaster had done but hadn't made any money at yet. Birdie raised gourds in her garden and made some mighty fine gourd dippers which she found a market for. Hoppy had one in his water bucket, which he'd swapped her three shows for, and he can tell you, even though he might not know much else in this world, that water drunk out of a gourd dipper tastes a right smart finer than what's drunk from a tin dipper.

Hoppy brought his truck to a stop beside the gas pump at Tollett's General Store, and that gave all the kids and dogs who'd been a-chasing him a chance to catch up with him. Everybody, including the grown-ups and the womenfolk, was raising a hullabaloo like he was quite a shucks and Santy besides, even though he was still several years short of thirty, and his hair, unlike the ghost-white of the real Hopalong Cassidy's, was just a sort of dirty yaller. But he wore his big black ten-gallon just like Hoppy's, and that covered most of his hair anyhow. Thinking of the real Hoppy, he couldn't offhand honestly recall a single Hopalong Cassidy pitcher show in which everybody had been so glad to see their hero as they was to see him right now. He had to keep his arms at his sides because if he lifted them everybody would rush into him, the dogs too.

Ewell Tollett came down off the porch to fill Topper's tank and get himself six straight free shows into the bargain. "Don't reckon it will rain tonight," he had to shout conversationally over the ruckus everybody else was making. "What's a-showing first?"

Everybody hushed their racket so they could hear Hoppy's answer. "It's called 'Hills of Old Wyoming,'" he announced.

Ewell looked doubtful. "Has it got Hoppy in it?"

"Of course," the fake Hoppy said. "Don't they all?" Hoppy had learned long since, and from all the different towns along his route, that first of all, everybody wanted to watch a rootin-tootin shoot-'em-up, and, second of all, any giddyapper that didn't star William Boyd as Hopalong wasn't worth watching. One time last season his distributor had sent him by mistake a movie called "It Happened One Night," which had not one single horse in it. It starred Clark Gable and Claudette Colbert falling in love on a country bus trip. Hoppy watched it and greatly enjoyed it, and felt satisfied with himself and the world afterwards, but that was one of only two times that his audience had demanded a refund, the other time being when his projector broke down completely.

Now, on the porch of Tollett's store, having already negotiated with miller Handy Tharp to use the broad meadow alongside the mill for the setting up of his mobile theater, young Landon "Hoppy" Boyd smiled at the mob of kids, grown-ups and womenfolk who surrounded him on all sides of the porch as if he were The Second Coming and he wondered if they worshipped him because of himself or simply because of the treat of entertainment that he provided. He might never learn the real answer to that, but there was a bigger question that haunted him and would occupy his hours during the time he sat in the back of the truck operating the projector to provide that treat of entertainment: did he hate himself so much just to balance out the way these folks adored him?

Because he did hate himself. That seemed to be the only thing he knew for sure. He lacked the easiness to get close enough to somebody else and ask them, "Do you ever hate yourself?" and thus he did not know, nor could he scarcely imagine, that just about everybody, at one time or another, searches their soul and comes to the conclusion that they did something, or failed to do something, that they feel real sorry for.

He didn't hate himself for any one thing in particular he'd done but just for all kinds of reasons. He even rued that this story here, like all the movies he showed, was all in black and white, every bit of it, although it deserved to be and there was no way that color could improve it. Several of his customers had never seen even a black and white pitcher show before, let alone knew that there was such things as color pitcher shows, which cost a lot more, not just to make but to get in to see. In Memphis one afternoon last winter he had seen a pitcher show in color himself, but once his eyes had got adjusted to the loudness of the color he had determined that color doesn't do anything for a story. Good stories, whether they are the ones we hear from our elders or the ones we invent in our own dreams, are never in color. At least we don't remember them as being in color. Color doesn't have any connection to suspense or building a climax or even to spinning a yarn. No, the shadows and flickers of black-and-white are a good story's meat and bones. You can take it home with you and remember it. Black is the color of the night. And the page of your mind, like this page right here, is white. One without the other is nothing.

But he didn't feel sorry about taking their money. That was one thing that he could live with that might have given him some regret at one time or another during this so-called Depression but not any more, not since he'd had that argument with that circuit-riding preacher, Brother Emmett Binns, who had accused him of robbing these poor folks of their pennies during a period when times were hard and nobody had any money…except that preacher, who still managed to take up collections at every little town he preached in the Ozarks, although his collections had dwindled somewhat because of the sum the folks spent at the pitcher show, which was the real reason the preacher had got into the squabble with him, and the reason he'd decided he had no call to hate himself for taking folks' money.

"They just have to make a choice," he'd told that preacher Binns. "You claim that they have to drop their nickels and dimes into the collection plate so they can buy their way out of their miserable life with a ticket to heaven. My claim is that their nickels and dimes can buy a ticket out of their miserable life for a little while right here and now."

No, he didn't feel any shame for taking their nickels and dimes. And his admission prices were reasonable, a bargain compared with the Stigler Brothers, who ran the route east of his and charged twenty-five cents for adults and a dime for kids; those prices were also charged by Captain Thomson, who ran the route west of his. He'd had a run-in with Cap Thomson, a big feller who'd accused him of trying to steal some of his towns and also of charging too little, just a dime for adults and a nickel for kids. But he never reproached himself for his admission prices, up or down.

He hated himself for other sundry and assorted reasons: for his unreasonable fear of heights, which made travel on the high roads a terrible ordeal; for his inability to laugh, in contrast to the real Hopalong Cassidy who laughed all the time when he wasn't shooting desperadoes; for his weakness in not being able to follow the same kind of backbreaking work that earned other folks their nickels and dimes in these hard times, like picking strawberries at two cents a quart or tomatoes at five cents a bushel, or hacking ties at twenty cents each, or scrubbing laundry on a rub board at fifty cents a day. He was too soft to bend over all day long picking strawberries or tomatoes, or swinging a broadax, and too impatient to pick enough berries—a hundred quarts a day—to earn any real money, and nobody was buying railroad ties any more anyhow. He refused to chop cotton, let alone pick it. He couldn't plow behind a mule. One thing he had in common with the real Hopalong Cassidy who he was going around pretending to be was a dislike for horses: supposedly William Boyd the actor who played Hopalong had to have somebody do his fancy riding for him because he plain and simple didn't like horses and didn't know how to ride one. But he had that mighty handsome pure white horse named Topper, who was just as important to him as Silver was to the Lone Ranger, and was the inspiration for this here truck being named Topper.

Hoppy rolled himself a cigarette but didn't have to light it because three or four people had their matches lit under his nose before he could even stick the cigarette in his mouth. There were other things the two Hopalongs had in common, besides their last name and their white means of transportation: they never drank nor smoked nor cussed in public, ole Hopalong was clean on the screen, but they sure did a lot of each in private, and Hoppy considered Tollett's store porch pretty private. The screen Hopalong got his name from the fact that he'd been wounded and walked with a limp; our Hopalong the traveling movie showman had jumped off a barn at the age of nine, thinking to see if he could really fly, discovering he could not, and breaking one ankle so badly he still had a limp much worse than the screen Hopalong, who in some of his later pitcher shows forgot that he had a limp anyhow. Neither Hopalong ever wore cowboy duds, not even a hat, when off the job…although the other Boyd supposedly liked to dress up really fine off the job, fancy suits and all, whereas Landon Boyd would just as soon wear a plain pair of overalls and a cotton shirt with the top button buttoned. And even when he was on the job, pretending to be Hopalong because everybody expected him to, he never wore the full outfit of fancy black duds with six-shooters in a holster and silver buckles and a silver longhorn clasp on his bandana; he wore the black ten-gallon hat, that was all, but that was enough, the peak of that hat moving through the crowd was enough to send shivers of delight up the spines of all the kids and maybe even throbs of the heart to some of the girls, although it wouldn't get him anywhere, because the worst thing he had in common with the cowboy Hopalong was that they never enjoyed any pleasure with the ladies. The real Hopalong could save the gals from villains and restore their loss of life's savings and rescue them from cliff edges and roaring trains, but he always had to ride off into the sunset without ever enjoying their fleshly favors. He never even got to kiss one. Nor did poor Landon Boyd, who was only half the age of William Boyd, young enough to be his son, and hadn't yet kissed anybody. Now right here on this store porch was a bunch of gals who'd jump and quiver if he offered to kiss them, but he couldn't. He just couldn't, to save his soul. His whole experience with the opposite sex had been limited to a few times previously when he was still a teenager and he had attempted what he supposed could be called intercourse with two different gals, neither one of whom had enjoyed it, owing to his ignorance, which was one of the main things he hated himself for and still kicked himself for, although it had been five or six years now since he had last embarrassed himself in that fashion.

In every town on his route—and there was a total of twelve pretty little towns on his circuit, running from Osage in the north to Oark in the south, Wesley in the west to Tilly in the east—in every one of those towns there would always be a bunch of girls who would flock around him as they were doing right now, openly flirting with him though he never knew what to say to them, and then later, after the pitcher show or even during it, one of them was bound to ask to be allowed to "jine" him. Of course *jine* was the way he pronounced join himself, just like everybody else. But it rhymed with shine and repine and thine and sign and divine and he'd been tempted to write a song or two about it, especially about one of those gals whose name was Clementine, but writing songs about it was the only thing he could bring himself to do, and he sang the songs only to himself.

He couldn't accept any of their offers, not even from the ones who came right out and said something like, "Hoppy, honey, why don't I climb up there and keep you company while the pitcher show is a-running?" How could he answer that truthfully by saying *If we was to recline with you supine and our laigs intertwine, you might opine that your design was mighty fine but mine was out of line?* He never said any such as that. All he could say was to tell them that it might be dangerous for them to climb up onto the truck bed amidst all that machinery with his delco pumping away to generate the electric to run the show, and besides he couldn't fool around while the show was running (which was just an excuse, because most all of the time he didn't have anything to do except change the reels). Then he'd have to close the door in their face, the door to his truck's back-end that served as projection booth and home, and hide behind the door with his jug of Chism's Dew, needing several swallers to still the beating of his thwarted heart.

And sometimes what the girl meant by jine was not simply to get together with him for the purposes of jining themselves together carnally, but actually hooking up with his tour, becoming, depending on who said it, his assistant, his helper, his sidekick, his partner, his slave, or his wife. He didn't need any of those. One pretty gal once said she wanted to "ride shotgun" with him to whatever town he was going to next.

Now Hoppy studied the girls around him, trying to select, in his imagination, which one of them might make him an offer tonight. They weren't all pretty; a couple of them were mudhens, and one was a clock stopper. The girls went on a-chattering amongst themselves, not saying anything straight to him although it was pretty clear they were saying everything *for* him. All of these people knew that he didn't have any gift for gab, which was another thing he hated himself for: he had never learned how to chaw the rag, swap yarns, or toss words. He had to be content to listen to others. By and by, the girls joined the womenfolk in taking their leave from the store porch in order to go home and start supper, and the men were able to reclaim their seats upon the empty nail kegs, rails, captain's chairs and other furniture of the store's porch. The kids remained standing or squatting in the dirt of the road beside the porch.

They never took their eyes off of him, and eventually he stood up, stretched, yawned, and declared quietly, "I reckon I could use a few of you'uns to help me set up the seats." He climbed back behind the wheel of his truck and drove it on over the meadow beside the mill, behind the store, and parked it in the spot where it would remain for the duration of his run of shows, with its rear end facing the broad swath of meadow where he would set up the seats and the screen. Soon Billy Millwee parked his little wagon right alongside in the same position. Hoppy needed three kids to help him lug the screen out of the truck, unfold it and unroll it and hang it between a couple of elm trees at the end of the meadow. It was just several bedsheets sewn together side by side, and painted with a chalky white paint called alabastine, a gallon of which was among the supplies cluttering Topper's interior. He needed the other kids to scour the neighborhood in search of tomato crates to support pine planks and form the benches for the audience to sit upon. The kids scattered and returned by and by lugging a total of maybe thirty tomato crates, and carrying, two by two, a dozen long pine planks.

When they were finished setting up the seats, Hoppy gave each of the kids a paper ticket that had the word "Admission" printed on it. It was the same kind of ticket, printed by Weldon, Williams and Lick of Fort Smith, that was used in all the big town theaters, and Hoppy had several rolls in two colors, green for kids, red for adults (although, this story being in black and white, you can't really tell the difference).

Hoppy knew that before the week was over, one of these kids would ask to go with him. Turning down the gals might have filled him with sorry regret, but turning down the kids sometimes broke his heart, and he could have killed himself. He was a hero to those kids, and one of his sorry life's biggest pleasures was to see their faces light up at the first sight of Topper as he drove into town: the kids would laugh and shriek and clap and carry on like the dickens, and somehow every last one of them who couldn't earn a ticket by helping out with the setting up and the cleaning up afterwards managed to scrape up enough pennies or a nickel to pay the five cents not just once but each of the six nights that he would play a village. Sometimes when they'd already spent the one free ticket he gave out for helping set up and clean after the first show, he'd think of other ways they could earn a free ticket: he told them if they would collect a jar full of houseflies he'd let them in. That made the grown-ups and womenfolk happy too, getting rid of all those houseflies. Once or twice he had let them collect lightning bugs, but they couldn't do that and watch the show at the same time; that is, as soon as it got dark enough for the lightning bugs it was dark enough to start the show.

He knew that when the last show was shown on Saturday night, the last episode of the serial, and it was time for him to get ready to move on to the next town, there would always be more kids than big gals who asked to go with him. He knew their dreams: they'd seen the magic of the pitcher show, they'd entered for a spell a world where the people are more real than real at the same time they're more fantastic than fantasy, and somehow the kids thought that if only he would let them go with him they could stay in that world forever or even become real cowboys with lavish attire and handsome horses, or at least movie actors pretending to be cowboys. He knew that dream, because when he was nine he had run away from home to join a circus. They'd turned him away, and not long after that he'd jumped off that barn to see if he could fly. He remembered those hopes and expectations.

Usually, because he simply didn't have the time or the patience to try to explain to the kids that there just wasn't any world beyond that screen, that that screen was just a bunch of alabastine-coated bedsheets sewn together and the world projected on that screen was pure-dee make-believe, and that the next town he was heading for wasn't really no different from this here little town, he'd tell them that his life was hard and lonesome and uncomfortable, riding his beat-up old truck Topper all over the roughest kidney-busting roads and scary mountain trails, the food was lousy and scarce, the pay was practically nothing, and besides the whole life was just seasonal, warm weather only, nothing to do during the cold months. He could usually scare them off with a frank picture of his existence, if need be showing them the complicated machinery of his projector and his delco, but if that didn't work he had to throw in something else made up, such as that he had a disease, the exposure to all them electrons generated from his projector had left him with a bad case of the cathodes, which is contagious and could only be helped by the large amount of good corn liquor that he had to consume.

These things were said to them when they begged or politely asked to go with him. But there had been times when they didn't ask; a kid would just hide himself somewhere in the back of his truck, even under his bed, and he wouldn't discover him until he'd started to set up in the next town, forty or sixty mile down the road, and then all he could do would be to tell the boy what a mistake he'd made and hand him over to some officer of the law, whilst the tears would be a-streaming down the boy's face and welling up in Hoppy's eyes. It always broke Hoppy's unhappy heart, but he knew he didn't have any room in his life or his truck for somebody else's child. He'd unstopper his jug of Chism's Dew to take away the pain, even though it was not generally his practice to imbibe before the last customer had headed off home after the show.

Sometimes he wondered if he might hate himself even more if, as he lived in either hope or threat of doing, he came across some kid he couldn't say no to, some kid who was just right, some kid who reminded him of himself when he was a kid wanting to run away from home. Some kid like Billy Millwee, only several years older.

Chapter two

It wasn't every day that somebody asked him to supper, let alone dinner. He reckoned that if he'd acquired a name for being a bright and breezy table-talker, he might've got more invites, but the word had probably got around that he was a pretty dull feller when it came to making chitchat. He didn't exactly hate himself for this, no, not out-and-out teeth-grinding loathing, but there was little in this life that he disrelished more than having to sit at the supper table with the menfolk and boys while the womenfolk and girls hovered around, and all eyes watching every bite he bit and every chew he chawed, and everyone waiting for him to say something clever. He'd much rather eat in the back of his truck, right out of cans, and pass up the pies and cakes so as just to eat in peace without having to say nothing. And usually he did, but on his first evening in town, having spent most of the day traveling, driving the truck over those kidney-busting roads, he was ready to take it easy and let the womenfolk wait on him, as they still did in the time-honored tradition, unlike these here big towns among the flatlanders where it was rumored that womenfolk actually sat down at the table with the menfolk.

Besides, Birdie Woodrum set out a swell supper, not just

leftovers from noon dinner as most folks had, but a supper that was practically a dinner itself, with freshfried chicken and freshmashed taters and freshstirred gravy and all. Him and Leaster Woodrum was the only ones at the table; the other boys had flew the roost, and so had most all the girls, so that only the baby remained to help her mother wait on the men. The girl, Ila Fay, maybe seventeen, wasn't a knockout but she didn't give you an eye-ache either. Like all the other girls in town, she thought Hoppy was some feller. Her prince, her eyes said. He couldn't set down his gnawed drumstick before she'd offer him the platter.

"Don't seem to me," said Leaster Woodrum with his mouth full of mashed potatoes, "that it'll come a rain this week."

Some moments drifted by before it occurred to Hoppy that he was expected to offer his opinion on this matter, and then he had to ponder what the best opinion would be. No rain, at least not at night, meant better attendance at the pitcher shows. But was Leaster hoping for some needed rainfall? It was hard to tell. "I reckon it might could," Hoppy said, and allowed Ila Fay to ladle some more green beans onto his plate.

There were no less than four desserts offered up, a sweet potato pie, an egg custard pie, a lemon layer cake, and some strawberry shortcake. Hoppy knew he'd have to have some of each, not that he didn't care to, so Birdie would feel happy. Birdie was known to have spells of deep downheartedness. Leaster himself was none too happy ever since the bottom fell out of the market for railroad ties. It occurred to Hoppy to attempt conversation. "How's the chairs coming along, Leaster?" he asked.

Leaster looked surprised, probably because he'd never heard Hoppy ask a conversational question before. Last year Hoppy had given Leaster a foot-powered turning lathe that he'd picked up in exchange for a week's worth of tickets for a whole family of Biddles over in Mt. Judea, and Leaster had started using his stock of white oak timber, formerly hacked into railroad ties, to turn into chair posts and rounds for frames whose bottoms he braided from bark, making a real easy chair that was good to look at. "I sold three of 'em last week," Leaster said. "Dollar and a quarter each." He finished his pie and shoved away from the table. "So I figure I can afford tickets every night for the pitcher show."

"Aw, I'll just let you in free," Hoppy offered, but Leaster wouldn't hear of it.

While Birdie and Ila Fay sat down to have their supper, Leaster and Hoppy went out to sit on the porch and smoke. Sitting out there, Hoppy could also watch the slow but steady arrival of folks heading for the mill meadow to attend the pitcher show. Some of them were driving cars, a Model T and a couple of Model As, some were on their mules or donkeys, but most were on foot, and they all waved real big to see Hoppy sitting there in his black ten-gallon hat.

Leaster studied the glowing end of his hand-rolled cigarette for some time, as if it were a strange insect, and then he cleared his throat and said, "Hoppy, where are you from, anyhow?"

Sometimes he got asked that question, but not too often. Most folks who asked it just wanted to be reassured that Hoppy wasn't some furriner from the next county over. It wasn't too hard to answer, so he did. He was born in Stay More, a remote, lost town in the deepest wilds of what became his territory for the showing of pitcher shows, and Leaster Woodrum had heard tell of it but had never been there, mainly because it wasn't on the way to anywhere. He had heard tell that it ought to've been called "Get There" instead of "Stay More," because the former was a lot tougher to do than the latter. Hoppy didn't want to include Stay More among the dozen little towns he visited on his tour, not because it was so hard to get to, nor because its population was dwindling, nor even because of all his unhappy memories about growing up there—or trying to. He tried to explain to Leaster that Stay More was not *on* the circle of his circuit, that it was more in the center, that if his circuit of twelve towns was like the face of a clock then Stay More was the center pin where the hands were attached. But that was just making excuses. More than once he had asked himself, when he had nothing better to ask, as so often he did not, just why he couldn't set up his shows in the town of his birth. The best answer he could come up with, and it wasn't an answer so much as one more lame alibi, was that he didn't want any more folks telling him about his grandpa.

15

The last few times that he had stopped in Stay More just to say howdy or to buy the fixings for smokes at the store or a demijohn of Chism's Dew from Luther Chism, or to check his mailbox at the P.O. (he never got nothing that amounted to nothing), or just to heed the pleading of the town's name (which supposedly had been bestowed by an Indian early in the nineteenth century), he always turned out having to listen to one more tale about Grandpa Stapleton. He thought he had heard them all, but there was always a new one waiting for him whenever he nodded his head in response to the question, "Say, aint you Long Jack's grandchild?"

He was told there was a clear family resemblance. The few remaining old-timers who had actually known Long Jack Stapleton always said, "You kind of favor him." If there weren't any ladies present or eavesdropping, one of the men might boldly make a crack in the way of hinting that maybe Hoppy was endowed, or rather unendowed, with the same shortcoming which had given Long Jack his ironic nickname. He had heard all the tales about that too, speculations about just how Long Jack had wound up unendowed: the doctor who had circumcised him had been drunk; the organ had been bitten off by a dog, or by a wolf, or by Long Jack himself during a nightmare; or Long Jack in a moment of conscious frustration or shame—or maybe accidentally—had hacked it off with an axe. There were lots of sawmills in those days where it could have happened. Whatever the real means of amputation, the shortcoming did not hinder Long Jack in his marital relations: he fathered several children, one of them Landon "Hoppy" Boyd's mother. On his Grandmother Stapleton's side, Hoppy traced his ancestry back to Jacob Ingledew, who had founded the town of Stay More. Hoppy may have resembled his grandfather Long Jack in some ways—the gentle face capable of animation and compassion—but Long Jack Stapleton had been a huge man with red hair and a bushy red mustache. Of course this here is all in black and white so the color of Long Jack's hair and mustache can't really matter. But Hoppy was more inclined to blondness: not the sort of white blondness that made the real Hopalong Cassidy silver-haired at the age of forty but a kind of straw-colored fair-hairedness. And he was tall, taller than the real Hopalong, but not gigantic like his grandfather. He remembered as a small boy asking his grandfather if he would ever grow as big, and his grandfather said, "If you believe it, you can."

He did not remember very much about his grandfather, not because little was memorable but because he had for some reason forgotten most of the details of his childhood, not because it was too painful to remember but because your progress through the perils of the life you've got here and now ought not be hampered by the baggage of the life you used to have. So most of what he knew about his grandfather came from what he heard from others, including his mother and including all those old men who loved to sit on the store porch all afternoon whittling sticks into flinders, passing the jug of Chism's Dew around, and telling endless tales about the way things used to be when things were always more lively and interesting than they'll ever possibly be again. Hoppy didn't believe half of what he heard but he liked to listen anyhow. No, he liked to listen *because* he didn't believe half of what he heard.

And he knew this fact about the nature of pitcher shows: they are man's attempt to make believable—because they're *showed*—the most unbelievable things.

Long Jack Stapleton had been a preacher, not necessarily a regular minister of any particular Christian denomination but at least a purveyor of the Word as found in the Bible, both old and new testaments. He had been a circuit rider, or itinerant, just as his grandson Hoppy was now an itinerant, albeit in black and white, a purveyor of black and white pitcher shows in a life without color. Unlike Brother Emmett Binns, the current circuit rider, he had not been out for profit or glory or gratification of the flesh. Nobody knew just where Long Jack Stapleton had come from. He was a furriner, that is, not a native of Stay More. Possibly he came from one of the selfsame towns that now comprised his grandson's itinerary. Leaster Woodrum hadn't heard the name before, but Hoppy had encountered the name Stapleton among some of his customers in other towns. In the middle of the coldest winter that Stay More had ever known, Long Jack had appeared, riding the biggest horse that anyone had ever seen, big enough to support not only huge Long Jack but also the girl, or young woman, clinging to his back, both of them dressed up all in fur: bearskins and coonskins and beaver skins. Because the girl's hair was the same fiery red as Long Jack's it was assumed at first that she was his daughter, but as it turned out she was his "baby sister," Sirena, destined to marry John Ingledew and become the mother of the large family of Ingledews who dominated Stay More in the first half of the twentieth century.

Their first night in town, Long Jack treated his hosts, the Dinsmores, to a sort of preview of coming attractions of his special powers, although Hoppy felt that all the stories about this had to be greatly exaggerated. It seems that somehow Long Jack supposedly had a gift of words, a tripping silver tongue that allowed his audience to visualize his narratives almost as if they were watching a pitcher show! Not simply visualize, no. They could not only see but also hear and taste and smell and touch. It was incredible, or magic, or both. According to the legends, in the beginning Long Jack had told the Bible's love stories, the romances of Abraham and Sarah, David and Bathsheba, Jacob and Rachel, Ruth and Boaz, etc. etc., so graphically, almost like the images that Hoppy possessed on one private reel of contraband film that he showed only to himself, that the deacons of the churchhouse had decreed that the people could no longer attend such shows, and they banned Long Jack from the churchhouse. In time, Long Jack, especially after he fell in love with Hoppy's grandmother, Perlina Ingledew, and married her and could enjoy all those salacious scenes in his own bedroom and therefore didn't need to narrate them to his congregations, promised the deacons he would never again project an "undecent" picture and was allowed to use the churchhouse again, where his "pitcher shows" were strictly of the Bible's action and violence, scenes of bloodshed and gore, flashing swords and decapitation, torture and pillage and scourging and mutilation. He packed the people in. People came from all over Newton County to watch his pitcher shows, and the meeting house wouldn't hold them all, so he had to give matinées in the afternoons and candlelit productions at night. The freewill offering he collected at each performance in time allowed him to build a modest house east of Stay More for the growing family that he and Perlina had, and eventually to retire there in comfort.

He had been retired for many years when Hoppy was born, so Hoppy had never seen him deliver one of his magic sermons. He heard about the sermons from his mother and from his uncles and aunts, who had been children themselves when Long Jack gave up the practice, or the ministry, and had not yet been born themselves when the deacons forbade the preacher from speaking any more blue movies. There were a few oldtimers who sat on the store porch whittling and spinning windies who claimed to have witnessed one or more of Long Jack's improper shows, and Hoppy's innocent young ears eavesdropped on their attempts to recall, almost with nostalgia, the erotic excitement of Long Jack's depiction of Adam and Eve driven from the Garden, giving themselves over to their urges almost desperately, as if bodily pleasure could compensate for the loss of Eden.

On the same long journey to Memphis when Hoppy had acquired his first reels of westerns for showing to his various audiences, he had met a distributor who had offered to sell him, for an indecent price, a single reel of a pitcher show which had no title, just a label, "Assortment." After sampling a few scenes, Hoppy was compelled to buy it. He had, in the past couple of years, watched it alone too many times already. It was grainy, jerky, black and white of course, silent, and unlike his grandfather's magic sermon pitcher shows made no pretense of having any relation to significant persons of any sort, or having any plots, or making any points other than that sex is an intensely compelling business. True to its label, it was a mixed bag of assorted combinations, men with women in several positions, including the substitution of the mouth for the genitals, sodomy, pederasty, and one brief but curiously stimulating encounter between a curvaceous lady and a German shepherd. The whole reel had seemed unbelievable the first time Hoppy had watched it, and he found himself trying to imagine what his grandfather's spoken blue "pitcher shows" had actually sounded like. Hoppy's reel was *real.* It projected—always on the secluded wall of the inside of his little mobile dwelling-place—actual albeit flickering, jumping images leaving nothing at all to the imagination…except the imagining of oneself into the position of one of the performers, as all motion pictures invite our vicarious participation.

But for an orator to select certain words and to enunciate them in such a certain way as to make the listener actually experience what was being described or narrated—that was almost beyond the range of belief.

Almost. Although Hoppy had buried most memories of his grandfather just as he had buried those of his childhood, he would always remember the one time that he himself had had a fleeting glimpse—a trailer, he guessed you could call it—of his grandfather's power. It was not long before Long Jack Stapleton died, of natural old age. It was right after Hoppy (who of course wasn't called Hoppy in those days but just Landon) had broken his ankle jumping off the barn, and Doc Swain had put a plaster cast on it, so he couldn't get around very well, and spent a week or so in bed, and Grandpa Stapleton showed up one afternoon, saying, "Landon, boy. Heared tell you was ailing." And sat down beside his bed. A minute passed, then Grampa asked, "Can I fetch ye anything?"

Landon had never before had his grandfather offer to do anything for him. Months earlier, Landon had run away from home to join a circus that was showing in the county seat of Jasper, leaving home not just because of the glamour and excitement of the circus but because he truly had come to believe that nobody cared for him or cared about him, least of all his grandfather, who was an old man, his fiery red hair and beard turned snow white in keeping with the black-and-white of this story, who had so many grandchildren scattered all over creation that he really had no time for any of them, who seemed to live in a world of his own, a world hidden behind his kind, compassionate face. Now here he was, not only paying attention to Landon but offering to fetch him something.

"I don't reckon I need nothing," he answered his grandfather.

His grandfather looked sad, or disappointed, or both.

After a while, Landon offered, "You could tell me a story."

His grandfather smiled. "What kind of a story?"

"What kind of story did you used to tell folks that made them think they were really watching it?"

His grandfather laughed, which Landon had never heard him

do before, or not that he could remember. "Stories from the Bible, mostly," Grampa said.

"Then tell me one of those," Landon said.

His grandfather sighed. "I've done went and used up all of those. I don't have them in me any more. But I reckon I could tell ye a Jack Tale, if ye want."

"Could you tell it so's I can see it and hear it and taste it and smell it?"

"I doubt it, but I could try."

Hoppy couldn't remember just how the story went. Just as the details of so many movies once seen are eventually dissolved into the drab fabric of our memory, Long Jack Stapleton's recitation of that Jack Tale to his grandson that afternoon in 1919 is but a blur. But it was something about this fellow named Jack, a simple but smart country youth, who is about to marry a wealthy farmer's only daughter, Betsy. But he discovers that Betsy and her parents are terribly silly folks, and he takes a vow to leave and never come back unless he can find in this big world three sillies more silly than those three sillies.

Up until that point, Landon, try as he might, couldn't really hear or see Jack, the hero of the story, let alone smell or taste or touch anything, and he thought he himself was just as silly as those sillies in the story, and so was his grandfather. But as he kept on listening to his grandfather, and the story involved Jack's discovery of the first of the three sillies, a woman trying to capture sunlight in boxes to brighten the inside of her windowless home, he suddenly realized that he was experiencing a pitcher show, the first he had ever seen, for not even the silents had come to Newton County yet. By the time Jack encounters the next silly, a family of milkmaids who have trouble counting to five, he was so engrossed in the picture he could count the teats on the cows. And when Jack meets the man who spends hours each day trying to put on his pants, Landon was so involved in the picture he involuntarily spoke aloud, telling the man what he was doing wrong. By that time Jack is convinced that all these sillies make Betsy and her family seem positively intelligent, so he returns home and marries her.

Landon could not swallow what his grandfather's mere words had done to him, and he demanded to know the trick of it, just as later he would discover in all his sideshow performances of magic that served as overtures to his pitcher shows that somebody would always insist upon being told just how he had accomplished certain feats or sleights.

"They's not exactly any trick," his grandfather said. "But words is little miracles, don't ye know? If you use 'em right, you can do anything with 'em."

Chapter three

Hoppy hated himself a good deal because he couldn't do anything with words. From the time that the first customers arrived for the pitcher show until it finally got dark enough to show the show—and nowadays it was nigh on to nine o'clock before it was dark enough—Hoppy had an obligation to provide some form of entertainment for the people, a kind of sideshow to the pitcher show, and he had long since developed and cultivated two routines, neither of which required him to do much if any talking. First, during the time he was selling tickets, he juggled. Sounds difficult, doesn't it, but it wasn't. He had a set of six juggler's balls (although he'd never got beyond five at a time) that he could toss up and keep in the air until the next customer came along, and he could do a bunch of tricks with those balls, clapping his hands once or even twice while the balls were in the air, and he hardly even seemed to interrupt himself to sell a ticket, and make change if need be, although if the customer had no cash but could only barter something like eggs, butter, a slab of bacon or chickens he had to do some extra juggling with the barter. Since he had to take off his black ten-gallon Hopalong Cassidy hat in order to do the fancy juggling, he just used that hat to hold the rolls of tickets and the cash and change, but if somebody brought eggs he'd have to stack them in a box he kept for the purpose, and as for live chickens he'd just put 'em under a upside down tomato crate.

Now, on this night, Billy Millwee tried to imitate Hoppy's juggling using green hickory nuts, but the most he could keep in the air at one time was two. It occurred to Hoppy that maybe he could hire Billy to sell tickets and collect eggs and chickens and such. But was Billy old enough?

Just about the time folks began to get bored with even the fanciest of his juggling, which was about the time that the last customer showed up and the last ticket was sold, but there was still too much light to start the projector, he switched from juggling to magic tricks. His props were limited and he didn't have a live rabbit to pull out of his ten-gallon hat, but he could sure make all kinds of things disappear and reappear; he could do tricks with coins and dollar bills and strings and rubber bands, he could make things float, he was a master of illusions. He might lack his fabled grandfather's power to make words become real images, but he could make people believe they were seeing something that wasn't there. Wasn't that a good-enough substitute for not being able to do things with words? Then why did he have to keep on being down on himself for not mastering words? By the time he finished, it was starting to get dark, and the dark helped his illusions. If there was enough light left, why, he would even hypnotize a couple of folks and get them to do hilarious things.

Naturally there were several customers who weren't customers, that is, they hadn't paid for a ticket and were hiding or sitting over on the edge of the meadow, hoping Hoppy wouldn't see them. He saw them but knew he couldn't do anything about them. Probably they were just so poor they didn't have a dime or a nickel for admission, nor even anything to barter.

He looked around and estimated the size of the audience, paid as well as unpaid, which was another of his talents, being able to tell almost to the person how many folks were there. Tonight there were seventy-nine, which was only about half a dozen short of the whole population of the township. He knew the others, the absentees, were folks who probably had to get up early the next morning to milk the cows.

If this whole story weren't just in black and white, even those colored balls that Hoppy juggled and the green nuts that Billy tried to juggle which had to be plain sepiatone at best, then along about now there would be some real pretty blue, which was the color all the air had got to be at the moment that Hoppy climbed up into his booth on the back of the truck, fired up the delco to generate some electricity, and turned on the projector, a 35 mm Western Electric IA which he'd already threaded in advance.

The first thing to show up on the screen of the alabastine bed-sheets was a big number "8", and everybody started clapping, and then a "7" and a "6" and so on until there was a "0" and the clapping stopped. Then the screen showed what looked like an Indian chief atop a paint horse atop a mountain crag shooting an arrow and below that "Republic Pictures Presents." From the loudspeaker which Hoppy had set atop the projection booth there swelled up some grand fancy music, and then it said on the screen "The Painted Stallion." This wasn't the main feature but just the first episode of the serial. For five nights Hoppy would show the first five chapters in the serial, each one of which ended in a real cliffhanger, and then on the last night instead of a feature he'd just show the remaining seven chapters of the serial, back to back, better than a feature in a way, although it didn't have Hopalong Cassidy in it.

"The Painted Stallion" is about a whole bunch of folks taking the very first wagon train out of Independence, Missouri to Santa Fe, in the year of 1820 when the western country was still infested with Indians on the warpath, as well as white bandits, who constantly try to ambush the wagon train and would've killed everybody except for some help from a mysterious Rider on a painted stallion who turns out, several episodes later, to be a woman. The woman is played by Julia Thayer, whose real name was Jean Carmen, and Hoppy had a powerful crush on her.

Ray Corrigan stars as our hero, Clark Stuart, the chief scout for the train, who also is carrying a secret trade treaty from the government to Santa Fe. On the steamboat arriving in Independence, he befriends a young stowaway, a freckle-faced lad of ten or eleven, who turns out to be Kit Carson, who would later become a famous scout himself. Sammy McKim, who plays Kit and even looks a little bit like Billy Millwee, is so lovable and also heroic that all the kids in the audience are crazy about him. Although he can't get permission to join the wagon train, he hides in the back of one of the wagons, and when he is caught and taken to the wagonmaster, played by nice old Hoot Gibson, all he can say is, "If you don't want me, I guess I can make myself scarce."

And Hoot the wagonmaster says, "I guess maybe we better see the cook and get you some supper. You see, a scout for this train's got to keep his strength up."

"Yes, Sir!" says beaming young Kit, and all the kids in the audience rise to their feet and holler YAY!

The first episode, "Trail to Empire," ends with all the audience wondering if the wagon train is doomed, with the wagons circled and the furious Indians riding and shooting all over the place, and everybody wants to come back the next night to see the second chapter and find out if the mysterious Rider (who no one knows yet is a woman) is able to save the wagon train or not.

Hoppy had watched all twelve episodes more than once and knew the ending would be happy. He also thought that the whole thing, although it had some flaws (such as repeated footage in which the same action happened twice or more) could be looked upon as if it stood for life's journey itself, or even his own particular journey with his mobile pitcher shows in particular, encountering difficulties along the way and overcoming them, and even if he hadn't yet discovered the equivalent of that strange Rider on her painted stallion becoming his guardian angel there was no telling but what she might show up in some form one of these days.

He also admired "The Painted Stallion" because it wasn't really real. Of course all pitcher shows are flights from reality but most of them try to imitate life as we know it, or life as it looks, but there were things in "The Painted Stallion" that just couldn't possibly *be*. It just wasn't possible that Davy Crockett and Jim Bowie could have been there together with the great Kit Carson as a boy. And then of course that guardian angel, a luscious white woman dressed in Indian garb with a full chief's headdress. It just wasn't possible.

By contrast, the main feature was completely realistic. He started it now, and it would run for an hour and nineteen minutes and require five reel changes. In "The Hills of Old Wyoming," somebody's been stealing the cattle from the Bar-20 Ranch that Hopalong Cassidy and his sidekicks operate, and they suspect it might be Indians who live on a reservation nearby, so they take off towards the reservation to find out.

Once the first reel was running good, Hoppy wandered over to the edge of the woods to relieve himself. He could've done it right beside his truck and nobody would have seen him because all eyes were fixed on the screen, but he wasn't taking any chances. He'd just started a stream running when he looked down and there was Billy Millwee taking a leak right alongside him. Hoppy chuckled, but then he said, "Billy, I wish you wouldn't copy every little thing I do." Then he had another chuckle when he imagined that right up there on the screen Hopalong Cassidy might need to unbutton his britches and water the sagebrush. Hoppy was always doing this: imagining things on the screen, filling in what the pitcher show left out.

Sometimes while the show was running Hoppy liked to mosey down towards the screen just so's he could turn and study folks' faces. Now, when the shooting started as Hopalong Cassidy captured the half-breed rustler Lone Eagle, Hoppy could watch as the audience hollered and whooped and whistled, and a lot of them used their fingers as six-shooters. Hoppy was also able to identify the several people who had never seen pitcher shows before, because they weren't making a ruckus, they were just sitting there with their mouths wide open and their eyes like saucers. Hoppy liked to try to recall the first time he himself had ever seen a pitcher show, when he was twelve, the same age he'd had his first wet dream, and he honestly hadn't formed an opinion as to which was better.

If their looks didn't say anything about how they were taking the show, Hoppy liked to just study them anyhow, to see how many of them he could recognize by name. This being his third annual trip to this town, he knew most of them by now, although there were a couple of pretty girls he couldn't recall having seen before, or maybe they had just grown up and blossomed since he'd last seen them.

Known or unknown, these people in this audience were his family, and he felt a great fondness for them one and all. Most of them sat together as families, although the kids preferred sitting on the grass or blankets right down in front of the screen. There were a few loners who weren't sitting next to anybody. There was Mercy Boonlatch, a widow-woman who earned her living carding wool from the few sheep who still wandered these pastures getting cockleburs in their wool that Mercy had to pick out after the shearing. And over there was Clemmie Whitlow, likewise a widow-woman, who knits the yarns spun from Mercy's wool into stockings and gloves and sweaters. In cool weather, Hoppy wears a sweater she'd knitted for him two years ago in return for just a week's worth of tickets, ninety cents worth, a good price for such a nice sweater. Hoppy couldn't understand why Clemmie and Mercy weren't the best of friends, and he intended to find out, one of these days. Clemmie had a reputation for being the meanest woman around, and Hoppy had heard too many tales of her sorry life and ways.

Yonder sat Billy Millwee's folks, Bardis and Ruby, who ran the feed store, or tried to, since Bardis was the town drunk and Ruby wasn't very bright. Hoppy'd eaten dinner at their house once last year and told them just half-joking that he was gonna steal Billy one of these days when he got to be old enough to travel. "You're welcome to him," Bardis had said.

During his inspection of the audience, Hoppy always kept one eye on the screen, watching for that little white cue spot in the upper right corner which warned that the end of the reel was near, and when he saw it he ran back to the truck to change the reel. He hoped that next year he'd be able to buy a second projector so he wouldn't have to stop the show while changing the reels, but meanwhile he had got his movements figured out and timed them so he could thread the new reel into the projector and have it running in less than a minute after the old one ran out. Even so, there would always be some folks, mostly kids and teenagers, who would get impatient and restless during the changing of the reels and start cutting up, starting horseplay and roughhouse, usually inspired by the fighting that had been happening on the screen. The same bunch of rambunctious rascals were also inclined to tussle whenever the screen showed anything romantic, like when Hopalong's good-looking sidekick Lucky Jenkins starts gallivanting around with the ladies.

But tonight, because "The Hills of Old Wyoming" has some cowboys singing in it (as a rule Hoppy hated the whole idea of the singing cowboy, but here was an exception), whenever Hoppy changed reels the audience broke into song, singing the words from the movie:

> Let me ride on a trail in the hills of old Wyomin
> Where the coyotes wail in the gloamin.
> For it's there that my heart's at home
> In the night let me rest with the blue sky for my ceilin.
> 'Till the wind's lullaby comes stealin
> From the hills where my heart's at home.
> Wake with a song! Wake with the sun!
> Saddle to mend, cattle to tend, plenty to be done.
> Let me live on the range where a man has room
> In the hills of old Wyomin. In the hills of old Wyomin.

Of course they couldn't finish all of that during the minute it took him to change reels, but he slowed down a little so they could at least sing the last part of it. It sure was a pretty song, and Hoppy liked the idea of a man having room to roam in, which he himself sure did.

This kind of pitcher show always ended with somebody, usually Hopalong Cassidy himself, riding off into the sunset. Hoppy had seen it happen so often that he would have been shocked if the show ended any other way. The real reason for the riding-off-into-the-sunset was obvious: our hero couldn't afford to stick around and get permanently involved with anybody; he had to make himself available for future adventures elsewhere. But Hoppy (our Hoppy) understood the symbolic reasons as well: the sunset is a climax, and it's in the far distance, and you want to bring a story to a close by moving from the here-and-now into the there-and-whenever. Hoppy wondered if, when this here story itself comes to an end, he'll be a-driving ole Topper off into the sunset somewhere. (Of course nothing's stopping you from flipping to the last page and finding out, which is a privilege that readers have over pitcher-show-goers.)

Everybody got up to go, moving real slow as if they couldn't bear the thought of leaving. Hoppy relished watching this part: the men stood taller and looked more manly and distinguished; the women all wore toothy smiles and held their heads up as if each one of them knew she was the best and the purtiest. The kids were each ten years older. The impossible became possible for a little while.

It was late, almost eleven o'clock. None of these folks were used to staying up that late, and many of them who had come on foot had a long way to walk to reach home, maybe an hour or more, and most all of them had to be up at dawn, but it was like New Year's Eve, a special occasion. Watching the lights of their lanterns, flashlights and headlights twinkling like lightning bugs and disappearing into the darkness, Hoppy knew that they'd all be back the next night, and the next, until he was gone.

It was quiet. Then somebody cleared their throat, and he turned to see in the dim light Ila Fay Woodrum, attempting to speak. Her folks, Birdie and Leaster, had done already headed off for home with their lantern. Ila Fay hadn't opened her mouth when Hoppy was having supper at their place, and now here she was trying to speak. She took a deep breath and let it out all in a rush, "Don't you reckon you could use me as a magician's assistant? All them tricks you do? Don't you need somebody to help? Or be your juggler's assistant? Hold your balls or whatever? I'd go with you wherever. I'm ready to go whenever. I just get so tired of being called 'Leaster's least'un,' and I aint all that least, now, am I?" As if to emphasize her lack of leastedness she thrust out her chest, and Hoppy had to notice that her bosom was well-furnished.

For a long moment Hoppy had a fantasy of taking Ila Fay with him and teaching her how to levitate or disappear or conceal things, or at least to juggle. He probably could use a magician's assistant, and he thought it was real clever of her to call it that. She wasn't all that ill-favored to look at; in fact, she was kinda cute. And she could cook, no doubt about that. He was plumb tired of his own breakfasts, let alone his suppers. The trouble was, he didn't want to abduct the last remaining child of his friends Birdie and Leaster. Oh, heck, that wasn't his main reason for turning her down. No. He tried, in his fumbling way with words, to express his main reason. "Ila Fay, hon, some'ers out there in this big wide world is a feller who is bound to be your man someday, and I sure wouldn't want to keep you from him."

"Maybe he's you," she said.

"I'd never ask my woman to live the life I have to live," he declared. "You just caint imagine what it's like. All this roaming. Most folks on the road has somewhere to get to, but I don't. I'm just a nomad. Do you know what that is? I'm just a no-man nomad, and you'd specially be disappointed in the no-man part of me."

"I don't know what you mean," Ila Fay said.

"I just aint able," he said. There. He'd said it. It was the same words his grandfather Long Jack Stapleton had said to his grandmother Perlina the first time she'd tried to get him to lay with her. Hoppy's equipment wasn't imperfect like Long Jack's but his management of it apparently was.

Ila Fay didn't need to ponder the matter very long before she seemed to understand, and that was another mark in her favor: she wasn't dumb. "Well," she said at length, "let me know if you change your mind."

"It aint my mind that needs changing," he said.

And after she was gone (she was halfway home in the dark before it hit him that he should have offered to light her way home for her with his flashlight), he really overindulged the moonshine, and overindulged his hatred of himself, hatred not for anything he'd done but for what he had neglected or failed to do. Landon Boyd's motto, private and awful, was: *If I had only done what I had ort to've done.* He stayed up late, got pickled on his jug of Chism's Dew, realizing that he didn't have to get up early in the morning like all these other folks did (another reason for having no use for himself). He was just sober enough to turn the projector to face the wall and thread it with his private reel, "Assortment," and then to recline on his bunk and watch as the various naked people performed various mating postures and procedures. He was either too drunk or too filled with self-abomination to play with himself properly, and after a brief flogging of his tired member he fell asleep. After a while the Delco generator ran out of gasoline and stopped producing electricity, and the projector died.

Chapter four

The heat woke him. The scorching day was already afoot, and the pitiless sun was blazing through his window. Hoppy hated daylight almost as much as he hated Landon Boyd. It was too hot inside his truck-shack to start boiling water for his coffee, so he set the kerosene stove down off the truck, and put it beside Billy Millwee's wagon, left where he'd parked it the night before.

He poured just a dollop of dog hair into his coffee, and that made him feel a little better, although his head was still pounding. He took his fish pole and tackle and went off down the creek to try his luck, but didn't get a nibble.

After a dinner of crackers and sardines, he walked on over to Tollett's General Store. He didn't wear his Hopalong hat but just an ordinary old farmer's straw hat. There were already several men gathered there wearing similar straw hats, lounging around easy-like, leaning back with their hands behind their heads or whittling several sticks into flinders, chewing tobacco, and jawing about this, that, and th'other. Hoppy had his own keen Barlow knife and he started in to shaving a stick right along with the others.

"Don't reckon it will rain tonight," Ewell Tollett said. The white sky was cloudless and blank—appropriate, Hoppy thought, for a story that's all in black and white.

"I wouldn't be so sure," Hoppy remarked. And, since Tollett did a pretty fair business in his store and was probably the richest feller in town, Hoppy offered, "I'll bet ye ten dollars it rains tonight."

"Haw!" Ewell retorted. "You're on. It aint rained a drop this month and it aint never gonna rain on yore pitcher show."

Was Hoppy still a bit drunk? Or just a reckless gambler? No, he simply had good reason to believe, on the basis of previous experience, confirmed more than once, that whenever Chapter Two of "The Painted Stallion" was shown, an episode that ended with a cloudburst, there was always a real deluge in the actual here-and-now world. It had happened three times already on the three Tuesdays in the three towns where Hoppy had shown that episode. The impossible had become possible so certainly that Hoppy had told himself he could probably earn a living as a traveling rainmaker, one of those fellers (most of them con men) who visit drought-stricken areas with showy equipment that makes a lot of noise and is supposed to create rain, but never does. Hoppy could get away with it, and all he'd have to do is show Chapter Two of "The Painted Stallion" wherever they needed rain. But he didn't even need to remind himself that he wasn't in this racket for the money he made.

Several other men wanted to make bets with Hoppy on the ridiculous notion that it might rain, but they couldn't afford to lose their money as easily as Ewell Tollett could. So the subject of talk was allowed to change, and before they got around to swapping their favorite dirty tales, they spent some time talking about that strange Injun on the painted stallion in the serial who seemed to be a guardian angel for the pioneers. Hoppy wouldn't think of giving away the fact that the Injun was actually a pretty white gal, although he found his thoughts drifting to just who she actually was, which is never revealed throughout the serial. Had she maybe been a white captive of the Injuns? How could she tell the difference between good fellers and bad fellers so that she could be the guardian angel of the good guys? Where did she spend the night, or eat, or fix herself a new supply of the keen arrows that she was shooting all over the place to warn the good guys or kill their enemies? Wondering about these questions, Hoppy allowed his restless mind to fantasize about Julia Thayer (or Jean Carmen), who played the part, a most desirable specimen of womanhood. He entertained himself with fantasies of how Julia would cure him of his hopeless case of not being able to last more than a minute in the act of love.

He was so caught up in this sexual reverie that he didn't mind too awfully much when the men proceeded right into their hour of dirty tales, a contest to see who could tell the funniest and bawdiest yarn. Hoppy wasn't able to compete in the contest, not because he didn't know any lewd stories (he had heard hundreds on store porches elsewhere) but because he was simply incapable of narration.

The dirty stories trickled off when a bunch of kids came running to the store porch to admire their hero. To amuse them, Hoppy performed a few sleights of hand and hocus-pocus, and that helped make up for his complete failure at telling dirty stories to the men, or telling any kind of story for that matter. It wasn't just because he was not much for talking, and it certainly wasn't because he was uncomfortable with dirty tales, which he greatly enjoyed so long as somebody else was retelling them, but he simply didn't know how to *make* a story, how to begin it, how to walk it or lead it, and above all how to give the ending a real thump. Maybe it was just like his failures in sexual relations. He couldn't satisfy a girl. He couldn't satisfy a listener. So he had to let his pitcher shows do it for him. And serial pitcher shows, like "The Painted Stallion," were a kind of long drawn-out, stopping and starting, almost coming but postponing, snatching grabbing jarring bumpy act of love. Especially if every episode has a strange helpful bare-armed lady in an Injun's war bonnet romping atop a mighty paint horse.

Later that evening, Hoppy got his tarp out of Topper and unfolded it and erected it as a canopy with Topper supporting two corners and a couple of poles the other two. Usually the tarp, which was made of heavy duck cloth painted with alabastine too, served as a screen when the wind caused the bedsheet screen to flutter too much, but he had learned to offer the tarp to his audience as protection in case of rain, although few of the audience had ever accepted it.

Experience had taught him to expect exactly what happened this night: when Chapter Two, "The Rider of the Stallion," was getting close to its end, after The Rider had saved our hero Clark from being mobbed by the bandits, and the long wagon train was approaching a river (the Arkansas?) to cross, the dark heavens opened to the sound and sight of thunderbolts and the downpour began, both on the screen and on the audience. But nobody got up to run for cover, even though his tarp was there, and he was standing under it keeping dry himself. Everybody watched the episode right down to its cliffhanging end, when our hero Clark, driving the wagon across the swollen river, was conked from behind by the same hooligan who menaced him throughout the story, and fell unconscious into the covered wagon as it capsized in the water.

While Hoppy was changing the reel to start the main feature, Ewell Tollett, soaked to the skin, stuck his head through the door and said, "I aint got ten dollars on me. But you could take it out in trade over at the store."

The next night, the third episode of "The Painted Stallion," like each episode, began with an exact repetition of the closing scenes of the previous episode, and so was also in a downpour, but strangely enough this did not cause any further rainfall in the here and now of this real world. Unaccustomed as he was to public speaking, Hoppy made a brief announcement to the audience beforehand, assuring them that no further rain would fall. Several men in the audience spoke up, thanking him for the rainfall of the previous evening, which was badly needed for the parched crops, and assured a good second haying.

That wagon train faced many perils as it braved repeated attacks from the bandits hired by the deposed lieutenant governor of Santa Fe, who was bent upon keeping the settlers out of the territory. The villain, Dupray, aided by his ruthless confederate Zamorro, would stop at nothing to foil the efforts of the wagon train to reach its destination and fulfill the storyboard: "Westward! The trail to Empire! From Independence, Missouri to Santa Fe, dogged pioneers fought to penetrate a wilderness of savage Indians…massacres of death. Even worse were the white renegades…outlaws and bandits unscrupulous in their greed."

The most impossible thing about the story, more so than the heroics of the goddess on the painted horse and the presence of such heroes as Davy Crockett and Jim Bowie and the kid Kit Carson, was that Zamorro and his henchman were constantly riding on into Santa Fe to report on their progress or lack of it to their boss Dupray, and then riding back out, hundreds of miles, to wherever the wagon train had reached. Hoppy allowed as how distance had no meaning in a good story.

Hoppy was happy that whoever made the film never ran out of ideas for ending each episode with a cliffhanger, including one which was actually that, with our hero Clark hanging onto a puny little shrub sprouting out of the side of a bluff (from which he was rescued eventually by the mysterious helpful Rider who dangled a rope down and tied it around the painted stallion to pull him up). The serial was packed with hazards and dangers—gunpowder wagons exploding and ambushes and runaway stagecoaches and trapdoors to fall through—and even though you knew in your heart that somehow the good guys would escape in the next episode, it was always a breath-stopping thrill when it happened.

The gender of The Rider was not revealed until the eighth episode, although there were some keen-eyed watchers who guessed earlier that she was a woman, and even some conjecture among the bawdy men on the store porch as to whether The Rider was actually fuckable.

It was Hoppy's custom to show all the remaining chapters of the serial, one after the other, on Saturday night, and because everybody couldn't hardly wait to see how it all turned out there was a better attendance on Saturday night than any other night. He had shown four other full-length Hopalong movies, "Hopalong Rides Again," "Borderland," "North of the Rio Grande," and "Rustler's Valley," none of them very different from "The Hills of Old Wyoming"—same people, including Hopalong, same sidekicks, Windy Halliday and Lucky Jenkins, same ugly mustached villains, same settings mostly with lots of desert mountains, same thundering hooves and blazing guns and all. Hoppy couldn't have told you, if his life depended on it, the difference between one pitcher show and the next. But the serial rolled right along each night as the wagon train got closer to Santa Fe and the desperadoes grew more desperate to stop them and the lovely Rider performed miracles of rescue with her painted stallion.

It was close to midnight when the last episode of the serial came to its conclusion and our hero Clark rode off into the sunset but with that Lady on the Painted Stallion right beside him! Everybody clapped as hard as they could and cheered as loud as they could, and if they couldn't they just come out with a mighty "Ah!"

Several folks stopped by the projection booth on their way home to say something like "I wush we didn't have to wait a whole year for the next time you'll be coming around," and "Why don't ye just stay more with us instead of going some'ers else?" and "You'd better just come home and spend the night with me and not never go anywheres" and "It's sure going to be lonesome and tiresome when they's not any more pitcher shows to watch."

The next morning, Ewell Tollett violated the Sabbath by opening his store long enough for Hoppy to bring in and redeem the various items he'd accepted in barter for tickets: about twenty dozen eggs, four gallons of butter, eight slabs of bacon, a dozen chickens, and a lamb. With part of the proceeds, along with the ten dollars Tollett owed him, Hoppy also stocked up on various supplies to get him down the road.

At noon of that Sunday, there was a dinner-on-the-grounds at the schoolhouse, which was also the church, and although the circuit-riding preacher Emmett Binns had given a fiery sermon denouncing pitcher shows and condemning the audience for the waste of money, Hoppy had slept late, as had quite a few other people, and did not attend the church services, going instead to redeem his barter with Tollett. But he showed up in time for the dinner, which was mostly in his honor. In fact, even that preacher Binns showed up, long enough to eat and to make faces at Hoppy. There were several platters heaped high with fried chicken, and every single pie and cake known to man...or done by woman.

When it was all over, Hoppy sure did hate to leave. They gave him a paper poke full of leftover fried chicken to take with him, as well as his choice of pies and cakes. When he got behind the wheel of Topper and started the engine, Ila Fay Woodrum came rushing up and jumped on the running board and said to him, "Have you thought about it? Have you thought about me? I'm ready to go. Just say the word."

"The word," he said, "is *'sorry.'* I sure am sorry."

When he backed out into the road, and turned, with everybody waving at him, he started off slowly, knowing that nobody would watch him drive out of sight, which is very bad luck according to an old old Ozark superstition. He noticed that Billy Millwee with his little wagon was attempting to follow him. Hoppy wasn't sure whether Billy wasn't just imitating him in his leaving. He hollered at Billy, "Next year, when you're bigger, I aim to take you with me."

"Promise?" Billy said, with tears running down his cheeks.

But Hoppy had never made a promise in his life, and he was forced to push his foot down on the gas pedal and leave Billy in the dust. He wasn't riding off into the sunset, which wouldn't set for a good little while, and he wasn't riding west but east, but he was sure riding off and this was THE END as far as that town was concerned.

It was only sixty miles or so to the next town on his route, but those sixty miles were rough going, up mountain trails with hairpin switchbacks and off along sheer craggy ridges whose height made him terribly nervous, and through dark woods with rarely a sight or sound of any critter of any kind. He didn't have to be anywhere until Monday and he was tempted to camp out if he came to a good fishing stream, but the dense forests were kind of spooky and he decided to get on.

It was nigh onto suppertime when he saw the cluster of buildings down in the valley, and he lifted his bugle and stuck it out the window and commenced playing his taps-like tune that said "From far yonder up the mountain road here he comes again, folks, Hoppy Boyd, the happy moving showman of moving pitchers to show you another good'un."

One by one and two by two they all came a-running, even the grownups and womenfolk, and every dog in town, and followed him as he slowed down along the main road. He didn't stop at Bedwell's General Store but drove on over to the schoolhouse meadow, where he would park his rig and set up his outdoor show, so that the screen could be hung from the side of the two-floor schoolhouse. Right and left he had to decline invitations to supper, on account of he was already well-supplied with leftovers from the previous town. He did a little juggling and some hocus pocus and answered their questions about the names of the shows. Tomorrow night after the first installment of a fabulous serial called "The Painted Stallion" they would all be treated to a fine Hopalong Cassidy movie called "The Hills of Old Wyoming." Several folks, womenfolk too, asked him why he couldn't just have the first show tonight, but he had to remind them it was still Sunday and he didn't ordinarily ever show a pitcher on the Lord's Day. He had to turn down several invitations to come go home and spend the night. One by one and two by two they left him alone.

He climbed up into his home in the back of his truck to fetch his jug of Chism's Dew, and damned if there wasn't a kid sitting on his bunk. Not just a kid, either, but a well-growed boy. His first thought was that the boy had just climbed up there as soon as he had stopped and parked, but then he realized the kid must've stowed away at the previous town and ridden all those sixty miles back here. If that was the case, then Hoppy would have to fetch some officer of the law to see to it that the kid got safely back home.

Chapter five

In spite of himself, his voice was gruff. "All right, you," he said. "Climb down off the truck." The kid lifted up his toesack passel, just a rag bundle that probably held all his worldly goods, and climbed down off the truck, out into the light where Hoppy could see him. He wasn't a little boy; he was tall, with what seemed a full body inside his loose-hanging overalls, maybe fourteen or fifteen, with a pleasant freckled face and fine-boned features beneath a stained felt hat, and his overalls were old and had been patched and repatched by his mother or his sister. He even looked like the young Kit Carson in "The Painted Stallion" although he was older and prettier. His first words to Hoppy, in a voice that hadn't even broken yet, were, "If you don't want me, I guess I can make myself scarce."

So he had done already seen that first episode of "The Painted Stallion"! Hoppy's first thought was to say, gruffly, "Then you'd better make yourself scarce," but instead he said the same words that Hoot Gibson, or Walter Jamison, as the wagonmaster was called, had said to young Kit Carson, "How long since you've eaten, son?"

"Well, I et a lot at that dinner-on-the-grounds, so I aint hungry."

"So then I caint say, 'I guess maybe we better see the cook and get you some supper. You see, a scout for this train's got to keep his strength up.' Since I caint say that to make this conversation go the same way it did in the pitcher show, I can only say, 'This aint a wagon train and you aint a scout and we're not heading for Santa Fe.'" Hoppy surprised himself by talking so much; it was the most words he had said in one stretch in quite some time.

"No, sir," said the lad sadly, instead of the happy "Yes, sir!" that Kit Carson had said. "But don't you reckon you could use me as a magician's assistant? All them tricks you do? Don't you need somebody to help? Or be your juggler's assistant? Hold your balls or whatever?"

"Say!" Hoppy interrupted. "Are you a friend of Ila Fay's?"

"I know her." The boy had a very pouty mouth.

"Know her, hell. You just quoted her, word for word."

"Well, I was listening in when she spoke them words to ye, sir. I was just a-fixing to say something like that myself, but she beat me to it. And then you turned her away."

"So if you were listening in, do you recollect what I said to her to turn her away?"

"Yes sir, first you told her that some'ers out there in this big wide world is a feller who is bound to be her man someday, and you sure wouldn't want to keep her from him. That don't matter to me, because I aint looking for a feller."

"But what I said after that?"

"You said you'd never ask your woman to live the life you have to live. You said that she just caint imagine what it's like. All this roaming. Most folks on the road has somewhere to get to, but you don't. You're just a nomad. You asked her, 'Do you know what that is? I'm just a no-man nomad, and you'd specially be disappointed in the no-man part of me.'"

"Don't you never forget nothing?" Hoppy asked in amazement at the boy's word-for-word recollection.

"Sir, you aint no more of a no-man than I am," he said. "That don't matter to me nohow. I just want to be your helper, sir, and your partner...and your friend."

Hoppy studied the youngster, who stood with a bearing that reflected his pluck. "What's your name, boy?" he asked.

"Uh, Carl, sir," the boy said.

"Carl what?"

"Carl Whitlow, sir."

"You any kin to Clemmie Whitlow the knitter?"

"Um, yeah, she's my aunt."

"Does she know you was fixing to try and take up with me?"

"Naw, sir, but she don't give a hoot."

"So you're from that *there* town but you don't know nobody in this *here* town?" Hoppy didn't want anybody hereabouts recognizing the boy.

"I never been here afore, sir."

"It aint but sixty mile and you aint never been here before?"

"I never left home, sir," Carl said, and added, "before now."

"Son," Hoppy said, struggling to sound nice and gentle, "lookee out yonder. That town aint a bit different from the one you just came from. Schoolhouse is a mite bigger but the store's the same size. Now you may think you've escaped from something, but you aint. It's just the same little old two-bit hick town with the same old kind of folks in it, and if you was to be my helper you'd just be stuck here for a whole week, seeing the same old pitcher shows all over again, and then we'd go on to another town that aint a bit different from this one, and show the same shows all over again, and so on, and on and on, till hell freezes over."

"Sir, I'd never get tired of watching 'The Painted Stallion.'"

"So you really want to be like young Kit Carson, huh? You kind of favor Sammy McKim, which is the name of the actor who plays him. Well, I'm sorry to tell ye, but you'd never get a chance to do all them heroic deeds that he did."

"How do you know I won't?"

My, but the boy was full of spunk. "We might as well sit down," Hoppy offered, and fetched a chair off the truck for his guest to sit on. He sat on the folding steps that led up to the truck. He remembered that when he had discovered the boy he had been on his way to go and get his Chism's Dew, so he climbed up and got the jug. It's rude not to offer your guest something, regardless of how young they are. "Care to jine me in a snort?" Hoppy brandished the stoneware demijohn.

"What is it?" the boy wanted to know.

"It aint none of your rotgut roastin-ear wine," Hoppy declared. "The Chisms of Stay More has always made a superior firewater." He poured some into a glass and held it out. "It aint even white," he pointed out.

"I never had none afore, sir," the boy said.

"And I reckon you don't smoke nor cuss neither, do ye?"

"I've cussed some," Carl claimed.

"Let's hear ye," Hoppy decreed.

"Damn," Carl said, and waited smiling for Hoppy's approval, which was not forthcoming.

"You cuss like a girl," Hoppy said. He poured himself a generous splash of the Dew and clanked his glass against Carl's. "Here's down the rathole," he toasted, and drank his off in one swallow, but Carl only took a timid sip and made a face. "You'll get used to it," Hoppy told him, but then realized that made it sound like Hoppy was going to keep him around long enough to have a chance to get used to it, so he added, "But I'm afraid I might not have any use for you. Can you drive this truck?"

"Oh, gosh, sir, I wouldn't want to try."

"Can you change a flat?"

"A flat *what*, sir?"

"Carl, this aint the army. You don't have to call me 'sir' every other word. A flat *tire*, dammit. I don't reckon you've ever messed around with any kind of a vehicle, now have you?"

"My maw...I mean my Aunt Clemmie, she has a wagon, and many and a many a time I've hitched the mule to it and drove it."

Suppertime came and went, and although Hoppy had stuffed himself at that dinner on the grounds he reckoned he'd better have a bite or two at least to keep his stomach from growling at him in the middle of the night, so he fetched the poke of fried chicken parts, and he and Carl finished off a few of them, and then a sample of some of the pies and cakes, and Hoppy had a few more slugs of Dew although Carl didn't manage to finish his first one. Hoppy found himself talking more than usual. There was just something about the boy that squeezed the words out of Hoppy. "You want to know the real honest-to-God reason I caint let ye jine up with me?" he said. "See if you caint understand it. When I play a town, like your town, everybody there is my family, and that town is my home for a whole week, and even though I am, as you would soon find out, a very hateful feller, leastways in my own eyes, I generally manage to feel that I am somehow doing some good in that town, so that it hurts me to leave it. But I have to leave it, I have to move on, you know, and I caint take anything with me. I have to start all over again in another town. I have to take that town and put it out of my mind. If I was to let ye jine me, I'd be hanging onto something I have to lose, I'd be dragging yesterday into tomorrow. It would be like…you know what 'blackberry winter' is, don't ye, when they's a late cold spell in May or early June, when the blackberries are blooming but it feels like January?"

"We had a real blackberry winter last month," Carl said.

"Well, then, you'd sort of be a blackberry winter to me. If you was to jine me, I'd probably take to callin ye 'Blackie.'"

"I don't keer what ye call me," Carl said. "Call me anything ye like. Just keep me."

"You ort to know I couldn't pay you nothing. I'm saving up every penny I earn from admissions to buy myself another projector so's I don't have to have a gap between the reels."

"I aint looking for no wages," Carl declared.

"Well, just *what* are you looking for, son?"

"You don't have to call me 'son' cause you aint that much older'n me."

"How old are you?"

"Take a good guess."

"Fifteen?"

"Close enough. I'm sixteen. How old are you?"

"Ten years past that."

"I would've taken ye for older'n twenty-six, but not much."

"So answer my question. Just what are you looking for? Excitement? You won't find it hereabouts. Adventure? We aint going anywheres interesting. Education? I could learn you all I know between now and bedtime."

Carl took his first generous swig of the Dew, and coughed a bit. Then in a voice quieted by his cough or the significance of what he was about to say, he whispered, "I just need somebody to take keer of me."

"Your maw wouldn't do that?"

"I didn't have a maw."

"Your Aunt Clemmie, then. I know she's poverty-pore but couldn't she feed ye?"

"I aint talkin about food, or money, or clothes, or a roof overhead. I'm talkin about *keer*. About somebody to belong to. About somebody who gives a damn. Could I have some more of that Dew?" Hoppy obligingly tilted the demijohn over Carl's glass, and Carl took a brave swallow and asked, "Hoppy, do you believe in ghosts?"

Hoppy snorted or scoffed, or both, but said, "I've never seen one, personally, but I've heared plenty about 'em, and I aint fixing to deny 'em. They don't scare me, though. Do they scare you?"

"No, they don't try to. They do keer for me, and they come at night and take me out into the woods to talk and to dance and play."

Hoppy gave Carl a sharp look, though it was getting too dark to see the youth's face clearly. He was beginning to think that Carl might be a little touched. "What do these here ghosts look like?" he asked. "Anybody you know?"

"No, they're not like folks. I mean, they're little people. No more'n *that*," Carl used his hand to indicate a dwarf's height. "I caint tell if they're gals or fellers, but somehow it don't matter. And some of them have wings like butterflies. Or dragonflies. And all of them are so light and pale and ghostly you can see right through 'em."

"Sounds like fairies to me," Hoppy declared.

"Oh, do you mean there is such things? Have you seen fairies?"

"Not when I was awake. Do your fairies talk like everbody else talks, or in some strange language?"

"They sound just like everbody else, only…only more songlike sort of."

"So you're trying to get away from them, is that it?"

"Aw naw, they're my friends. And they said they'd always be with me wherever I go. I'd like to know iffen they've follered me."

It was full dark now, and Hoppy glanced around, as if he might see some of Carl's fairies cavorting in the moonlight. Even if the young man was someway not right in the head, Hoppy was thoroughly enjoying his company. There was another hour or so to kill until bedtime, even assuming he might care to go to bed at a reasonable hour, and Hoppy knew he'd have to invite the kid to spend the night. He could put the folded sheet-screen on top of the folded tarp to make a pallet on the floor of Topper, and that would be fairly comfortable. Hell, he was halfway tempted to offer the boy his own cot and sleep on the pallet himself. But meanwhile they could just sip their Dew and enjoy some conversation. Hoppy considered trying to explain to the boy what was obvious to Hoppy: that the boy had just cooked up all those fairies out of his lonesome imagination, the same way all of us have made up imaginary playmates at one time or another. But wouldn't it be better to let the boy go on believing whatever he wanted to believe?

One thing was for sure: Hoppy knew that he wouldn't be able to get rid of Carl, not easily. For the first time in his long experience with runaways or would-be runaways, he had one that he might just keep. Whether Carl seemed like a kind of grown-up Billy Millwee, with a little Kit Carson thrown in, or whether he just had better reasons than Ila Fay or any of those other gals had, he had somehow won Hoppy over, even if he was a little peculiar in his notions about those sprites or elves or leprechauns or whatever. Hoppy knew that such critters had a reputation for being naughty and full of mischief, and he hoped Carl's fairies would behave themselves.

Hoppy rolled himself a cigarette and lit it, then with the same match he lit one of his kerosene lanterns, turned low, just enough so they could see each other. The dim light from the glowing wick made Carl's soft, pleasant face seem sort of ghostlike, and Hoppy was inspired to wind up and deliver himself of a rumination about ghostly aspects of the business in which he was involved, not just the images on the screen (and many times a newcomer to the experience of pitcher shows had been compelled to go behind the screen to see what was there, as if the ghostly image on the screen was not substantial), but the fact that William Boyd, with his white hair and white eyebrows (not to mention his white horse Topper) is a ghostlike presence in all his appearances as Hopalong Cassidy. Of all Hollywood's actors, Boyd was the palest, most unreal, most haunting of all the ghost presences on the silver screen...Hoppy paused to be sure his listener got the significance of that word "silver," because silver is the most ghostlike of tints. Carl listened raptly to Hoppy's ideas and digressions, and Hoppy was amazed at himself, that he was so talkative. He reflected, although not aloud to Carl, that a true friend is somebody who brings out the best in oneself, especially one's best words.

He had to remind himself, eventually, that this was supposed to be an interview of an applicant for the newly created job of all-round helping hand. Tomorrow he would find out if Carl had the ability to thread the projector and fire up the delco and maybe even juggle. But there remained a few questions to be answered tonight, so Hoppy could sleep on the answers. "Can you by any chance play a musical instrument?" he asked.

"I'm fairly good on the pianer," Carl said.

"Glad to know it, but we aint got room for one of them." Hoppy was aware that the long heritage of motion pitcher showing had once included a live pianist to accompany the silent pictures, but the smallest piano he'd ever seen was still too big to be lashed to Topper's tail end.

"I can play the banjo and the dulcimore too," Carl said. "But I never had ary of my own."

"Maybe we can find you one some'ers. Well now, I reckon they's just one more question I have to ask you, but it's a important one. Can you read?"

"Yes, sir, that's something I can do."

"The reason I ask is, you may have noticed all those words written out in 'The Painted Stallion.' Even though it's a talkie, there are all them there titles or captions, like in the beginning where it says, all capital letters, 'TO THE HEROES OF YESTERDAY! THOSE PIONEERS WHO BRAVED THE PERILOUS TREK WESTWARD, DEFEATED A HOSTILE WILDERNESS, AND BLAZED A GLORIOUS TRAIL ACROSS THE PAGES OF AMERICAN HISTORY.' Or like each episode has those words about each of the main characters, like 'Dupray—deposed official determined to destroy the American wagon train before it reaches Santa Fe.' Quite a few of these folks can't read, you know, and you probably noticed that some of 'em had to ask whoever was sitting next to 'em to read those things for them, but oftentimes whoever's sitting next to 'em caint read neither. I'd get out there and read those things for everbody myself, but I've got to be making adjustments on the projector early in the show, so what I need is for you to get up in front of everbody and read the captions for us. Do you reckon you could do that?"

"I aint never spoke in front of a crowd afore," Carl declared. "And my voice sure is shaller."

"It'll do." Hoppy wondered how much longer it would take before Carl's voice broke. Sixteen was pretty old to still be talking alto. "And maybe we'll find somebody who'll sell us a cheap banjo or dulcimore." Hoppy stood up and stretched, and declared, "Well, it's time to grab ourself a flop. I'll fix ye a pallet on the floor."

"That's okay, sir. I'll just sleep out here on the ground."

"The hell you will. You'd get drenched with dew and I aint talking about Chism's Dew. You'll be comfy on a soft pallet in the back of the truck."

Hoppy prepared the pallet, and then said, "Well, we'd best shake the dew off the lily, and I aint talking about Chism's Dew neither although that's what caused it, I imagine." He walked away from the truck a good little distance and unbuttoned his britches and started a stream, but Carl didn't join him, as Billy Millwee had once done. When he'd finished and shaken it and turned, he said, "Don't you need to shake your lily too?"

"I reckon not," Carl declared, and after they'd gone to bed, Hoppy couldn't help but wonder if the boy might wet the pallet. He was still awake some time later when he noticed the boy getting up from the pallet and going out. But he didn't return quickly, and Hoppy had to get up and go look for him. He found him at a distance from the truck, on the edge of the deep woods.

"Any of your fairies show up?" Hoppy asked.

"They did, but you scared 'em off."

Chapter six

Carl Whitlow sure did make himself terrible useful right off the bat. Hoppy woke to the smell of coffee making and bacon frying, and right short he had breakfast laid out on the little table, and damned if there wasn't even some fresh cream for the coffee, which cream, Hoppy learned, Carl had obtained from a cow in some nearby pasture. He had also obtained, from an undisclosed nearby source, a straw broom, with which he had given Topper a thorough sweeping, badly needed, not to mention a dusting and a wiping too. Hoppy wondered if Carl had had some help from his fairy friends. He was glad to see everything looking so freshed up but he was abashed that he'd allowed everything to get so crummy in the first place. And the breakfast was just right. How did Carl know the eggs was exactly the way Hoppy liked 'em, over easy? But Carl wouldn't eat with him, hanging back to wait on him like womenfolk did until Hoppy was done. Hoppy wasn't going to make a big deal out of it, because he'd already decided that Carl was a right peculiar feller. For instance, he wore that hat all the time, never took it off, and Hoppy wondered if he slept in it. It was just a old floppy felt fedora, a size too big and the band sweat-stained. It just barely cleared the ceiling. Hoppy knew that before long he'd have to get Carl some new duds, if they could find a store big enough, or else have to order from Sears Roebuck.

After breakfast, before it got too hot inside of Topper, Hoppy gave Carl some lessons on the equipment. The delco was fairly simple, just how to fill the gas tank and how to crank it and start it, and where to oil it, sometimes how to clean the spark plug. But the projector, that big old Western Electric, was something else. Hoppy not only had to point out all the gizmos—the film chutes, the sprockets, the idler, the stripper, the pad roller, the sound gate, the projector head and magazines—but the exciting lamps and how to focus them and how to change them if they burned out. Carl thought it was exciting that the lamps were called exciting lamps, because they were a source of light and as important to the show as the sun is to the earth. Hoppy felt obliged to give Carl a basic lesson on electrons, cathodes, anodes, and photo-electric cells. Carl was a quick study. Hoppy thought of himself, the projectionist, as a weaver, who wove the film from the upper magazine down through all those loops around the various sprockets and through the various gates into the lower magazine. You had to have nimble fingers, and as it turned out Carl's fingers were not only quicker but more sprightly than Hoppy's. The film may pass the light aperture with a controlled intermittent motion, but it must pass the sound aperture with an absolutely steady motion. Before the morning was over, Carl knew as much as Hoppy could learn him about the big projector, and was able to answer correctly any test question that Hoppy could throw at him, for example, what is the purpose of the loops in the film? What does the loop between the intermittent sprocket and the sound sprocket do? Carl said, correctly, it absorbs the intermittent motion of the film.

Before noon dinnertime rolled around, Carl wanted to be excused from the projector so he could start fixing dinner. Hoppy had to explain to him that unlike most folks who labor hard in the fields all morning and require a big dinner to get them through the afternoon, they hadn't done anything in the way of tough manual work, and therefore all that Hoppy ever had for dinner was just lunch: something like a can of Vienna sausages or sardines and a bunch of crackers. But Hoppy was pleased to know that Carl considered himself able to fix a regular dinner if need be. There was still plenty of leftover pie and cake.

When the afternoon heated up, as was his custom, Hoppy moseyed over to the general store's porch to sit and whittle with the other men, but this time he took Carl with him, and introduced him simply as his sidekick. Carl did not own a pocketknife, so Hoppy treated him to one for seventy-nine cents at the store. Obviously, Carl hadn't had much experience with whittling, but he got the hang of it. It doesn't take much skill just to shave the flinders off a cedar stick. Whitlow the whittler, the men jibed. Carl was by far the youngest man there, but he was a big-enough boy that nobody thought nothing of his listening in when the men got around to their favorite pastime of telling dirty tales and jokes. Hoppy watched Carl's face out of the corner of his eye, and some of the bawdy tales clearly didn't mean a gol-darn thing to him, so later, when they were back at Topper and Hoppy was training Carl in the juggling of balls, Hoppy asked him if there was anything he hadn't got in those jokes or tales, and Carl allowed as how he hadn't understood some of the words. What was "nooky"? Was it the same as "tail"? And what was "tearing off a piece" torn off of? The poor kid didn't even know that "screw" was something else besides hardware. But he caught on to juggling real fast, and in fact got to where he could juggle six balls at a time, which was one more than Hoppy could do. Hoppy worked out a routine where they could juggle together and catch each other's balls. When the customers started showing up that evening, Hoppy let Carl sell the tickets, although some of the customers were a little slow or cautious to give their money to a stranger who was just a teenaged kid not wearing a cowboy hat like Hoppy. But with Carl handling the tickets and some of the juggling, Hoppy could devote himself to the magic show, which was his specialty. He hadn't had time today to start giving Carl lessons on magic, teaching him the tricks and the secrets; eventually he wanted to use Carl as a prop in some of the tricks and maybe saw him in half or levitate him or something. Between them they were going to give these folks a real show for their money.

Carl was ready to start the projector showing the first reel of the serial but Hoppy wanted him out front to read the captions for the benefit of all those not blessed with the power of literacy. So Hoppy started "The Painted Stallion" himself and Carl stood up in front of the audience (it wasn't the whole population of the town and wasn't as large as the previous town's) and looked over his shoulder to read the words when they came on the screen. His alto voice was stuttering at first but he got over it, although he couldn't read the capital letters in a capital-letter voice but only a lower-case voice that was not audible beyond the first four or five rows: "trail to empire. westward! the trail to empire! from independence, missouri to santa fe dogged pioneers fought to penetrate a wilderness of savage Indians…. massacres of death…even worse were the white renegades…. outlaws and bandits unscrupulous in their greed…. across the western wilderness swept the legend of the painted stallion…. the rider of the painted stallion…. mysterious figure sworn to defeat outlawry…." At that point there was a close-up of The Rider with her bare arms and shoulders which ought to have been enough to let everybody know that she wasn't an Indian chief but a woman, although most folks never got it until the eighth episode. She shot the first whistling arrow to warn of the ambush and then she and her painted horse leapt over a perilous chasm.

Hoppy let Carl change the reels and he did it so quickly there wasn't time for any restlessness to break out amongst the audience: no time for horseplay or roughhouse and if there was Hoppy was right there to stop it.

After the show was over and everybody was gone, without even being asked Carl moved up and down the rows of seats picking up any trash that had been left behind. When Hoppy thanked him for that, Carl said, "Sir, you know, we could make even more money if we sold things to eat. Candy. Peanuts. Maybe even popcorn."

"Popcorn?" Hoppy said. It was a farfetched idea, eating popcorn at a pitcher show. But the more he thought about it, the more he was inclined to give it a try, so the next day he went over to Bedwell's Store and waited for the candy drummer to show up, the man who came to sell boxes of candy to Art Bedwell, and when the drummer came Hoppy told him he was in the business of showing pitcher shows and that was his truck right over yonder by the schoolhouse, and could he get wholesale prices on candy? He was able to buy a box each of Baby Ruths, Oh Henrys, Butterfingers, and Powerhouses. Art Bedwell sold him, also at wholesale, a thirty-pound sack of peanuts in the shell and a ten-pound sack of kernels of popping corn. Also two hundred little paper pokes for holding the peanuts and the popped corn. Carl suggested getting some salt to sprinkle on the popcorn so Hoppy bought a box. The whole outlay came to nearly twenty dollars, so Carl was going to be up the creek if he was wrong about refreshments for the customers. But that afternoon, among the loungers on the store porch, when the topic of conversation got around to the terrible heat of the day and the awful drought that had afflicted the area, Hoppy offered to bet anyone who cared to make a wager that it would rain this very night, and not only did Art Bedwell bet twenty dollars but various other men made bets ranging from fifty cents to five dollars, for a total of over forty dollars bet against Hoppy that it would not rain.

"Sir," said Carl on the way home from the store, "if we do make any money from a-sellin the candy and stuff, you'll lose it all on that bet, and then some."

"I wish you wouldn't call me 'sir,'" Hoppy said for the eleventeenth time. It made him feel old. "Don't worry. It's a sure bet."

Both bets were sure. At the show that night, at a table set up beside Topper with a sign hanging above it that Carl had painted to proclaim CONCESSIONARY, Carl sold everybody plenty of candy, peanuts and the popcorn that he had popped on the kerosene stove and then properly salted and even buttered with the barter-butter that they had in good supply. Hoppy noticed the distinctive smell of the popcorn and thought it made a nice fragrance for the night air. Hoppy tried some of the popcorn himself and discovered that it gave your hands something to do while you were watching the show. But you don't want your popcorn to get wet, so, as always happened with the second episode of "The Painted Stallion," when the dark skies on the screen opened up and poured down, the skies here in this real world darkened and dumped a goose drownder on them, and everybody rushed their popcorn protectively to the cover of the tarp or of trees or of whatever closed vehicles they might have come in.

The tarp had been spread out from Topper beforehand, and most folks crowded under it for the duration of the downpour, happily munching their popcorn et cetera through the showing of "Hopalong Rides Again." Inside of Topper, dry and cozy, Hoppy shook Carl's hand in congratulation. After the movie, the various men who had made bets with Hoppy were only too glad to pay up, because the rain would benefit their crops and their fields of hay.

And Carl proved his usefulness in another regard: whenever the girls flocked around Hoppy, as they did now, and one or more of them attempted to jine him, or kids came by who would ordinarily have wished to jine him, Carl pointed out to all of them that the position was already filled. So Hoppy was spared having to repeat his usual reasons for not accepting them, and thus was also spared that small but significant bit of self-hatred. In time, everybody in town knew that Hoppy the pitcher shower already had a perfectly capable sidekick who was a darn good juggler and a first-rate popcorn maker.

That night of the rain, the tarp had got too wet to be folded up and used as Carl's mattress, and Hoppy would not hear of Carl's request to sleep in the damp woods among his fairy friends. Despite the rain, the temperature was still very hot and the humidity was awful, so Hoppy, as was his custom on the hottest summer nights, decided to sleep without his clothes, and he offered Carl the use of his cot, saying he could just sleep naked atop a blanket or two on the floor. A nightcap of Chism's Dew made that all the easier. But even after Hoppy had undressed and put out the light, Carl wouldn't take off his own clothes.

The next day, when Hoppy suggested that they go down to the creek with a bar of soap for a dip that might be called a bath, Carl claimed that he just wasn't ready to be taking a bath. "I aint done nothing to work up a sweat," Carl said. In that case, Hoppy decided, he'd give him something to make him sweat. Hoppy went into the village and rounded up the necessary hardware, the loan of the tools, and the lumber to construct an upper bunk over his cot in Topper. He was a good carpenter, and he let Carl do some of the sawing, enough to work up a sweat, and between them they finished the job in a couple of hours. Now Topper had double-decker bunks, and Hoppy also found a mattress and pillow to put over the cords in the upper one. "Now you need a bath, boy," Hoppy pointed out to him. "Let's head for the creek." Carl dutifully followed him as he hiked along the creek until he found a secluded spot hidden amongst willows, but after Hoppy had stripped to the skin and jumped in, Carl said, "I'm sorry, I just caint. I'm just too shy, I reckon. Maybe when I get to know ye better, I could."

"*Know me better?*" Hoppy said, spreading his arms wide. "Here I am in my birthday suit, hiding nothing." But he understood. He went ahead and soaped himself all over and even washed his hair, while Carl just watched. Then he climbed out, toweled off, and handed the bar of soap to Carl. "I'll mosey on back to the truck, and you can rench off your sweat secretly." Hoppy dressed and walked away from the creek, but waited to give Carl time to undress or leastways to take off that hat, and then Hoppy crept back to spy upon him. But he was not there. He must have moved on down the creek a ways.

That night they showed "Borderland," one of the better Hopalong movies, and at eighty-two minutes the longest of them all. In it, Hopalong goes undercover in order to infiltrate a gang of outlaws, and the role allows him, usually a teetotaler, to belly up to the bar and toss back a few, and even to be mean to children, a sacrilege. Of course he redeems himself in the end. After the show was over, Hoppy brought out the demijohn of Chism's Dew, and invited Carl to join him, and after tossing back a few (to Carl's one) he opened up and decided that if Carl wanted to get to know him better he would tell Carl all about himself. So in the space of an hour before a late bedtime, Hoppy gave Carl a rundown of the key events of his wretched life, the roots of his self-loathing, the disappointments with women, the whole woebegone works. "Have you ever done it?" Hoppy asked him. But Carl wanted to know what he was to have done. "Gone to bed with a girl," Hoppy explained. Oh no, Carl said, he hadn't never done nothing like that. "Well, you aint missed anything, I can tell ye," Hoppy said. "You know, the first time I ever tried it, and I wasn't but maybe ten years old and she was the same, I thought I was supposed to put it into her belly-button!" Hoppy laughed. "And I tried and I tried. It took me the longest time to figure out where it was supposed to go." Carl joined Hoppy in his laughter and they drank their drinks and Hoppy was happy. Unlike the real Hopalong Cassidy, who was laughing all the time when he wasn't busy shooting an outlaw, Hoppy never laughed, and his laugh lacked the robust heartiness of his namesake's. "To tell you the truth," Hoppy confessed, "it wasn't until after I had left a couple of gals downright frustrated that I managed to figure out, all on my own, without any help from them, that gals is supposed to enjoy the whole business theirselfs and even have some kind of little fit at the end of it. Did you know that? Did you know that gals have fits in the last part of doing it?"

Carl gave his head a modest nod. "I've heared tell of it," he admitted.

"Let me show you something," Hoppy said. He got out his special reel called "Assortment," and turned the projector to face the wall, the part of the bare wall he had painted white with alabastine to make a small screen. He ran the reel through the projector until he found the place he was looking for, then fired up the delco and turned on the projector, and there on the screen was a scene that was one of his favorites because, unlike so many of the displays of sexual activity, it seemed to record the female's blissful reaction, mounting pleasure, and the throes of her fit. Of course the film was silent but you could tell from the woman's face and mouth that she was hollering her head off. Her back arched up and her whole body shook like an earthquake.

For the longest time Carl couldn't say a word, maybe because his mouth was too far open. Then he finally said, "Well I never." He sucked in a deep breath and said, "Boy. Gracious to heavens. Where on earth did you get this pitcher show?"

"A feller in Memphis sold it to me," Hoppy said, "for my own personal use. And now for yours, too, if you'd keer to watch more of it."

Hoppy showed a few more scenes, including the one with the German shepherd. He stole a glance towards Carl's crotch, to see if perhaps he was getting him a bulge in his britches, but it was too dark to tell. Hoppy himself, perhaps because of the effect of watching "Assortment" in the company of another feller, was feeling aroused.

Finally he was moved to ask, "What does watching this do to ye? Are you het up? Or does it bother ye some?"

"Never in my born days," Carl said, "did I ever imagine there was such things."

"Tell ye what," Hoppy suggested, "next time some of them gals comes flocking around, why, you just take your pick, and have your way with her."

"It's you they're after," Carl said. "Not me."

"We'll have to get you a hat like mine. And some new clothes. Let's us run down to Clarksville tomorrow. It aint but twenty mile or so, and they've got stores. And we've got money."

"Hoppy," Carl wanted to know, "do folks really do all them things? And with dogs even? And with their mouths and all? And all those positions?"

"If it's on the screen, you have to believe it," Hoppy said. It was getting on well past bedtime, so Hoppy finally yawned and asked, "Do you want the bottom? Or do you want to get on top?"

Carl giggled when he realized that Hoppy was talking about their bunks.

Chapter seven

I t's all downhill to Clarksville but the road twists and turns like
crazy, with such switchbacks as would make you think you're going
the way you came. Hoppy had taken the precaution of removing
the projector's exciting lamps, just so they wouldn't get jostled all
to hell.

He was in a good mood. Carl had fixed pancakes for their
breakfast, with blueberries in 'em, and Hoppy had eaten a whole
stack. All was right with the world…except Hoppy had to grip the
steering wheel tightly with both hands, and he wanted a cigarette
but couldn't stop to roll one, let alone put it in and out of his mouth.
"Could you roll me a cigarette?" he asked his companion.

The little poke of Bugler had its tab dangling from his breast
pocket, and Carl reached over to pluck it out and get the papers that
was under its band. "I never rolled one afore," he declared, "but I
reckon I've seen you do it so many times that I can probably do it
myself."

And sure enough, Carl did a pretty fair job of cradling a
paper in his fingers, sprinkling the Bugler all along it, rolling it and
licking it and twisting the end. The boy sure was handy. He even lit

the cigarette for Hoppy and placed it in his mouth so he could get a good draw on it.

"You ort to try one yourself," Hoppy suggested. "Won't kill ye, and I reckon you're old enough."

"One time I dipped some snuff," Carl declared, "but I just don't hanker after the taste of terbacker."

Hoppy was content to let the cigarette dangle from his lip as he drove, but whenever he wanted it taken out, like when the ashes needed to be tapped off, all he had to do was nod his head and Carl would pluck it from his mouth. Hoppy reflected that he wanted to learn Carl how to drive ole Topper, but not on this terrible dirt road. Besides the hairpin curves, there were some mean chuckholes and ruts that were jouncing the hell out of Topper, and wrenching the steering wheel beneath Hoppy's tight two-handed grip.

In fact, they weren't halfway to Clarksville when Topper hit a chuckhole so bad it knocked Hoppy's cigarette right smack out of his mouth. The cigarette landed on the seat between him and Carl. Hoppy had to keep his eyes on the crazy road to keep Topper from shooting off of it, and he couldn't make out what happened, but apparently that damn cigarette burned right through the leatherette seat and ignited the stuffing of the seat, and before they knew it there was a blaze a-flaming up.

"Godalmighty!" Hoppy exclaimed, struggling to bring Topper to a halt. "Piss on it, Carl! Piss on it!"

But Carl disobeyed him. Carl did not piss on the fire, which was starting to rage. Topper's rear wheels, locked tight, were clawing into the dirt. "Did you hear me?" Hoppy demanded. "Yank out your pecker and piss on the fucking fire!"

Carl burst into such tears as would have doused the fire if it were not out of control. "I don't have nothing to piss with!" he cried. "I don't have no pecker."

Hoppy at last had the truck motionless, and pulled up the handbrake, then stood on the running board and started in to pissing on the fire himself, and soon had it put out, but became suddenly and curiously very self-conscious. Was he maybe exposing his member to a member of the opposite sex? His member wasn't anything to be ashamed of, but it was a member, after all, even though Carl had seen it on a number of occasions, like yesterday's dip at the creek. But was this *Carl*?

When the fire was completely out, although the stink of his piss was magnified by being mixed with smoldering seat-stuffing, Hoppy sat and stared at Carl for a little while longer, long enough to ask, "What happened to your pecker? Did it get hacked off or something?"

Carl was still sobbing. "I never had none to start out with." His voice had changed from alto to soprano.

Hoppy reached over and grabbed Carl's hat and yanked it off, and her hair cascaded down her neck. "What's your real name, gal?" he asked, gently.

"Sharline," she said.

Even her eyes, out from under the shadow of the hat's brim, were suddenly more feminine, and sort of pert. "How come you've been deceiving me?" Hoppy wanted to know.

She was still weeping but not sobbing. "You wouldn't never of kept me if you'd known I was a gal. Ila Fay's much better than me, but you turned her away."

"Ila Fay aint near as pretty as you," Hoppy said.

"Thank ye kindly, sir. But you know you wouldn't have let me jine ye iffen ye'd thought I was a gal, now would ye?"

She was sure right about that. But now that she was revealed for the young lady she actually was, after all these days and nights they'd spent together, and all her usefulness to him, how was he going to get rid of her? Hoppy found himself blushing, thinking of what he had done in her presence, exposed his naked body, exposed his private reel "Assortment," belched and farted too maybe, and even cussed words that one doesn't speak in the presence of a female. And last night he had slept with her beneath him! Or, that is, after going to all that trouble making that double-deck bunk, he had taken the upper bunk because it was hotter up there and he slept naked and she didn't. How could he possibly go on sleeping that way? What was he going to do with her? Her toesack with all her meager belongings was still back there in the house part of Topper, and maybe he could get it and just put her out right here and now beside the road. No, that would be unkind, and he'd really hate himself for it. Maybe he ought to take her on to Clarksville and turn her over to the sheriff…but he could get himself in trouble if it looked like he had abducted her or something.

He was in a hell of a tight spot. Driving on down the road, he remarked, "I was a-fixing to buy ye a new pair of overalls. But it looks like maybe I'd better buy ye a dress instead, don't it?"

"You aint obliged to buy me nothing," she said.

"Oh yeah I am too," he said. "All the money you've earned, selling that candy and popcorn and such. All the work and help you've done for me."

"I'd just as soon have overalls," she declared. "You'd best be saving every cent to pay for that other projector."

Hoppy was touched at her thoughtfulness, and reckoned that she might be worth keeping. He wondered what other lies she'd told him, and on the rest of the drive into Clarksville, easier and smoother once they were down out of the mountains, he asked her to lay her soul bare and correct whatever other misconceptions he'd formed of her. For one thing, she wasn't sixteen, as Carl had supposedly been, but seventeen going-on-eighteen in another month or so. For another thing, Clemmie Whitlow wasn't her aunt but her mother, although they had hardly been on speaking terms with each other. Ila Fay wasn't exactly her friend, but she had agreed, in the event that Sharline was able to leave town with Hoppy, to break the news to Sharline's mother, not telling her however who Sharline had left town with but just saying that she had run away from home and would be all right. "She really don't give a damn where I went or who I went with," Sharline declared. "She rued the day I was born." All that stuff about fairies was true. Sharline really did have a lot of woodfolk little people who were her only friends. Until now. Hoppy was the first real friend she'd ever had.

"How come I never saw you when I was playing that town?" Hoppy wanted to know.

"You did. You looked right at me several times, and once you even smiled real big at me. But of course I was wearing a dress."

As it turned out, Clarksville had only one store that was big enough to carry a line of ladies' dresses, but that was good enough. To watch Sharline looking at Clarksville, you'd think he had taken her to St. Louis or even Chicago. She had never dreamed there would be a place with so many buildings in one spot, and that big courthouse, and railroad tracks with a real train on 'em! Before he took her into the store he just drove around town for a while, letting her soak it all in, getting a taste of urban life.

The little department store where he took her also filled her with such awe he had to nudge her to close her mouth. She couldn't believe that there were *racks* of store-boughten ready-made apparel, and the ladies' dresses was so lovely she never could make up her mind. The store clerk kind of sneered at Sharline's overalls, and Hoppy decided to get her an everyday dress too, one that she could put on right here and now to get out of those overalls, which she did, in the dressing room. When she came back from the dressing room with the old overalls folded up, she also had a stretch of a tire's inner-tube, which, she explained in a whisper to him, she had been wearing wrapped around her bosom in order to flatten her breasts, which, now freed, bulged against the calico cotton of her new dress. Then he also let her pick out another everyday dress for good measure before picking out her dress-up dress. Then he got her some nice shoes, and a purse. As well as some unmentionables, while he turned his back. Hoppy suddenly realized that it wouldn't do when they got back to the town they were playing for him to try to explain that he'd left town with a feller and returned with a gal, so he decided they'd best keep ole Carl around for the rest of the week until they got to a new town, and he bought the poor kid some good overalls. Sharline, protesting the expense, picked out a pair, and a work shirt to go with the overalls. The last thing he bought her was a ten-gallon hat like his own to keep her hair up in and eventually to wear as a complement to his Hopalong Cassidy hat. The whole works came to nearly sixty dollars. Sharline grabbed his arm and said, "*I don't know how to thank you.*" You already have, he said.

Before heading on back up the road, he treated her to lunch at a real café on the town square. It was the first time she'd ever held a menu. He suggested the steak, and had one himself. They barely had room for the cream pie afterwards.

After lunch he drove her around the square and they parked to take a look at The Logan, a genuine pitcher show theater. It wasn't open this early in the day, but they could see through the big door's round windows into the lobby, and they could read the posters for the current attraction, "Lost Horizon" with Ronald Colman and Jane Wyatt, and the coming attractions, including a comedy called "Topper" with Cary Grant. Hoppy wished he could take Sharline to the real pitcher show, just so's she could find out there were pitcher shows that didn't have horses in them, and in which you could sit with back support and a roof over your head.

She smiled all the way home, or, not really home but just the place where they'd be showing pitcher shows for a couple more nights. She really looked pretty in that dress. Were her good looks tying his tongue? He found himself unable to think of things to say to her. He stole glances at her whenever he could take his eyes off the road. There was something so out of this world about the fact that she was a female. Also it was out of this world that his good friend Carl no longer existed, almost as if he had died, and that made Hoppy a bit sad.

Thus he was almost relieved to bring Carl back for the duration of their stay at that town. Before they got there, he stopped and parked along the road so Sharline could climb into the house part of Topper and change from her pretty dress into the new overalls. She wrapped that inner-tube around her bosom again too. And then pushed her hair up into her new ten-gallon hat. "Howdy, Carl," Hoppy said to her. "Mighty proud to see ye again."

When they arrived at the schoolhouse yard where they'd been parking Topper, Hoppy was dismayed to see that his screen had been removed from the side of the schoolhouse and there were a group of men erecting poles and sticks and brush into a sort of "roof" over the seats his audience had sat upon. At first the brush pile struck Hoppy as the makings of a bonfire, and he wondered if the folks of this town were a-fixing to smoke him out. But then he recognized one of the men, not a local townsman but that circuit-riding preacher, Brother

Emmett Binns, with whom he'd had previous run-ins. Binns was dressed differently from the other men, all of them wearing farmers' work clothes and him in a suit and tie and black preacher's hat.

"Doggone," Hoppy said to Carl, or Sharline. "Looks like they're fixing to put up a brush arbor." She nodded as if she knew what he was talking about, so he needed to ask, "Do you know what a brush arbor is?"

"Yeah," she said. "Brother Binns put one up in our town last year. But he waited until after you'd gone. He even told us that was his intention, not to interfere with your wicked pitcher shows."

You didn't see brush arbors very much any more, but in the old days they was a common fixture of the revival circuit, when one or more preachers would hold weekday as well as Sunday meetings, the purpose of the brush being to shield the congregation from the hot midsummer sun, although some brush arbors met at night too, and always there was a lot of musical accompaniment for gospel singing with fiddles, mandolins, banjos, guitars, and even a piano.

Hoppy parked Topper where it had been before, and they got out and approached the men. "Howdy, Binns," Hoppy said. "Couldn't you have waited a couple of more days until we were finished?"

"Brother Boyd," Binns said, although he ought to have known that Hoppy wasn't of any religion, "all the folks hereabouts got the idee that you had done gone away anyhow."

Binns was a slick character, reminding Hoppy more of a traveling salesman than a minister of the gospel. "Heck, we jist took a run down to Clarksville to do some shopping. Didn't you see my screen a-hanging on the schoolhouse? You don't think I'd go off without my screen, do ye?"

"No telling what you fly-by-night fellers might do," Binns said. "Anyhow, these folks are ready for the Word of God, aint ye, brethren?" He looked around at the other men, and a few of them nodded their heads in agreement. Binns went on, "Everbody hereabouts is ready for an old-time brush arbor, which as you can see we're putting up."

"You're putting it up right over the seats for my pitcher show," Hoppy pointed out.

"Do you own them seats?" Binns asked. "Didn't you just throw 'em together out of boards and tomater crates that you found around here? Them seats belong to the Lord now."

Hoppy couldn't think of a quick retort to that, so he was surprised that his assistant could. "<u>Emmett Binns</u>," Carl said, "you've always been liable to just take whatever you please, whether it belongs to ye or not."

Brother Binns glowered at Carl, or Sharline, and looked him or her all over, and then peered closely at his or her face. "Well as I live and breathe," he said. "If it aint <u>Sharline Whitlow</u>! Gal, what are ye decked out in them men's togs for? And what are ye doing over here so far from home? Does your maw know you've took up with Landon Boyd?"

Carl's voice changed into Sharline's, right there in front of those men who were listening. "I'm his assistant," she said. "I'm part of the show. I can juggle and do magic tricks and norate the words on the screen and sell candy and popcorn and make myself useful in all kinds of ways."

"I'll bet," said Brother Binns. "And I'll bet you're living in sin with him right there in that truck-house thing."

"No, I aint, but I'd sure rather do it with him than with you!"

Brother Binns blushed; he got pretty red in the face, and looked nervously around at the other men and then lowered his booming voice. "Maybe we ought to be elsewhere," he said.

"The elsewhere you ought to be is plumb out of this town," she said.

"Or leastways," Hoppy suggested, "wait a couple of nights until we've finished our run of pitcher shows."

Brother Binns transferred his glower from Sharline to Hoppy. He could only look hard at him for a long little spell, trying to think of something to say. "Matter of fact," he finally said, not in his booming voice but just in a growl that Hoppy and Sharline could hear, "I was just about to suggest that you and me share this brush arbor until such time as your shows is over. You use it by night, I use it by day. But on second thought, that would be hypocrisy, since one thing I aim to do is preach against your sinful entertainments, to show these good folks that watching pitcher shows is not only against Scripture, it's not only a waste of their hard-earned nickels and dimes, it's also an *indolence* that is an abomination unto the Lord!" His voice rose with these last words, and he continued so everyone could hear, "When I get through with you, Boyd, they won't be a soul in this country who'd spend a penny to watch one of your shows!" His voice dropped again, "Now if you'll excuse me, I've got to help these good folks finish this here brush arbor." He turned to go, but turned back, almost whispering, "Listen. I don't know what she has told you, or what she plans to tell you, about me, but just so's you'd know, Sharline Whitlow don't live in this world, she lives only in her imagination."

He stormed off to rejoin the work on the brush arbor.

Sharline wasn't looking indignant. She had a big smile on her face. But she wasn't looking at Hoppy either. Maybe she was avoiding his eyes. Maybe she was just looking off into the distance, as if she might spot some of her elves to come and help her. Then she reached up and gripped the brim of her new ten-gallon hat and pulled the hat off, allowing her long hair to spill down across her shoulders, then she put the hat back on. She glanced at Hoppy. "I guess I aint fooling nobody," she said. And she climbed up into the back of Topper, and shut the door behind her.

Chapter eight

He seriously began to doubt that he ever would be able to get to sleep. It was bad enough, all the things on his mind that wouldn't dare let him alone; it was terrible that sleeping beneath him was a gal. Well, not *beneath* in the sense of underneath his own self, but down below in the lower bunk. And not terrible neither, not *because* she was a gal, but he was a feller and had never in his whole life slept in the same room, let alone the same bed, even if it was a double decker, with a gal. Those nights she'd slept down there as Carl didn't count, did they? And he wasn't too awfully sure that she was sleeping. He listened for her breathing, to see if it was regular, but couldn't make it out amidst the chorus of night sounds: crickets, tree frogs, katydids, cicadas, nightingales, whatever. For all he knew she might've snuck out in the dark to spend the night with her fairy friends…or even with Preacher Binns. He hadn't yet managed to learn the details of whatever had once transpired betwixt the two of them. He had hoped before bedtime to worm the truth out of her, but he'd been loath to broach the matter, and anyhow he couldn't be certain that whatever she told him would be the truth. Hadn't Binns said that she lived only in her imagination? *Maybe she's only imagining me,*

Hoppy thought, just one amongst a thousand rapid-fire thoughts that flitted through his sleepless skull; *Maybe I don't even exist except in her fancy.* He tried rolling over on his back and cradling his clasped hands under the back of his head. That was just a little more comfortable. It was awful hot, even with Topper's windows and the door wide open. Under ordinary circumstances in such heat Hoppy would be sleeping bare-ass naked, but of course he wouldn't dare strip down to nothing in her presence. And she was sleeping—if she was sleeping—in her slip, a silky thing she'd picked out in Clarksville that covered her up pretty well, although the glimpse he'd caught of her before putting out the lamp was like as if she had nothing on, her curves and all. It was some kind of wonder that they had wordlessly agreed to go on sleeping together, or, not together of course in *that* sense but in such proximity to each other. There was something terribly exciting about the situation, which was another contributing factor to Hoppy's sleeplessness. The thought that she was a real pretty gal and she was right down there below him made it impossible for his swollen member to unswell.

The only way he could force his busy mind to stop thinking about her was to rehash some of the items of the afternoon and evening. Fortunately there were enough citizens of the town who were caught up in the progress of the serial "The Painted Stallion"—of the wagon train on its way to Santa Fe—who wanted to know how it all came out, especially the latest cliff-hanger, and even wanted to buy some more of the popcorn, which the preacher had never thought to offer for sale at a brush arbor camp meeting, nor had any brush arbor ever had a concessionary attached to it. Even though the brush arbor overhead made viewing of the screen impossible from some of the seats, certain influential men of the town, prodded perhaps by their womenfolk and children, had persuaded Brother Binns to allow the brush arbor to be used during the evenings for the purpose of the pitcher shows.

Binns had been adamant at first. Even though he had told Sharline the year before that he'd waited until Hoppy's shows had left town in order to hold his meeting at her town, the real reason for that hadn't been out of any respect for Hoppy or even politeness but just the fear that he wouldn't be able to compete with the pitcher shows. And now, even though his brush arbor meetings were strictly daytime, he didn't cotton to the notion of sharing the meeting-ground with a worldly, sinful pitcher show. One of the men—in fact it was Art Bedwell, who ran the general store and was the upstandingest citizen in town—said to him, "Brother Binns, look at it this-away: by the time you get done with your service, and everbody has had their fill of singing and shouting and salvation and all, nobody will be able to stay awake through the pitcher show!" And all the other men laughed, Hoppy too, though he was mildly worried about the truth of Art's conjecture.

Brother Binns had scratched his chin and after a while had said, "I reckon we might tolerate just a couple more nights of pitcher shows." So the men had helped Hoppy put his screen back up on the side of the schoolhouse. The men also had rolled and lifted an old upright piano out of the schoolhouse and set it up beside the pulpit of the brush arbor for the use of the musicians who would be playing for the service.

When Sharline had come out of Topper again, she had been Sharline, not Carl, dressed in one of her pretty new dresses and her nice new shoes, and her long hair flowing out from beneath the ten-gallon hat, her one silent acknowledgment that she was still, like her boss Hoppy, a pitcher shower.

"No sense in trying to fool nobody no more," she had remarked to Hoppy. And then she had sat herself down at that piano and had commenced a-playing, and you never heard nothing like it. Hoppy had truly regretted that this whole story is just in black and white, because that music Sharline played on that piano had been full of reds and golds and blues and greens. And her beautiful long hair—its color, which wasn't dark but wasn't light neither, just couldn't be revealed in black and white. She had still been a-playing the piano when the first customers of the night showed up for the pitcher show, and they had all gathered around the piano to listen. Even Brother Binns had showed up. She had stopped playing in order to do her usual chores: selling tickets, juggling, the magic (and somehow a female magician's assistant is much more magical than a male), making and selling popcorn, starting the projector, and reading out the captions for the benefit of the illiterate. Hoppy had wondered just how he had ever managed to get along without her. She was just as efficient as Carl had been…and lots better-looking to boot. And now that musicianship had been added to her talents, she was absolutely indispensable.

To anyone who might have asked her, as some of them had done, "Wasn't you a feller last time I seen ye?" she had said by way of answer, "That there 'Indian chief' on the painted stallion is not a feller neither." And that had been the night, coincidentally and wondrously, that the episode of "The Painted Stallion" had made it clear that the magical guardian angel of the wagon train, despite her headdress and other Indian garb, was a woman.

Now Hoppy sighed, and realized that being on his back wasn't the best position for sleeping. He rolled over and squirmed a bit to get into a better sleeping position, and it caused the whole frame of the bed-bunk to shake. "Landon," she said, just barely audible above the crickets and other night critters.

"Yeah?" he said, just a little more audible.

"Are you awake?"

"Naw, I'm dead to the world," he said, and chuckled. "How about you?"

"Out like a lamp." She giggled. "But I must be talking in my sleep."

"Go right ahead," he said. "I'm a-listening to ye in my dreams."

But she did not say anything else for a while. Maybe he was just a-dreaming. If so, he wished that something noteworthy might happen. Most of his dreams didn't have any talking in them. And here she was, by and by, with the next thing she was fixing to say: "I guess you're wondering if Emmett Binns ever done anything to me."

Hoppy cleared his throat. "The thought has crossed my mind. Not that it's none of my business."

Another long silence from her. Then she said, "Not that he didn't try. Boy, did he ever try." Hoppy could hear her sighing over the memories. "But like he said, I don't live in this world, I only live in my imagination. Well, if that's true, and it aint, I confess to you that I have imagined what Emmett Binns could have done to me. He's not bad-looking, you know. And he's a great talker. Wait till you hear one of his sermons. And he did actually do Ila Fay Woodrum, and I had to listen to her brag about it and describe it and get me all hot with her words so that I did have to have some little make-beliefs of my own that he might have done me too. But he never did. That's the honest truth. You have to believe me."

"I believe you."

"I can't even imagine what it's like. If I live only in my imagination, then I must be dead as far as that's concerned, because I can't even begin to dream up what-all it would feel like."

Hoppy coughed. Whatever inclination he had for attempting to try to educate her was undone by the plain truth that he had no idea whatsoever of what it felt like to a woman, and even a pretty incomplete notion of what it ought to feel like to a man. He coughed again, and could only say, "Well."

"Ila Fay tried her best to tell me, and she said I could take a cucumber and warm it up in the oven and maybe get some notion of what it's like, but a cucumber without any feller attached to it just wouldn't be right, now would it?"

All Hoppy could think of to comment was: "I reckon not."

"Yours doesn't look anything atall like a cucumber anyhow," she said.

Hoppy assumed that was a compliment, but was embarrassed at the recollection of the number of times she, or rather Carl, had seen his equipment.

There was such a long silence, except for the chorus of night critters (and Hoppy knew they were making all that noise purely and simply to make known their desires), that Hoppy began to wonder if she might have finally fallen asleep. But eventually she spoke again. "You'll recollect I was listening when Ila Fay offered to do it with you and you turned her down on account of being a 'no-man,' you said. You told her you just wasn't able. But she didn't know what you meant, and I don't know what you meant. Can you tell me?"

Hoppy felt he owed it to her at least to make an effort to explain. He had already told her, when she was Carl, about his sense of leaving several females frustrated because he hadn't been able to make them experience the fit or attack which comes at the end of the deal. Now he said to her, "Last night I showed ye that blue movie of mine, the little reel called 'Assortment.' Of course I thought I was showing it to Carl, and I would never have showed it to ye iffen I'd known ye was a gal. Anyhow, you recall how some of them gals in those scenes would get so carried away, from all the inning-and-outing that the fellers was doing, that they'd finally just explode with a big spasm of delight? Well, I just aint able to keep on inning-and-outing long enough to give any gal that pleasure."

There was another long silence from down below, while Hoppy stewed in his self-loathing, before her words drifted up: "How come? Do you get winded or tired out?"

"Naw, but the rapture of it makes me shoot off my jism too soon, and once that happens I get too limp to keep on." He knew he was blushing, but it was dark and she couldn't see him from down below nohow.

"What's 'jism'?"

"Didn't Ila Fay never tell you about that? Didn't nobody never explain to you how babies gets made?"

"You must think I'm real stupid."

"Sharline, I don't think you're the least bit stupid. But most gals your age has got some notion of all the juices involved in the breeding of male and female."

"Could you show me what jism looks like?"

Maybe I don't even exist except in her fancy, Hoppy allowed, once again. She was having a weird dream and he was in it, and this was the part where he was supposed to whack off with his right and pour it into the palm of his left for her inspection. As quick as he was on the trigger, it oughtn't to take more than fifteen seconds of whacking. He hated himself because he wasn't bright enough to think of the idea of suggesting to her certain ways she might help produce the jism. That would come later in sad hindsight. "We'd have to get up and light the lamp for you to see," he said. "I could just try and tell ye. It kind of looks like buttermilk."

"Oh," she said. "It's not red like blood?"

"Naw, it's fairly white." He remembered that his "Assortment" contained one scene in which the feller's jism landed on the gal's bosom, and he was tempted to offer to show that scene to her. But somehow the thought of watching a stag film in the company of a doe was awkward, and nearly all the scenes showed how the fellers were able to go on and on and on forever before they shot off. Hoppy lost himself in meditation upon this woeful inadequacy of his and did not even notice that there were no further questions or comments from his audience down below. When at length he remembered that he'd been engaged in a spicy conversation with a member of the opposite sex, he bethought himself that perhaps she had at last drifted off into the land of Nod, and he certainly felt like joining her there. He yawned noisily, smacked his lips, rolled over again toward the wall, cradled his head in one arm, shut his eyes tight and tried his best trick for falling asleep: emptying his head of all thought. After a long while a thought forced itself upon him, and he realized he had never wished her a good night.

He whispered, although it seemed the chorus of night critters was quieting, as if they had fallen asleep themselves or were simply giving up in their efforts to advertise their horniness. "Good night, Sharline. You sure do play the pianer awful purty."

She did not even say, "Why, thank ye kindly." Or even "Good night yourself." She did not say anything, and for a while he bounced back and forth between two thoughts: one, she was already on the seventh of her forty winks and completely out, or two, something he'd said about jism might have offended her. Maybe she didn't care for buttermilk. He lay there for a long, long time before a third possibility hit him: she wasn't even there. "Sharline!" he said, not whispering but loud enough to wake the dead. It did not wake her. He climbed down off his upper bunk and felt around on her bunk but there was no body in it. He went to the door and looked out. Maybe she was just out there somewheres attending a call of nature. He was tempted to put on his pants and shoes and go off looking for her but he didn't bother getting dressed, he simply went on out there. He'd spent most of his childhood going barefoot, so it didn't bother his feet none. There was a moon, not full but waxing, and he could see well enough not to trip over anything. He walked all around the schoolhouse and even looked into the girls' outhouse (the boys didn't have one, as usual). He wandered through the brush arbor, which made him think of Emmett Binns and made him wonder if possibly Sharline had sneaked off to join the man. Where was Binns staying, anyhow? Probably with the Bedwell's in the town's best and biggest house, across the road from the general store. Unmindful that he was dressed only in his underclothes, Hoppy went to the Bedwell's house and walked around it. Dogs barked at him, and he retreated, but not before convincing himself there were no lights in the Bedwell house, nor anybody up.

Some time had passed, and it occurred to him she might have returned to Topper and gone back to bed, and he checked there, but she wasn't home yet. As long as he was awake, he fished his tobacco pouch out of his shirt pocket and rolled himself a cigarette, and while smoking it he recalled how Sharline on the first night—or rather Carl—had talked about fairies, and Hoppy had found him or her in the edge of the woods. So Hoppy explored the tree-line and for a while he stared off up the forested mountainside. The woods were shrouded in mist or fog, which seemed to glitter in the moonlight and amongst those shimmerings he caught a glimpse of what seemed to be a figure…or two or three. Nothing except heights had ever scared Hoppy since he was a little kid, but there was something spooky about those figures, whatever they were, which made Hoppy very reluctant to approach them. But he did, plunging into the woods and climbing the mountainside. Soon the various figures had merged into only one, which he clearly perceived now as the silken slip she was wearing (which was light pink, but in the black and white of this story was only a nice pale sepia). "Sharline," he said.

Then it seemed as if she divided into two or three other girls in slips, who drifted off into the mists. But there was one left, and that was her, and that was enough. And she spoke. "You scared me."

"You scared *me*," he said. "What in heck are you doing out here?"

"Dancing with my friends," she said.

"Your fairy friends?"

78

"If that's what you want to call 'em."

"I thought they were only Carl's friends."

"But I'm Carl."

"Why did you leave, without ary word to me?"

"All that talk we was doing. It just made me get too het up and light."

"So you came up here to cool down?"

"Sort of. My friends helped me."

"How'd they do that?"

"They helped me have that 'big spasm of delight' you was talking about."

"Oh. Did ye actually, now? How was it?"

"Just swell. Everything around me, all these woods, everything, just quit, just stopped being, and I had the all-overs right powerful."

"*All-overs,* huh? I reckon that's a good way to put it. Did your friends show you what jism looks like?"

"They don't have any."

"Why not? Aint some of them fairies fellers?"

"No, they're not males or females."

"Huh? Then how did they make you come?"

"*Come?*"

"That's what it's called, that all-overs business."

"It was more like went than came."

"Then how did they make you went if they don't have any tallywhackers?"

"Is that what you call them?"

"Or whatever. Peters. Peckers. Prides. Pricks. Privates. Penises."

"You don't have to have one of those to come. Or to help someone else get over the mountain."

"Who told you that?"

"They did. My friends. I told them about you, and they said your problem is that you live inside of your penis."

"My, my. Is that what they said? Well, that sure is clever of 'em, even if I aint so sure just what it means. It don't even sound like something you could make up out of your own fine head."

"But they also told me I ought to be happy because you do keer so much about me that what bothers ye most is the thought your penis would let ye down so's you couldn't satisfy me. They said that most fellers don't even keer about whether their gals can come or not. They said you feel you'd be a-cheating me if you came and I didn't. They said most fellers just want to get their own pleasure without giving any."

"They said all that? Well, I tell ye, they sound like they've got a good head on their shoulders."

"They told me to ask you how many times you've been kissed."

"Me? Well, come to think on it, that there is something I haven't yet tried."

"You went to bed with two or three gals but never kissed one?"

"I reckon it never crossed my mind. Nor theirs."

"Landon. Kiss me."

Chapter nine

Bright and early the next morning, folks started coming from all over. Word must've spread awful fast, and it made him jealous to think that all these folks were coming primarily to camp out for the brush arbor camp meeting, not to attend the pitcher shows, although Sharline tried to console him in that suspicion by pointing out that probably it was a combination of the two attractions: that those folks were coming to camp out for the brush arbor, sure, but they were also coming because they'd heard that the camp meeting would be including pitcher shows at night.

"Has anybody ever camped out for a pitcher show?" she asked him. It was one of these here *rhetorical* questions that he didn't have to answer, although the answer was no, nobody had ever been known to camp out for pitcher shows, whereas at camp meetings it was traditional for whole families to come into town with their wagons loaded up with all the supplies they'd need, plus a tent of some sort. The population of this town seemed to double overnight, the same night that he and Sharline had become more than just friends, had in fact become a twosome, and had slept so late that when they finally did step out of Topper it was to discover that dozens of strangers were setting up their tents around the perimeter of the brush arbor. Most of these weren't really *tent* tents, that is, they weren't made of canvas ducking or nothing, but just crude shelters of some kind, boards and stuff thrown together, more likely tied than nailed, that would make sleeping places for a family. It looked like a gold rush town or something, and a whole bunch of little kids was already surrounding Topper, so that when Hoppy put on his ten-gallon and stepped down from Topper, one of the kids asked him, "Are you the preacher?"

"No, I'm just the pitcher shower," Hoppy replied. He caught sight of Emmett Binns moving among the settlers of this tent city, and pointed to him. "That there's the preacher right over yonder, in the fancy suit."

But the kids did not leave. Another one asked, "What's a pitcher shower?"

"A man who shows moving pitchers," Hoppy answered. These kids all looked like they were from the deepest, darkest hollers of the mountains.

"What's a moving pitcher?" they wanted to know.

Sharline, dressed real pretty with her hair brushed nice, came down out of Topper. "Just wait till you see," she told them. She swept her hand across the screen tacked to the side of the schoolhouse. "You'll see horses a-galloping, and injuns a-whooping, and six-shooters a-blazing, and mountains much mightier than these."

"The heck you say!" one of them said. "How do you get the pitchers up there? How do you make 'em *move*?"

Sharline pointed to the square hole in the back end of Topper, beyond which stood the projector, and attempted to explain what a projector was, and Hoppy smiled with admiration and no little pride as his girlfriend put in plain words the complicated mechanics of the cinema. Hoppy realized she would make a good school teacher if they ever had to give up traveling and go to work for a living.

But the kids weren't completely satisfied. "Show us a pitcher!" they requested.

"It's daylight now," she observed. "We'll have to wait until dark."

"*Huh?* How can we see the pitchers in the *dark?*"

These kids and their families, Hoppy and Sharline were to discover, had come to town from the most remote parts of Johnson and Franklin counties; for some of the younger ones, it was their first trip to a town of any size. All of them, grown-ups too, were thrilled with what amounted to a holiday, at least a holiday from the backbreaking work of their poor homesteads in the far hollers.

Groups of people were already singing hymns, although they were conflicting with each other: one group here was singing "I'm Coming, Lord" while another group over there was singing "Happy Am I" and although both were in 4/4 time the melodies clashed.

Emmett Binns came up and said, "Sister Sharline, hon, we need you to play the piano. Do you know 'We'll Work till Jesus Comes'?"

"Hum a little of it and I'll pick it up," she said, and left Topper and Hoppy to go up to the piano beside the pulpit.

Hoppy wasn't none too happy to lose his assistant to the religious crowd, but he enjoyed watching and listening as her playing brought the whole bunch of them together in singing the same song, without conflict. Soon she was joined by a pair of fiddlers, a banjoist, a mandolinist, a dulcimoron, and three guitarists. And she hadn't even had breakfast yet, although most of these people were getting ready for dinner. As he listened to the music, Hoppy let his mind back up to the enchantments of the night before. You know, it was hard *not* to believe in those fairies she claimed she'd talked with and cavorted with. He didn't see how she, or any gal, could have made up some of the stuff they had told her. He still didn't quite understand what they'd meant by him living inside of his tallywhacker, but it was certainly something to think about, and, in fact, when he and Sharline had later attempted to become one, he had tried to get outside of his tallywhacker so to speak, that is, he had endeavored to quit thinking of that pestiferous appendage as a part of himself, or at least not the dominant part of himself during the firm but gentle moments of taking Sharline's virginity. And sure enough, it seemed to him, at least it *seemed* to him, that he had been able to last a little longer than he expected to, not nearly long enough to give her any satisfaction but not so all-fired speedy as to mortify him. He hadn't hated himself at all, and they had drifted off together to the land of Nod all entwined. Yes, there probably really were some sort of fairies out yonder in the woods, and he wouldn't be at all surprised if he eventually met up with some of them himself, if he managed to stick with Sharline long enough.

Later he took Sharline a plate he filled from the dinner-on-the-grounds, a feast which, he discovered, would be a kind of continuous part of the camp meeting. After they'd eaten, they joined the audience in the brush arbor for the afternoon's services. It was a scorching hot day, but the thick canopy of brush overhead filtered the sunlight that fell on them, and once again Hoppy was sorry this was all in black and white and couldn't do justice to the yellowish-green glow that the brush, filtering the sunlight, cast all over everything.

Sharline had to get up and return to the piano whenever a hymn was called for. There weren't enough songbooks to go around. Sharline had told him she couldn't read music anyhow; she could just play it by ear. For that matter, most of these folks, coming from the farthest reaches of the deep Ozark Mountains, couldn't read in the first place. So the congregation improvised, with the loudest voices coming from those who knew the hymns by heart, while those who didn't hummed or crooned under their breath. Even Hoppy was able to join in on the bass parts of "Amazing Grace" because he'd heard it so often, although it bothered him to declare himself "a wretch like me," even though it was the truth.

That was the last hymn, for a while, and Sharline got up from the piano and came to sit beside Hoppy while one of the elders delivered the opening prayer, thanking the Lord for the beautiful day and for bringing all these folks together here in this peaceful and holy place and asking the Lord to grant power and persuasion to Brother Binns in his efforts to lead the unrighteous to salvation.

Then Brother Binns mounted the pulpit, holding his arms wide in welcome after brushing back his slick hair. His voice was soft and gentle as he began, and Hoppy had to allow that he was a pretty good speaker. He hadn't said more than a dozen words when the first shouts of "Amen!" came from the audience, and soon Binn's every sentence was met with folks hollering "Hallelujah!" and "Praise the Lord!" and "Yes, Jesus!" and "Glory to God!" Sharline, who had apparently had one or more previous experiences listening to Binns in a brush arbor, whispered to Hoppy that this was called "getting happy." Hoppy figured out that the main drift of Binn's sermon was to convert the unsaved to repentance and baptism and salvation. But the preacher first had to spell out the sins and transgressions which required salvation, and these included drinking, smoking, lying and cheating, playing cards, disobeying parents, disbelieving the Bible, fornicating, dancing…and attending pitcher shows. Hoppy's hackles rose as he listened to Binns declaiming, "Bretheren and sisteren, lookee yonder at that big white sheet a-hanging from the side of the schoolhouse! Do ye know what that's *for*? Tonight after it gets dark, right here on this very sacred ground, right here in front of the innocent childring and womenfolks, a man who thinks he looks like a cowboy name of Hopalong Cassidy, and that's him a-setting right there, friends, that man is going to start up a machine that will throw up on that screen big pitchers of people actually moving around and doing things, nonsense about cowboys and all sorts of foolishness meant to steal your minds away from righteousness. And he's planning to make you pay cash money just for the right to look at it! If it wasn't so sinful for you to watch such foolishness, you could stay right in your tent and see it just as well without paying a penny. But he's going to try to get you to sit right where you're sitting now and pay for the privilege! He's going to sell you a one-way ticket to Hell!"

Some of the womenfolk in the audience stood and started shouting angrily in a tongue that wasn't English but wasn't any tongue known to man, either. Hoppy was taken aback at the audience's clamor, and looking around him he beheld the hostile looks of a bunch of tough fellers who seemed ready to lynch him. Sharline put her hand on top of his, where he was clawing his knee.

"Don't let me catch none of you good folks at the pitcher show tonight," Emmett Binns warned. "Just to make sure you won't be here for such as that, we'll all gather tonight at the river. They's a hole on the Mulberry not far from here where we can take our lanterns and have a night-time baptizing, while this pitcher shower stays here all alone."

"Except for me," Sharline said out loud, loud enough that the preacher heard her. He cast her a stern glance and seemed to be trying to think of a way to answer her.

"Bretheren and sisteren," he said to his audience, "most of you good folks who came here for this great revival meeting, some of you coming for miles and miles and planning to stay at least a week, you didn't bring any money with you anyway, did you? Hard times like these, you didn't have any money to bring, did you? Like the Good Book says, First Timothy six and ten, money is the root of all evil. So you don't want to give any of it that you might have to fill the pockets of this evil pitcher shower. Matter of fact, I think it would be a good idee if you took any money that you might have brought with you and get rid of it by putting all of it in the collection plates that Brother Dowdy and Brother Tharp are going to pass around right now! What do you say? Let me hear you, what do you say?"

"AMEN!" "HALLELUJAH!" "GLORY TO GOD!" The folks shouted. And they fished in their pockets and their purses and came up with whatever coins they happened to have on hand, which Brothers Tharp and Dowdy began to relieve them of. Sharline said to Hoppy, "There goes our gasoline money for the next town."

"Art Bedwell would fill our tank for nothing," he said to her.

"I told you he could preach, didn't I?" she said. "He could talk anybody into anything. But he couldn't talk me into his bed."

A feller sitting behind them tapped Hoppy on the shoulder and asked, "How much was ye fixing to charge for that pitcher show?"

"It's a nickel for kids and a dime for grown-ups."

"Maw," the feller said to the woman beside him, "hang on to some of that."

And sure enough, Hoppy could discern by glancing around him, not everyone was coughing up all their cash.

Brothers Tharp and Dowdy deposited their plates on the table beside the pulpit. "Is this *all*?" Emmett Binns asked of the audience. "Times is hard, yes, but that's a offering the Lord would look upon with sorrow. Are some of you holding back on me? I sure would hate to think that this tiny little collection is the best you can do." He ranted onward for another ten minutes about the evil of money and the fact that money wouldn't do a bit of good at a camp meeting. He finally got off the subject after declaring, "I just don't want to know that ary a one of ye paid ary a cent to see a sinful pitcher show."

Then he shrugged his shoulders, shifted his tone into full booming declamatory and began an exhortation to get converts to come down to the mourner's bench. These were the souls who would be saved at the nighttime baptism, and each of them did an awful lot of hooting and hollering in the process of declaring their readiness for salvation. Their spirit infected the whole crowd, and there was shouting and screaming from all over. Some folks were so seized by the spirit that they fell on the ground and kicked and thrashed as well as screamed. There were even kids among them, flat out on the ground, crying for mercy and weeping with joy. It didn't seem to Hoppy that they were "getting happy," but he had to allow that it was probably good for everybody, to get it all out. It was probably a way of letting off their troubles, their frets and frustrations. There had been many a time, before Sharline, when Hoppy himself had sure felt like he could use a good scream or two.

But it sure was a real spectacle. The man behind Hoppy remarked, "Who needs a pitcher show if we get to watch all this carrying-on?"

Sharline was needed to play the piano for the closing hymn, which was "I Am Thine, O Lord." Hoppy had noticed that Sharline never sang along with the others, but assumed it was just because she was just too busy pounding the keyboard. Later when they were alone again and getting their equipment and gear ready for the evening show, he asked her why she didn't sing along in the hymns, and she simply said, "I don't foller the words." And a bit later she smiled at him and added, "But I am *thine*, O Lord." His heart swole.

His heart swole even more that night when he discovered that their audience was bigger than ever. There were not only most of the people who lived hereabouts and had come to the shows and the first three episodes of "The Painted Stallion," but also a sizeable portion of the "furriners"—the campers at the camp meeting who had come from over the mountains—were in attendance, although some of the latter had requested either to be allowed to barter whatever foodstuffs or personal belongings they could for admission or else they tried to sneak in, an easy thing to do since there were no gates or doors or walls to stop them from it. Hoppy told his ticket-seller, Sharline, to just let the freeloaders in, at least for tonight. The more honorable spectators, who couldn't afford the admission but didn't want to sneak in, approached Hoppy with assorted offers of chickens, eggs, slabs of bacon, butter, the shirts off their backs, and even sexual favors. Since some of them had brought the family cow along for the trip, Hoppy was willing to accept a pail of fresh milk. Otherwise he just said, to the poor, as most of them were, "Be my guest," and let them all in.

One person he didn't say "Be my guest" to was Emmett Binns, who, having concluded the mass baptism on Mulberry River with spare time enough afterwards to change from his wet clothes into dry clothes—"civilian" clothes that left him scarcely recognizable—decided to, as he put it to Hoppy, "See what all the fuss is about."

"Ten cents," Hoppy said.

Brother Binns gave Sharline a dime and hung around to watch her juggling six balls and being made to disappear by the magician, but then the preacher found himself a seat in an inconspicuous spot outside the brush arbor where the rest of the people wouldn't notice him.

That night's show didn't make them much profit, especially since Sharline's concessions—the candy and popcorn, etc.—went largely unsold because most everyone was stuffed on the supper leftovers of the perpetual dinner-on-the-grounds.

When full dark settled in, before starting the projector, Hoppy asked Sharline if she could give the audience a kind of rundown of what had already happened in "The Painted Stallion" in the first three episodes that most of them had missed. She was glad to oblige. Standing at the pulpit in the light of a kerosene lantern, wearing her ten-gallon hat and her Clarksville dress, she delivered with the patience of a schoolteacher a summary of the beginning of the serial, which proceeded reasonably into her reading of the captions for the serial as it began.

As the first images unfolded on the screen, there was a reaction such as Hoppy had never before witnessed among his audiences: a group gasp, a noisy shared intaking of breath, and an assortment of exclamations of surprise and delight, each prefaced with "Well," an interjection of satisfaction: "Well, can you beat that!" "Well, as I live and breathe!" "Well, burn my clothes!" "Well, hush my mouth!" "Well, who'd've thort it!" If the hollering of the camp meeting was "getting happy," this was getting happier.

Hoppy wandered down the edges of the brush arbor, to relish their facial and verbal expressions. He had always enjoyed observing his audiences, but now he was watching a multitude who were having their first experience with pitcher shows. And were clearly beside themselves with pleasure. He couldn't help thinking of the night before, of Sharline's losing her virginity; most of these folks were sort of having their entertainment virginity taken away. He could easily discriminate between them and the townspeople who had already seen several pitcher shows: the latter were almost smug and gloating, knowing they'd lost their virginity but reliving the experience through the others.

Emmett Binns was doing his dead-level-best to refrain from expressing any reaction whatsoever. The only way he could do this was by fixing his face into a permanent scowl of disapproval. But as the serial ended and the main feature, "Rustler's Valley," began, Binns allowed himself to get transported into the story and to feel the same pleasant escape from this world as everyone else was feeling. He was even heard to remark, "How about that!" and "Head 'em off at the pass, fellers!"

When the show was all over, and folks were reluctantly making their way back to their tent homes (and even a few covered wagons like those in "The Painted Stallion") on the outskirts of the field, Binns hung around. "That shore is some kind of marvelment," he commented to Hoppy and Sharline. "If that don't beat all. If that don't skin the mule and hang up the hide."

To be friendly, Hoppy offered, "Care for a snort, Reverend?"

Binns looked around him to see if they were being observed, but everyone else had gone away. "I don't reckon a little one would kill me," he said.

Hoppy got out the jug of Chism's Dew and three glasses, and

they sat around and sipped, as the lightning bugs cavorted and in the far woods Sharline's fairies commenced dancing.

Binns was full of praise for the Chism's Dew, which, he allowed, put all other spirituous beverages to utter shame. After his third drink, Binns remarked, "You know, I've been thinking, me and you ought to go into partnership together. Instead of competing with each other, we ought to have combined camp meetings and pitcher shows all over the place. What do you say?"

Hoppy started to laugh but caught himself. "I'd have to sleep on it," he said.

Binns shifted his look to Sharline. "And you? Where are you sleeping?"

"Same place," she said.

Chapter ten

But it was harder to sleep than it had been the previous night. "There sure are a lot of them out there," Sharline observed, as they lay listening to the sounds of their temporary neighbors. Even though the closest one, a covered wagon, was parked at least a hundred feet away, it seemed that Topper no longer had the nocturnal seclusion that it usually had, and the night's usual chorus of crickets, frogs etc. was overlaid with the buzz of voices. Their words couldn't be understood, but there sure was a lot of talking going on. Hoppy imagined that most of them were discussing the pitcher show, either "The Painted Stallion" or "Rustler's Valley" or both. He doubted that anyone was talking about Brother Binns' sermon, and that was certainly a big advantage that pitcher shows had over religion: you could sociably discuss the plot and characters afterwards.

Hoppy was surprised at himself for not being able to dismiss, right off the bat, Emmett Binns' offer, and during the mighty long time it would take him to fall asleep he would weigh the pros and cons of it, and come up with a line of reasoning such as that Binns was seeking to capitalize on the popularity and memorability of pitcher shows in order to draw and keep a larger audience for his revival meetings. Binns had the power to pull folks out of the most remote corners of the Ozarks, folks who would trek long distances to get religion but wouldn't make such a trip just for pitcher shows, and maybe there was something to be said for the idea of using Binns as a drawing card.

Hoppy and Sharline did not make love that night. It might have helped them get to sleep easier if they had, but Sharline was still a bit sore from the tear in her maidenhead, and both of them were too conscious of being surrounded by the tents and shacks and covered wagons holding the population of the camp meeting. So they were content to hold each other closely, as the narrow lower bunk required them to do, and to whisper at length their night thoughts and their expressions of great nearness to each other, as well as their opinions on Emmett Binns' offer.

"I don't like him," Sharline said. "And I sure don't want to travel with him. What town are we going to next?"

"Deer," he said.

She kissed him. "You're a dear, too. Where do we go from here?"

"*Deer*," he said. "That's the name of the town, up in Newton County."

"Let's not tell him, or anybody else, in case it might get back to him."

"Okay, but why not?"

"We don't want him a-follering us."

"You don't think it might pull in a right smart of a bigger audience if we jined up with him?"

"Tomorrow," she said, "I'm going to buy some paint at Bedwell's store and paint us a sign on both sides of Topper, and I don't want that sign even to mention Emmett Binns."

"All right," he said, "but I told him we'd sleep on the idee, so who knows what we might decide after a good night's sleep. You have sweet dreams, hon." He gave her a squeeze and closed his eyes.

"Landon, if you wake up along in the night and I'm not here, don't get riled. I just might have to go out and visit with my fairy friends."

"Promise me ye won't go out in just your slip," he requested.

But if she ever did get up and go out during that night, other than to heed a call a nature, he didn't know about it. When he woke up, at last, it was to the sound of the furriners' various roosters greeting the morn, and Sharline wasn't there, but she was right outside of Topper, fixing breakfast on the kerosene stove. Hoppy decided one of the nicest things about her was fresh readymade coffee with ham and eggs and biscuits all set to eat.

After breakfast, he walked with her over to Art Bedwell's store, where he got himself some makings of cigarettes and she bought a pint can of black paint and a two-inch lettering brush.

He had one request: "Don't make the letters too big." He liked all that empty white space that covered Topper, and he didn't think Topper would appreciate being marked up with black paint.

She kept the letters just big enough to be seen from a distance, and here is what they said:

HOPALONG'S ROAMING PICTURE SHOWS

MOVING PICTURES ON THE MOVE

And in much smaller letters, down below, she painted:

Landon "Hopalong" Boyd, prop.

Sharline Whitlow, ass't.

She duplicated the sign on the opposite side of Topper. Her lettering was very neat. It was so clean and sharp, Hoppy reflected that if they had to quit traveling and go to work for a living and she didn't want to teach school, she could earn a fair living as a sign painter. And he told her how much he admired her work.

But she had another talent too that he would never have guessed. A bunch of folks came over to look at the new sign painted on Topper's sides, and among the folks was Emmett Binns, who said "Good morning, Brother Boyd, and good morning, Sister Sharline.

Right nice sign you got there. Sister, I was wondering if you'd have time this morning to give me another haircut."

All Hoppy could think was: *another?* Sharline replied, "It'll cost ye two bits, same as usual."

"Where do ye want to do it?" Binns asked.

"Why, right here's good enough, I reckon. Let me get my scissors." She climbed up into Topper and fetched from her toesack bag of possessions a pair of scissors and a comb. She got a spare sheet to cover him with. He sat in one of their chairs in the yard beside Topper, and she went to work, and Hoppy felt more jealous than he'd ever felt in a right smart spell. But it didn't take very long, not even as long as it'd take a woman to make love to a man. She did a good job, and Binns was left looking more presentable.

As he paid her the quarter, he asked of Hoppy, "Well, did ye get a chance to sleep on my offer last night?"

"Yeah, we did, but we aint made up our mind yet." Hoppy appreciated the first person plural he was using. And he appreciated not coming right out with a flat turn-down but instead leaving Binns wondering.

Binns was studying the new sign on Topper's side. "Are you two actually living together inside of that?" he asked. Sharline merely gave her head a slight nod, and Binns said, "I could marry ye, so it would look respectable and wouldn't be such a sin."

It took Hoppy a moment to realize that Binns meant performing a marriage service, not marrying Sharline his own self. Then Hoppy said, "We'll have to sleep on that notion too," and gave Binns such a look as would tell him to mind his own business.

"Suit yourselfs," Binns said. "I just hate to see such open sinning going on right here in the camp meeting."

"You don't have to see," Sharline said. "Nor nobody else neither."

Binns reached out and touched her name where she had lettered it on Topper. "You're advertising right there that you're *with* him," he pointed out. The paint was still wet and he smeared her name and got some paint on his fingertips. "Oops," he said. They did not offer him anything to wipe his fingers with, and he didn't want to use his best handkerchief, so he went off in search of a rag or a place to wash.

Hoppy and Sharline inspected the smeared sign. "Let's just wait until it's dry," Hoppy suggested. "And then we'll get some white paint to cover it and you can start over and do it again. And maybe you ought to put at the bottom, 'Haircuts, twenty-five cents.'" He hadn't meant to be funny, but Sharline laughed. "You never tole me you was a barber," he said.

"You aint jealous, are ye? Do you want I should do you?"

"Might as well," he said. "But I won't pay ye two bits."

So she gave him a haircut, the first he'd had since early spring, the first he'd *ever* had from a female barber, which was real exciting, even arousing. He did indeed get jealous, wondering if Emmett Binns had experienced the same arousal beneath her hands.

"Do you think we ought to get married?" he said.

She did not say anything. Her hands stopped working on his head. He had to crane his neck to see behind him, to see what her face was doing. She was just looking sort of bemused, but with a teeny smile on the edges of her mouth. At length she spoke. "Is that a proposal?"

"Since the preacher brought it up, I just wondered what you thought of the idee."

"Some day," she said, "when I get to know you better, I'd sure be proud to hear you make a proper proposal."

"Some day I just might," he allowed.

Hoppy helped her wash the dishes and tidy up around Topper, and he took their water bucket off to the spring to refill it. The spring, which was in a sort of ravine at the foot of the mountain, was in steady demand by the many campers, and Hoppy had to wait in line to get his chance to fill his bucket. The spring appeared to be drying up in the drought and his bucket took a while to fill.

Sharline cooked a couple dozen fried apple pies to contribute to the dinner-on-the-grounds, and then there wasn't too much left of the morning to kill before dinnertime, but the two of them went out in their ten-gallon hats and wandered amongst the crowd of folks who were finding ways to kill the morning. Groups of kids surrounded them and tugged at their hands and wanted to know what was going to happen in "The Painted Stallion." Would that there wagon train ever make it all the way to Santa Fe? Would the injuns get 'em all? Would that Injun chief on the paint horse save the good guys? And what kind of pitcher show would they be showing tonight? Some of the older kids had more complicated questions about how did they manage to capture all those things on the celluloid that ran through the machine. How could they get the sound on that celluloid? It sure was a wonder. What was the world a-coming to?

They watched for a while as some of the kids played a game of "washers," which involved trying to pitch large metal rings into one of three holes, the nearest hole worth five points, the middle hole ten, and the fartherest fifteen points. Other kids were playing the classic mumble-de-peg with their jackknifes, a game Hoppy had played as a kid, and he took the trouble to explain to Sharline how the game got its name, from the penalty suffered by the loser of the game, who was required to kneel down and pull a matchstick out of the ground with his teeth, or "mumble the peg."

Promptly at noon the ladies of the town began arriving with covered platters and dishes for the dinner-on-the-grounds, and quite a number of the ladies of the campground also offered various plates and pails of food. All of these were spread out right on the ground, on top of tablecloths or coverings of some sort, and the older boys were appointed the task of shooing away any dogs, cats or pigs who tried to get into the food. But the boys had their hands full with the animals and couldn't do anything about the human freeloaders, nearly all of them furriners, who helped themselves freely to the dinner without having contributed any dishes of their own. These spongers were voracious and they fought among themselves and even the townspeople, crowding and jostling to get first helpings of the meats and pies.

Art Bedwell remarked to Hoppy, "My old womarn was up at the crack of dawn to start fixing food for this here dinner, and I shore do hate to see these peckerwood leeches jist a-helping theirselfs."

In fact, the freeloaders had pretty much cleaned off the food before Hoppy and Sharline could get their turn at it, and Hoppy was particularly irritated to discover that Sharline's platter of fried apple pies was empty. He had been looking forward to having one for dessert. He was going to remember what most of these deadbeats looked like, and he was going to refuse them all admission to that night's shows unless they had money to pay.

The camp was steadily growing in population, with new people coming in their wagons, on horseback, on foot, and a few cars. The brush arbor wouldn't hold a fraction of them for that afternoon's services. Fortunately for Sharline, among the new arrivals was a woman who Binns introduced as "the unbeatable pianer player of these parts," who knew all the hymns by heart and would relieve Sharline of her thankless stint at the keyboard.

Hoppy and Sharline decided they didn't want to sit through another sermon by Binns anyway. They returned to Topper, but the yard around Topper was filled with people, and there were folks sitting on Topper's steps and running boards. "Let's get away from here," Sharline said to him. "But I want to get something first." She went up into Topper's rear end and came back with fistfuls of some gauzy stuff.

When they had hiked a distance up the mountainside, she showed him what she had. "Last night a woman swapped me these for admission to the show for her whole family. I've got an idee for using them but I need to try them out and see what you think." She showed him the scarves, if that's what they were: soft sheer lengths of see-through fabric that were light as gossamer. She threw one of them up into the air and it floated around before she caught it. Then she threw two of them up, and three of them, and got the first and re-threw it before the others came down. "If I can just learn to throw all six of them, it will be a kind of juggling."

She led him to a glade in the forest where, she said, her fairies dwelt...but only by night. And there, with the grace and lightness of a fairy she began to practice with the gossamer scarves...or "fascinators," as Sharline said they were called. They sure did fascinate, and he wished he could mention their colors, of which each was a different one. He was envious of the dexterity and the light rhythm with which she whipped the chiffon fascinators around, sent them tossing in the air this way and that, and eventually reached the point where she could keep all six of them afloat and adrift and whirling and spinning. Her whole body swayed and pitched with the movements of her plucking at the fascinators. Hoppy had the notion that her dancing was being watched admiringly by her fairies.

She practiced for a full hour. "You've got my balls licked," he commented, then realized the double meaning and said, "I mean, I could never juggle them balls the way you're a-juggling them scarfs. It's going to be a real hit with the crowd tonight."

She draped the chiffon around his neck and gave him a big long kiss. She was pressed tight against him and whispered in his ear, "Everbody's down there, and we're up here, and nobody would see us if we commenced to be jined."

"Your fairy friends are probably watching," he pointed out.

"If they are, they're admiring us," she said.

So they did it right there in the broad daylight on the leaves of the forest floor, removing just enough of their clothes—his pants and her panties—to make it possible. This was practically the same spot where they had first kissed the other night. But then they had returned to the comfort of the bunk in Topper to actually jine theirselfs together. Now, when he felt their jinedness beneath him, he forgot to remember what she had said her fairy friends had told her about his living inside of his penis, and he made the mistake of living there again, living in such luxury and wonderfulness that in consequence, partly also because of being right out in the open air in this glade, he became too powerfully transported with the pleasure of being inside of her, and that finished him off in no time, although with the greatest coming he'd ever felt, so mighty that it took everything out of him and he could only collapse on his back and lie there panting for breath. His only thoughts were two: he hated himself again for not being able to give her the all-overs, and he wondered how much danger there was that his jism inside of her might leave her in a family way. "I'm sorry," he said.

"That's okay," she said. She snuggled her head into his neck, but after just a moment she rolled the rest of her body up on top of him, and before his tallywhacker had a chance to shrink and sleep she had got it inside herself again. He had never heard of a woman being on top, although it had happened in his private pitcher show, "Assortment." Somehow it seemed unnatural, even perverse, like some of the other goings-on in "Assortment." But as she began to move, moving in a way she couldn't have moved on the bottom, he began to understand that maybe it was even better this way. And it also made it easier for him to step outside of his penis and not live in it for a while, and to enjoy completely what was going on without worrying about coming too soon. Now she was moving very fast. He began to move himself, as much as being beneath would allow him to do, and pretty soon they were both really smacking against each other, and he was surprised to discover that for the first time in his life he was on the verge of coming again. He had never heard of such a thing, but somehow it didn't seem unnatural, and he decided that if it was going to happen he might as well just let go and get the most out of it. When her all-overs finally arrived, truly all-overing her everywhere, he all-overed himself, with a force he would never forget.

A long while later, as they still lay in a tight embrace, their sweat beginning to cool and dry in the late afternoon as a breeze began to waft through their glade, she commented, "Boy howdy, that was the nicest. That was just *too* nice."

When they were finally ready to leave, they discovered that the breeze had scattered her gossamer fascinators, and they spent a while tracking them down and gathering them up. One was hung on a tree limb he couldn't reach, and he was afraid of heights, so she scampered up that tree like a squirrel and fetched it for herself.

Making their way back to the camp, they came upon no less than three other couples, teenagers, hither and yon, who were also using the woods for acts of lovemaking. They were tempted to pause and watch but realized that these kids weren't doing anything that they themselves hadn't just done.

That night, Sharline performed the juggling of the fascinators while the audience arrived and after Hoppy had done his own juggling. Her nimble tossing and catching of the scarves caused everyone to say *Ooh!* and *Ahh!* almost as if she were doing stunts on a daring trapeze. He stood back and admired the otherworldly gracefulness of her movements without being able to resist the thought that such beauty actually *belonged* to him. It was almost enough to make a man believe in God.

"Makes you want to thank the Almighty, don't it?" a voice said at his ear, and he turned to see Emmett Binns. The preacher was leering. "I tell ye, Brother Boyd, if you don't want to marry her, I'd be mighty proud to make her into Mrs. Binns."

Chapter eleven

He was to discover that Emmett Binns had not just been making polite chitchat when he made that remark. Binns began to tail Sharline, keeping it sly at first but eventually right out in the open, like a puppy dog attaching itself to a new master. There would even come a time, once when Binns was nigh on to drooling as he sought to help Sharline gather up her fascinators, when Hoppy would be moved to say, "Down, boy."

And for the remaining two days of their run in that town, the preacher seemed to look for every chance to be in Sharline's company. Binns declared his disappointment that she was no longer attending the brush arbor services, and he invited her back to play the piano for the hymns, saying he'd get rid of "the unbeatable pianer player of these parts" and restore Sharline to the position of accompanist. But Sharline wasn't interested, although for want of anything better to do she and Hoppy sometimes attended the services, not sitting in the brush arbor because it was packed full but standing in the shade of a tree within earshot of Binns' sermons. Binns always glanced in their direction whenever he railed against fornication. He never lost a chance, in his orations, to put in a word or two about the supreme sin of unchastity outside the sacred bonds of marriage, and he never lost a chance whenever he was with Sharline to hint that he sure would like to go for a little walk in the woods with her.

But his greatest hypocrisy continued to be his attack on the evils of pitcher shows despite the fact that he himself continued to watch them, although he went to great lengths to avoid being seen, and even appeared in disguise, wearing a fake beard and mustache that he had obtained god-knows-where.

Pitcher shows, he declared from the pulpit, were a violation of Psalms 101:3: "I will set no wicked thing before mine eyes: I hate the work of them that turn aside; it shall not cleave to me." That simple verse was good for an hour or so of oratory. Furthermore, we are told in the fifth chapter of Ephesians, verses 3–7: "But fornication, and all uncleanness, or covetousness, let it not be once named among you, as becometh saints; Neither filthiness, nor foolish talking, nor jesting, which are not convenient: but rather giving of thanks. For this ye know, that no whoremonger, nor unclean person, nor covetous man, who is an idolater, hath any inheritance in the kingdom of Christ and of God. Let no man deceive you with vain words: for because of these things cometh the wrath of God upon the children of disobedience. Be not ye therefore partakers with them." All of these things, Binns pointed out, are found in pitcher shows, and we are clearly asked not to partake of them.

Hoppy couldn't recall a single scene in any of the Hopalong Cassidy movies, or in all the episodes of "The Painted Stallion," which would fit that description…except possibly some of the foolish talking and jesting. But he supposed that you could find something somewhere in the Bible that would condemn just about anything, which was one reason he'd never had much use for reading that particular book. Come to think of it, the only books he had read, apart from his schoolbooks years ago, were a few paperbacks by Clarence Mulford upon which the Hopalong Cassidy pitcher shows were based—*Heart of the West, Three on a Trail,* and *Call of the Prairie.* Comparing the novels with the film versions, which had been in his repertoire the previous year, had been an unsettling experience for Hoppy. The experience of actually watching on the screen what he had created in his own way upon the screen inside his head while reading the novels convinced him that there was either something terribly wrong with pitcher shows or else something terribly wrong with novels, and he had decided that since he owed his livelihood to pitcher shows he had better take sides with them, so he had given up reading.

For three nights now, following each show, when the campers had returned to their tents and the townsfolk to their homes, Emmett Binns had come to Topper, had taken unbidden the one sitting-chair, had removed his beard and mustache, and had accepted, because it would have been rude of Hoppy not to offer it him, a glass of Chism's Dew. Hoppy wasn't able to determine whether Binns really liked the whisky that much, or was just using this conviviality as an excuse for being near to Sharline, but in any case, Sharline usually found a good excuse for absenting herself from the two men. Hoppy guessed that she might be going up the dark mountainside to join her fairy friends. But in any case he was left to make conversation with Binns, not too difficult as long as he let Binns do the talking, and Binns hardly ever shut up. Hoppy decided there was one thing Binns craved more than Sharline, or Chism's Dew, and that was the sound of his own voice.

Binns' favorite topic was the possibility that he and Hoppy would become partners and combine their enterprises in the future, and he was full of ideas about the project, such as riding on ahead (he owned not a mule like most circuit riders but a fairly recent-model Ford coupe) in order to "set up" certain towns and post public notices of their coming. He was convinced that together he and Hoppy could draw crowds such as had never been seen in these parts before.

Hoppy didn't mind listening to Binns run on and on about this grand scheme, and there were even times when he was tempted to tell Binns that he'd be willing to give it a try. The only time he spoke up himself was to remark, "Preacher, it seems to me that if this here particular crowd we've got at this camp meeting is anything at all like what we'd expect down the road, I aint so sure I'd want to see any more of such."

"Don't worry," Binns said. "I reckon most of these folks are poor appleknockers and peckerwoods from the furthest backwoods, and the towns I've got in mind for us are a little more civilized."

Sharline was gone a long time. At least Hoppy didn't have to worry about her being in the company of Emmett Binns, because he was right here. Although it was close to midnight, the camp was still alive, and they could hear the sounds of folks talking all over the place, and even somebody playing a mournful harmonica. Hoppy poured the preacher another drink, and realized he might have to revisit Stay More sometime soon in order to replenish his supply of Chism's Dew.

Both men got more mellow than was good for them, even to the point of swapping some bawdy tales. Since Hoppy wasn't good at narration, he kept his joke short, and in return got a complicated yarn from the preacher about a wicked feller that died and went to Hell but discovered that it was a real nice and pretty place with flowers and pretty girls, and he was even able to talk them into the bushes. But, as the preacher's punch line put it, "Goddamn it, the girls here aint got no cunts!"

Binns and Hoppy had a good laugh and helped themselves to the Dew. After a while, Hoppy invited, "Preacher, would you care to see a *real* pitcher show?" He led the preacher up inside of Topper, and turned the projector to the wall to project upon it his "Assortment."

The preacher sure was flabbergasted with what he saw in that particular pitcher show, and he grunted his appreciation and moaned his approval throughout. They were both so absorbed in the scenes of "Assortment" that they didn't notice Sharline returning. She stood in the door and watched the two men, her lover and the preacher who had wanted to be her lover, both of them drunk and enjoying a very wicked pitcher show. "Jesus God," Emmett Binns was remarking, "I never even knew that a feller could put it in *that* hole!"

Hoppy spied Sharline but gestured for her to remain quiet. She fixed herself a glass of Chism's Dew and resumed watching the men watching the spicy antics on the wall. Hoppy caught her eye and gestured at the preacher's groin, where an enormous bulge rose in his britches.

At length the preacher said, "This is driving me nuts! The trouble with most pitcher shows is that they make you want to be *in* them. The trouble with *this* pitcher show is it makes you want to be *in* a gal, any gal, Goddammit!" He stood up, making no effort to conceal the huge swelling in his pants. He turned, and caught sight of Sharline. He stared at her, and then at Hoppy. "I'm a-dying," he declared, whining. "I've just got to have me some cunt!"

"It's Hell, aint it?" Hoppy observed.

"Couldn't I do nothing or say nothing?" Binns asked of Sharline. "Give ye anything? Promise ye anything? Couldn't ye have mercy on me? Out of friendship?"

"I think you're drunk," she said to him. "And *you*," she said to Hoppy, "are *bad*." And she walked down from Topper and disappeared into the night, taking her drink with her.

Hoppy turned off the projector and killed the delco. "Well," he said, "surely they's other gals in this camp who'd love to lay down with the minister."

Binns finished his drink in one swallow and said, "Thanks for the stupendous show." Then he too disappeared into the night. Hoppy hoped that he wouldn't be reappearing in the same place that Sharline went.

When Sharline eventually returned, she was upset with Hoppy. "You didn't have no call to be a-showing your private reel to the preacher," she said.

"Heck, he's always preaching about how sinful pitcher shows are," Hoppy said. "I wanted him to see a *real* sinful pitcher show. And he sure did relish it!"

It was very late. They took off their clothes and went to bed and relished each other.

There was no brush arbor meeting the next day. Hoppy learned from Art Bedwell that the preacher had been taken to the county jail at Clarksville, and the rumor was that he'd not only been caught with an underage female who had not been willing, but had also been intoxicated. This rumor had spread throughout the camp, and some of the campers had already departed. This did not include any of the spongers, who raided the dinner-on-the-grounds as if it were any other day.

But the pitcher show went on as scheduled. Before it began that night, after Hoppy and Sharline had done their juggling and magic tricks, Art Bedwell asked Hoppy's permission to make an announcement. The way he made the request gave Hoppy and Sharline the feeling that he had something important to say. Bedwell stood up in front of the screen tacked to the schoolhouse, and Sharline had the idea of turning on the projector without film in it, just to make a kind of spotlight for the storekeeper while he delivered his speech. Although a number of campers had decamped, the brush arbor could scarcely hold a fraction of those who remained. Not very many of them had actually paid admission, but Hoppy didn't know how to enforce payment among a crowd that large. Sharline was able to refuse pokes of popcorn to anyone who didn't have money to pay or something to barter, but she couldn't stop them from snitching the candy she'd spread out on the concessionary table. The whole situation was so bad that it convinced Hoppy he would never have been able to join forces with the preacher. Camp meetings and pitcher shows simply wouldn't mix.

Art Bedwell wasn't a practiced public speaker but he was the town's leading citizen and his duty in making the announcement gave his voice an authority he didn't know he had. He shielded his eyes against the glare of the projector and said, "Folks, the camp meetings and these pitcher shows has sure been a boon to one and all. On one hand we've seen a many and a many a soul get moved to repent and accept the Lord. On the other hand we've sure had some real pleasure watching these exciting shows. Refreshment for the spirit all around.

"But folks, it has all just got out of hand. Most of you good people are law-abiding and considerate of one another, and do your share to keep everybody happy. But there are some no-good rascals and devils amongst ye who are just out for themselves, taking whatever they can get. The womenfolk of this town have complained to me that they have to work and slave to fix the food for everyone, and they don't even have time to attend the sermons and the shows themselves!

"And I've heared tell of things missing. You know they's not a house in this town that has a lock on the door, because most folks don't even know what locks are. Why, the doors to my store don't even have locks on 'em, and I've commenced to notice things gone. Somebody has been just helping theirself to whatever they want, all over the place!

"Considering that the camp meetings is supposed to be dedicated to the glory of God, and to bring salvation to the wicked, there has been an awful lot of transgression and mischief a-going on! And I aint even gonna mention what might have become of the preacher hisself. Others have committed not just thievery but drunkenness and cussing and fornication! Why, they's no telling how many babies has been conceived out of wedlock!

"My friends, is this a camp meeting dedicated to God or is it a den of iniquity? I aint pointing any fingers, and like I say I aint even gonna mention the preacher hisself. He might have had his weaknesses but he wasn't responsible for the troubles that this gathering has had. I aint a-blaming Hoppy Boyd neither. It aint his fault that his pitcher shows has attracted undesirable elements like a cow turd draws flies.

"But me and some of the other respectable citizens of this town, including Deputy Sheriff Higgins, who's a citizen of this town hisself, has talked this over and we have decided that we're going to have to close down this whole thing, just as soon as the last episode of 'The Painted Stallion' is shown tomorrow night.

"Meanwhile, it is our duty to ask the bad'uns—and you know who you are—to get out of town! Before sun-up! If tomorrow there is one more act of thievery, or freeloading, or of drunkenness or other misconduct, including fornication, we will shut down this whole proceeding on the spot!

"Sure, I know the whole country is suffering hard times, and lots of you folks don't know where your next nickel is a-coming from. But that don't entitle you to just take whatever you can get.

"So we might as well start right here and now with all of you'uns who has come to this pitcher show without paying anything for it, not even barter. I want to ask such of you'uns who has sneaked into this show to kindly get up and walk out!"

Art Bedwell put his hands on his hips and waited for a response from the audience. Hoppy was tempted to speak up and say that he didn't mind letting some folks in free, since it was the next-to-last night anyhow, but he was no good at all at public speaking. Along with everybody else, he could only tremble beneath Bedwell's oratory.

Few folks left, anyhow. Art went on standing there with his hands on his hips, looking around him at dozens of people who had scoffed the admission, but just a handful actually stood up and walked out, and several of those could be seen later, after the install-ment of "The Painted Stallion" began, standing on the edge of the crowd. Among those on the edge of the crowd, Hoppy recognized the unmistakable fake beard and mustache of the disguise of the disgraced preacher, who, Hoppy assumed, had been released or made bail.

The show went on. In the projection booth, Sharline asked Hoppy, "Are you and me fornicators?"

"Honey, we sure are," he said. "But I don't think Art means that we have to get out of town on account of it."

"I'm glad he spoke up," she said. "They've cleaned me out of candy, and one woman tried to grab my fascinators."

Hoppy told her that he had seen in the back of the crowd a figure who was unquestionably Emmett Binns in his disguise. "I reckon they let him out, for some reason," Hoppy said. "But we don't have to worry. They's just one more night to go, after tonight," he said. "And then we'll leave all these 'Christians' behind us."

Just as the pitcher show, "North of the Rio Grande," was build-ing up to the showdown between the good guys and the bad guys, the sewed-together bedsheets tacked to the schoolhouse suddenly developed some strange glowing rectangles which, Hoppy realized, were the windows of the schoolhouse behind the screen, and were glowing with light. A few of the audience realized the source of the glow, and someone shouted, "Fire!" which you should never do in a crowded theater, even if the theater is out of doors.

The two-story wooden schoolhouse began to blaze. Hoppy figured that whoever had started the fire must have used some gaso-line to help it along. Very quickly the whole building was engulfed in flames, and Hoppy's bedsheet screen became burning rags that fell to the ground.

People ran hollering every which way. A bucket brigade was organized, and Art Bedwell furnished all the galvanized pails he'd had for sale in his store, and all the dwellers of the camp furnished their buckets, and a long line of men ranged down to the spring to fill the buckets and pass them from hand to hand. The spring, however, was practically dried up. The line of the bucket brigade was shifted to Bedwell's well, but that too was quickly dried up. The flaming schoolhouse ignited the brush arbor, and although the brush was still green the fire consumed it and roared out of control and quickly spread to the camp of tents and shacks and wagons, and people scrambled to save whatever possessions and livestock they had. Hoppy drove Topper up the road a safe distance from the fire, where, along with everybody, including the futile bucket brigade, he could only watch as the site of the schoolhouse and the brush arbor and its camp was leveled.

Art Bedwell remarked to Hoppy, "I reckon I didn't need to make that announcement after all. The Lord is taking care of the situation, and driving the transgressors out."

"The Lord wouldn't burn down your schoolhouse," Hoppy observed.

Fortunately the town had one doctor, who was able to treat the numerous people who suffered burns, although two or three had to be transported to the hospital in Clarksville.

Hoppy remained suspicious that Emmett Binns might have been the arsonist. Later that night, when the fire was finished and nothing remained but smoldering piles that would continue smoking all night, an effort was made to find places for everyone to sleep. Hoppy moved Topper back into a part of the meadow where there was no smoke. He checked all of his film to make sure that none of it had been damaged by the heat, taking each metal reel down from its rack on the wall and opening the can and running a length of the reel through his fingers. This took a while. Then he and Sharline prepared for bed. Just as they were turning in, Topper's back door sprang open, and there was the preacher, still wearing his disguise.

He pointed his finger at Hoppy. "Satan!" he said. "You're the devil hisself or else you're one of Satan's deputies, sent to tempt me and try me and bring me to ruin. You liquored me up and took away my good sense and then you showed me that lurid pitcher show to inflame my loins and force me into evil! Yea, though I have repented and asked the Lord's forgiveness, yet am I determined to avenge your wickedness."

Hoppy stood up to him. "How do ye aim to do that?" he asked.

"Tomorrow at the meeting I'll confess what you done and what you made me do, and I'll ask the congregation for their pardon for my misbehavior, and then I'll ask them to stone you out of this camp!"

"This camp?" Hoppy said. "Look around out there, preacher. There aint no camp no more. You burned it to cinders!"

"What?" Binns said, then softened his tone. "Do folks think it was me that set the fire? I swear, it wasn't me done it. What cause would I have had for doing such a thing?"

"Burning your bridges," Hoppy suggested.

"Huh? No, it wasn't me, I swear to ye. It must've been some of those riffraff that got riled up by Art Bedwell's little speech."

"Well, the camp meeting has been burned out," Hoppy observed. "If you want to preach against me tomorrow, you'll have to do it to a standing audience in the hot briling sun. All the seats burned."

"Are you fixing to finish the pitcher shows?" Binns asked. "What will folks sit on?"

"Well, they'll be so eager to see the last episodes of 'The Painted Stallion' that they won't mind sitting on the ground."

"We'll have to see about that," Binns said.

Chapter twelve

T he next day Emmett Binns made a sorry spectacle of himself. Most folks who had come from a distance were headed on back out of town anyway, having decided not to stay around for the last episodes of the serial. Most of the town folks agreed with Art Bedwell that God Himself had brought down the fire upon them, to burn out the evil and wrongdoing. Emmett Binns made an attempt to stop some of the families departing, telling anyone who would listen that the camp meeting would go on, the brush arbor would be rebuilt, and he himself had not only repented and received the Lord's blessing but would solemnly promise never to touch another drop of liquor nor to lust after any females. But all of his haranguing of the various departers failed to persuade a single one of them to stay.

Of course there was no dinner-on-the-grounds. Any people still remaining were responsible for feeding themselves, and Hoppy wouldn't let Sharline fix him a dinner but was content to revert to his customary lunch of Vienna sausages with crackers.

At what would have been the usual time for the commencement of the brush arbor meeting, Emmett Binns stood on the blackened earth where the pulpit had been and held his arms aloft and boomed, "My friends! Forsake me not! Come and listen to a sinner beg for mercy!" A couple of dogs and one small boy observed him, but were his only audience. Binns mumbled onward for a while, then gave up.

He ambled over to where Hoppy and some kids were hanging the alabastine duck canvas between two trees to make a screen for the night's show. "I hope you get a better crowd than I did," he said morosely.

"I reckon a few will show up," Hoppy said. "At least I owe it to 'em to show the rest of the serial."

"And then where are you going?" Binns wanted to know.

"Uh, I don't rightly know. I reckon me and Sharline will just hit the open road and see where it takes us."

"North, south, east or west?" Binns asked.

"I don't rightly know that neither."

"Have you give up entirely on the idee of me and you becoming partners? I know I've disgraced myself as far as this town's concerned, and probably as far as all of Johnson County is concerned too, but there are other towns all over the Ozarks where nobody knows what a fool I've been, and I could make a fresh start and build a new brush arbor, and bring in folks from far and near to hear me and to hang around for your pitcher shows."

For a moment Hoppy told himself that Binns was absolutely right, and that a partnership with Binns might possibly bring in a fat lot of coin for both the camp meeting and the pitcher show. But then he had to remind himself of two things, one, that he wasn't in this racket for the money, and two, Sharline didn't like Binns. "Preacher, I just don't think it would work out," he said. "Sorry, but we're fixing to go our own way."

Binns glowered at him. "Don't you feel no guilt for putting me in this jam?"

"Naw, because you put yourself in it."

"If it hadn't been for your whiskey and your goddamn obscene pitcher show, there'd be hundreds of people in this meadow right this minute listening to me lead them to salvation."

"Maybe not. Maybe the feller that started that fire was feeling insulted by what Art Bedwell said. Maybe the camp would've burned out regardless of the trouble you got into."

Binns hung around for another hour, arguing with Hoppy and practically begging for a chance to go with him to whatever town he was going to next, just as a "trial," to prove that it would work, that Binns would draw a huge crowd, that they could get along just fine, and everybody would live happily ever after.

By and by Sharline joined them. She listened to Binns ranting on about going with them, and then she said to Binns, "Do you recollect the first thing I said to you when you showed up to make your brush arbor just the other day? I said, 'You've always been liable to just take whatever you please, whether it belongs to ye or not.' And now you're trying to take *our* next town, wherever we go from here. Mister, you've got another think a-coming to ye."

"Slut!" he said to her. "If it wasn't for you, I'd have no trouble at-all getting Hoppy to be my partner."

"He's already got a partner," she said.

And that should have been the end of the discussion. But Binns got the last word. "I'll ruin you'uns yet!" he declared. "The day will come when not a town in the Ozarks will want you and your miserable shows!" And he stormed off.

But he showed up that night for the final run of episodes in "The Painted Stallion," and even paid his ten cents to get in. He didn't bother to wear his fake beard and mustache. Some of the town's kids had gathered and rounded up more tomato crates and planks to make benches replacing those lost in the fire, and Sharline had given them free tickets. She gave another performance with her chiffon fascinators. When it came time for their final magic show, she told Hoppy he ought to make Binns disappear. Hoppy laughed and said, "We're going to disappear ourselves in the morning."

There wasn't a considerable crowd, mostly just townspeople, but that included everyone who had attended the first episode of "The Painted Stallion" and were now eager to see how the whole journey of the settlers to Santa Fe would turn out. Sharline remarked to Hoppy while the last episode was showing, "Their journey was a little like ours."

He thought about that, and understood what she meant. "And you're the pretty lady on the painted horse, who has been our guardian angel," he said. "And we're going to ride off into the sunset together."

The next morning, sleeping late, they missed the chance to ride off into the sunrise. It was Sunday. Although the town was large enough to have its own doctor, it didn't have its own parson, and Emmett Binns offered to conduct the worship services, but Art Bedwell let him understand that he wasn't welcome. That ought to have been enough to send the preacher packing, but he still hung around, and Hoppy knew he was just waiting for a chance to try to follow Topper to the next town they were going to.

Just as he had done in the previous towns on the last Sunday of his stay, Hoppy took all of the various things he'd collected for barter—dozens of eggs, gallons of butter, chickens, slabs of bacon and two live piglets—to Art Bedwell's store in order to redeem them. Bedwell topped off Topper's tank with gasoline and gave Hoppy thirty dollars and enough credit for Sharline and Hoppy to have a pleasant hour wandering around the big old general store selecting odds and ends of foodstuffs and house wares. After they'd loaded all this loot into Topper, Art Bedwell invited them to Sunday dinner, a substitute for the dinner-on-the-grounds that was usually held in Hoppy's honor as his last meal in all the towns he visited. "We've had enough of them," Bedwell remarked. Mrs. Bedwell was happy not to have to feed a multitude, and she gave Hoppy and Sharline a real fine roast pork dinner. As they were finishing up the various desserts—custards and cobblers as well as cakes—Art Bedwell went to the dining room window and looked out, and remarked, "He's still out there, parked right behind Topper."

"Sure," Hoppy said. "He's just waiting for us to take off, so he can foller us to the next town."

Bedwell suggested, "I could get Deputy Higgins to detain him for something, if it would help give you'uns a head start."

But when dinner was all over and they said their long good-byes to the Bedwells and got into Topper's cab, Binns was no longer around. His Ford coupe had completely disappeared. Still, as Hoppy drove east up the road that would take them to Catalpa and Salus and thence into Newton County, he stopped occasionally and waited to see if the black Ford might be following. Once, because there was plenty of time, he pulled off into a side road that was concealed from the main road, turned around with Topper pointed toward the main road, and they waited there for a while, maybe half an hour, to see if Binns would come along. But he didn't.

"Maybe he's given up on us," Sharline said.

They had a pleasant Sunday afternoon drive up into Newton County, passing through some real pretty country. Late in the afternoon, halfway to their destination, Hoppy stopped along the road and set the brake and said, "Hon, it's about time you learned how to drive this rig."

"Oh, *no*," she said. "Don't I do enough different things to help out? Why do I have to learn how to drive?"

"Are you planning to stick with me?" he asked.

"Like molasses," she said.

"Then you never know when the time might come someday that you'll need to take Topper yourself and go somewhere. Or leastways help out with the driving from town to town."

So Sharline got behind the wheel, but she was clearly flummoxed. Hoppy explained each of the things she'd have to use—the starter, the choke, the gas, the clutch, the brake. There wasn't any other traffic on the highway, which was truly a *high* way, with views far off into the mountains of Newton County.

It took her several attempts to learn how to let out the clutch while pressing the gas at the proper rate, and Topper lurched and bucked all over the place. And once she got it going fairly smoothly, she couldn't master the proper turning of the steering wheel to stay on the road. She slammed on the brakes. She stared at Hoppy. "I wet my dress," she announced.

He laughed. "That's better than you could do that time the seat caught on fire."

They spent an hour on Sharline's practicing the operation of Topper, but she never could get the hang of it. Hoppy reasoned to himself that Sharline was loaded with so many talents in so many different things that maybe she just didn't have any room left over for the management of a complicated piece of machinery like a motor truck. "Don't feel bad," Hoppy consoled her as he returned to the driving himself. "I can't play a lick on the pianer. I've been doing all the driving myself for so long I reckon I can just go on doing it." Soon the highway crested a plateau that afforded a fabulous view to the north, miles and miles of mountains, blue mountains behind green mountains and misty gray mountains behind the blue mountains. He pointed. "Right up yonder way is Stay More. You can almost see it from here." Sharline wanted to know if he would ever take her to his hometown. He told her he'd have to go there sometime soon just to get another jug or two of Chism's Dew, and to check his mailbox, although he never got anything of significance in the mail.

Before reaching their destination, Hoppy handed her his bugle. "Let's see if they's one other thing you can learn to do. Let's see if you can't blow a tune on that." She put it to her pursed lips and tootled, but couldn't create a tune. Hoppy took it back, driving with one hand, and played for her his tune which went *From far yonder down the road here he comes again, folks, Hoppy Boyd, the happy moving showman of moving pitchers to show you another good'un.* She watched him, and just as she could learn to roll cigarettes from watching him do it she could learn how to press and purse her lips and puff her cheeks to get a tune out of that bugle. She practiced for a while until she got pretty good at it, although the tune she finally came up with was more like *From far yonder down the road here they come again, folks, Hoppy and Sharline, the happy moving showmen of moving pitchers to show you a bunch of good'uns.*

"That'll do just fine," he said, as they came into the outskirts of the village. "Now stick the bugle out the winder and give it all you got!"

So their arrival in the town was just as heralded as any of his lone arrivals had been. And as in all the other towns, one by one and two by two they all came a-running, even the grownups and womenfolk, and every dog in town, and they followed Topper as he slowed down along the main road and came to a stop at Faught's store. Unlike Ewell Tollett and Art Bedwell and many other storekeepers of

Hoppy's acquaintance, Arlis Faught was a fairly young feller, a real good-looking young man, and he was postmaster besides, or rather his mother was, and he ran the place for her.

The store was closed, because it was late in the day and also because it was Sunday, but Arlis Faught came a-running from his house across the road and acted like Hoppy was his long lost brother. The two men were about the same age and even looked alike, although Hoppy thought that Arlis was a darn sight sightlier than himself. Hoppy introduced him to Sharline, and couldn't help but notice the sparkle in Sharline's eyes, probably caused by Arlis' good looks as well as by his courtly manner. The various young ladies in the crowd were giving Sharline such jealous looks as would have damaged a lesser gal.

"Hop, a whole year is just too blamed long," Arlis Faught said. "Tomorrow when the post office opens I'll show ye the calendar, that has got the days marked off since you was here last. I just caint tell ye how tickled to pieces we all of us are to have ye back again!" But he didn't have to try to tell. The kids were clapping and the dogs were barking and some folks were dancing a jig.

"Same place as last year?" Hoppy asked Arlis.

Arlis nodded. "Right out back." There was a broad meadow right behind the Faught store that made a great theater. It had a steep slope to it, but that was almost an advantage, with the screen at the lower end. As Hoppy drove around to the meadow, with Arlis hanging on to the running board and everybody else following, Sharline used her new-found flair for the bugle to blow a rousing rendition of "The Battle Hymn of the Republic."

When Topper was parked in the place where it would remain for a week, Arlis said, "Never mind that it's Sunday. Let's us have the first show tonight!"

"You know I caint do that," Hoppy said. "But if you waited for a whole year, you can wait for one more night."

"Then come on over to the house and let Maw feed you some supper and spend the night with us in a good feather bed!"

Hoppy laughed, thinking that Arlis' phrasing made it sound like Arlis and his mother and Hoppy and Sharline would all get into one bed together. He knew that Arlis was just being polite anyhow and didn't really mean the invitation. It was Hoppy's duty to say, as he did now, "I thank ye kindly, but I reckon we'll be fine enough right here with Topper." He really liked Arlis, though, and wouldn't have minded having supper at the Faught place.

After Hoppy answered the crowd's questions about the first show, "The Hills of Old Wyoming," and prompted Sharline to give a verbal preview of "The Painted Stallion," the crowd dispersed.

"This is a right nice old town," Hoppy said to Sharline, before they climbed up inside their truck-shack.

"It's all up so high," she observed. "Not like the last two towns that are down in a valley surrounded by mountains."

"We're right on top of a mountain here," he remarked. Then he suggested, "Why don't I drag the stove out here into the yard so we can fix supper out here?"

He climbed up into Topper to get the stove. Inside, he saw at once that something was wrong. Something was missing, although it took him a moment to figure it out. Then he couldn't believe it. All of the cans of film were gone from their rack on the wall! He searched all over the floor, thinking they might have got jostled out of their perch. But there was no mistake: every last reel of film he owned had been taken...except for the reel for the last episode of "The Painted Stallion," which hadn't been taken out of the projector when it was finished. He looked under the bed, and there, wrapped in the towel he kept it in, was his one private reel, "Assortment." But all the other reels were gone.

He jumped down. "Sharline, goddammit," he said. "We are in one hell of a fix. Somebody has took all the film!"

"No!" she said. "How could they do *that*?"

"He could have climbed up into Topper while we was having dinner at the Bedwells."

"Emmett Binns?" she said.

"I don't know who else," he said.

They both thought back, and recounted the last time they had been inside of Topper and any other times they might not have been watching the truck. They reflected upon the fact that Topper, like all the houses in the Ozarks, had no lock on the door. They reflected upon the fact that theft was practically unknown in the Ozarks…until it had started happening at the camp meeting and perhaps had become infectious and contagious. Mostly, they reflected upon Emmett Binns and his mean, low-down, misbegotten motives for having taken several hundred dollars worth of pitcher shows.

Then all they could do was reflect upon what could possibly be done. Hoppy wanted to go right away right back to where they'd come from, where the films had been stolen, and he even started up Topper and got it out on the road before Sharline could talk some sense into his head and persuade him there wasn't any point in going back *there*, because Binns would be long gone.

So he stopped Topper and turned it around once again, but not before Arlis Faught had seen him and come a-running. "Thought for a second you was a-leaving town!" Arlis exclaimed to them.

Hoppy broke the terrible news to Arlis, and said he didn't know what to do but there just weren't any films to be shown.

Arlis took the news worse than Hoppy himself had. He was frustrated and furious. "Yeah, I know that preacher Emmett Binns," he said. "And I wouldn't put it past him. Where do you suppose he might have headed?"

"They's no telling," Hoppy said. "That's the problem."

"Tomorrow I'll round up the boys," Arlis said. "They's about eight or nine fellers in this town who has got fairly good vehicles, and we'll just make up a posse. Yes, just like in the Hopalong Cassidy pitcher shows where the posse tracks down the rustlers and the robbers. We'll catch that son of a bitch. Pardon my language, Sharline."

That was some comfort to Hoppy and Sharline and helped them get through the sad night. Neither of them felt like sleeping. Hoppy speculated on what might be done if the posse couldn't catch up with Binns. Hoppy didn't have the money to order a whole new set of pitcher shows, and even if he did it would take an awful long time to mail off the order and get the films delivered. If he had the money, it would be quicker just to drive all the way to Memphis, but that was a horrible thought, and he wasn't sure that Topper could stand a trip of that length.

They might just have to give up showing pitchers and go to work for a living. Sharline would make a good schoolteacher or a good sign painter or a good barber or just about anything she set her mind to, and Hoppy could...well, Hoppy could find something to do, although his hatred of himself returned in full force when he realized that he really wasn't good for nothing except showing pitchers.

It was a perplexity, a sore kettle of fish such as had never confronted Hoppy in all his born days. He never would have got to sleep that night if Sharline hadn't thought to do something about it. First, she went out in the moonlight into the woods and besought her fairy friends. Then by and by she came back and made Hoppy get into the bed, where she loved him for so long in so many various ways that he finally fell asleep.

Chapter thirteen

Word spread quickly all over south Newton County that a no-good scoundrel of a circuit-riding preacher name of Emmett Binns had robbed Hopalong's Roaming Picture Shows of all the pitchers. People coming to Faught's store and post office to get their Monday morning mail made a huge outcry over the news of this crime, and by late morning Arlis Faught had organized his posse: he himself would drive his good Chevy Cabriolet roadster, and he invited Hoppy and Sharline to ride with him. Eight other men driving various vehicles, half-ton pick-up trucks as well as coupes, sedans, and a touring car, would also eagerly join the determined posse.

The difference between Faught's posse and those of, say, the posse in "The Hills of Old Wyoming" that went out in search of the rustlers, was that a western posse customarily stuck together in their search for the evildoers; Faught's men agreed to split up and fan out, going east, south, west, and north to cover as much territory as possible in their search for a certain black Ford coupe containing a runaway preacher and a couple dozen reels of motion pitcher film.

"Let's git 'im, boys!" Arlis shouted to his men as they started their engines and sped away. Two of the other vehicles accompanied Faught as far as Fallsville before they split off at the fork there, one heading south, the other west, while Arlis turned northward. From his discussions with Hoppy about Binns' earlier movements, Faught had decided the best bet would be to hunt through western Newton County and up into Carroll County.

It was a fine auto Arlis had, and speedy. That little roadster had white-wall tires, even, with the spare attached to the rear trunk, which actually was a rumble seat. There wasn't a back seat, so all three of 'em had to sit crowded together in the front seat, with Sharline in the middle. Arlis loved to talk while he drove, which was fine with Hoppy, so that Hoppy didn't have to talk any himself except to make an interjection now and then about Faught's palaver. Mostly what Arlis talked about was pitcher shows and how much they meant to him and how he wished he could see them more often than the one time a year that Hoppy came around. Arlis knew more about Hopalong Cassidy than Hoppy himself knew. He even knew lots about the career of William Boyd the actor, who had already been a popular Hollywood star before an accident of destiny gave him a chance to become Hopalong Cassidy. He even knew the story of how Clarence Mulford, the author of the many Hopalong novels, had become furious at William Boyd for changing Hopalong's appearance and character so thoroughly from what Mulford had intended.

Arlis, in his monologue about pitcher shows, even got somewhat poetic, which made Sharline smile with pleasure. "Up in these mountains, ye know, it gets mighty lonesome most of the time, with nothing much to do. Most folks don't know nothing except that they're a-living. And a life has got to be got through, with whatever can be found to pass the hours and the days and the nights, and they's just not nothing that will kill off the tedious hours easier than a good pitcher show."

"I know what you mean," Sharline said. "My life was empty and worthless until Hoppy came along."

"Where'd you meet up with ole Hop?" Arlis asked her, so Sharline was allowed to contribute to the chitchat for a while, talking about her family and where she'd grown up and how she stowed away on Topper in disguise as a boy, and so on. She even told things she hadn't told Hoppy, such as that when Sharline was a child her mother Clemmie Whitlow had kept Sharline shut up in the corn crib all the time in order to keep her from having any contacts with people, who in her mother's firm belief were hurtful and monstrous. Sharline's revelations of her childhood prompted Arlis to talk about his own childhood, and before long Arlis and Sharline were swapping all kinds of stories about what a miserable growing-up they'd endured.

Whenever they came to a town or a village, Arlis would stop at the post office, where he usually knew the postmaster or postmistress, and he would inquire if anybody had seen Emmett Binns or heard tell of his coming or going, and to request that Arlis be contacted at once if anybody did catch sight of Emmett Binns or his black Ford coupe. After stopping and getting out at one town, and stretching awhile because of the way they were crowded into the front seat, Hoppy declared that he'd never ridden in a rumble seat before and he offered to sit back there. So Arlis opened up the rumble seat and Hoppy climbed in. As they drove on, he noticed that Sharline kept sitting right where she had been sitting, in the middle of the seat with her shoulder up against Arlis', and Hoppy wanted to tell her that it wasn't necessary, that she could move over and give Arlis more room to drive. Through the back window, Hoppy could see that ole Arlis never did stop talking. Hoppy enjoyed riding open-air in the rumble seat although it was a bit dusty.

By late afternoon, when they hadn't caught a clue to Binns' whereabouts, they decided they'd covered enough territory for one day and had better turn around and head on back, taking a different route home. The last town they came to before turning back was Omega, up in Carroll County, and there Hoppy discovered that Captain Thomson's Pitcher Shows had set up to play the town. Hoppy had never got along well with his competitor, whose route to the west of Hoppy's was more extensive than Hoppy's, and who had a much larger collection of shows which he showed on twin projectors so there would be no pause between reels. He also showed inside a big tent almost like a circus tent, with hundreds of folding chairs. Hoppy and Cap Thomson had once bickered over two towns in the west of

Hoppy's route which Thomson wrongly claimed belonged to him, although Hoppy had been playing them for the previous couple of years. Hoppy really wasn't in the mood for stopping to say howdy to Cap Thompson, but a thought suddenly occurred to him, and he hollered for Arlis to stop.

Cap Thompson had a house-trailer home that was separate from his huge tent. He didn't smile when Hoppy climbed out of the rumble seat and said howdy. He said, "If you think I'll let you have Omega, you're bad mistook."

"Nossir," Hoppy said. "I don't want Omega, which is pretty far out of my part of the country. We're just passing through, trying to find a preacher named Emmett Binns."

"Sure I know that rascal, but I haven't seen him lately."

"Well, he stole all of my pitcher shows."

"You don't say. That's terrible. He must've had a good reason. I've heared him preach about how sinful pitcher shows are. How did he come to take 'em from ye?"

"It's a long story, and you don't want to hear it. But he has put me out of business, and what I want to know is, do you have any extry pitcher shows that you would sell me or rent me or loan me the borry of?"

"Whenever I'm through with a show, I ship it back to the distributor in St. Louis. I don't have any to spare that I'm not showing."

Hoppy eyed Cap Thompson and wasn't too sure that he was telling the truth. But he said, "I just thought I'd ask. Thank you." Hoppy turned to go, but paused. "If you should happen to run across Emmett Binns, tell him he's broke the hearts of a lot of good folks down in Newton County. Hell, maybe he'll try to sell my shows to you. I had a bunch of good Hopalong Cassidy shows."

"My crowds only want to see Gene Autry and Roy Rogers and Tex Ritter."

"Singing cowboys ought to be rounded up and shot," Hoppy said.

They stopped at a store to get something to eat, and then they headed back by a different route, stopping at Osage, one of the towns on Hoppy's circuit, where he was due to appear later in the summer. Hoppy told his old friend storekeeper Sammy Sturgis the story of what had happened, and said that he might not be coming after all, if he couldn't find Binns and get his pitcher shows back. Sturgis took the news as if it were the end of the world, and said he'd personally organize all the able-bodied men of Osage into another posse to hunt for Binns. That would pretty much cover the northern part of the Arkansas Ozarks.

When they got back, and met at Faught's store with the other members of Arlis' posse, not one of whom had found any trace of Binns, it was full dark and time for what would have been the showing of "The Hills of Old Wyoming." A pall settled upon the town and its inhabitants, almost as if Christmas Day had arrived without any evidence of Christmas. As some sort of consolation Hoppy and Sharline gave a performance of all their juggling acts, including Sharline's dazzling tricks with the chiffon fascinators, and then they also put on a show of all their magic tricks, including levitation, disappearance, and hypnotism, but it just wasn't the same, and there were long faces all around.

Arlis Faught said to the assembly, "Well, as long as we're here, and itching to watch some good stories, why don't we just have some tale-telling?"

So folks sat around and took turns telling all their favorite old stories, omitting the off-color ones because children and womenfolk were present. It wasn't bad. In fact, Hoppy himself, who through long exposure to all of his own pitcher shows had become more or less immune to their enchantment, was thoroughly beguiled by some of the stories he listened to. Even Sharline took a turn, telling a couple of old ghost stories she'd heard and couldn't forget. In fact, she did such a good job of narrating, with proper pauses and inflections and delivery in general, that Hoppy could almost see the things happening, just like in that one time he had listened to his grandfather, Long Jack Stapleton, giving a demonstration of his fabled power to tell stories that became visible.

Before bedtime, Hoppy said to her, "Tomorrow you can change the sign on Topper so it says, 'Sharline's Roaming Pitcher Stories.'"

She looked at him to see if he might not be kidding. And maybe he wasn't. Maybe they could really make a living at it. He was so pleased with the thought that he put a little extra interest into satisfying Sharline in bed. She was becoming unquenchable, but he did all he could to quench her.

The next day, the members of the posse met at Faught's store and with the help of roadmaps planned the territory they would cover that day. Several of them commented to Sharline on what a fine storyteller she was. Arlis Faught informed them that he had an appointment that day with the postal inspector and didn't know just when he was arriving, so regretfully he wouldn't be able to join the posse. He offered Hoppy the use of his Chevy roadster, but one of the other members of the posse, Teal Buffum, who planned to head eastward into Searcy County, offered to take Hoppy and Sharline with him. Hoppy told Sharline she didn't have to go with them. It would be a long and tiring trip over some bad roads, and there wasn't any sense in both of them going. So she could stay behind if she felt like it. Hoppy had been worrying about what might happen if they actually did come across Emmett Binns. Hoppy was ready to strangle him, and he didn't want Sharline to witness the violence.

Only later, after he and Teal Buffum were on the road, did it occur to Hoppy that there might be a risk in leaving Sharline alone with Arlis Faught, who had charmed her the day before, not just with his good looks and courtly ways but his smooth tongue. Hoppy knew that he and Sharline were practically a married couple, or at least a couple, and she would always be faithful to him. But would she? Teal Buffum, as they drove, did hardly any talking at all, which left Hoppy's mind free to wander, and he had a few unsettling thoughts about the fact that Sharline was, after all, a very lusty gal who sometimes surprised Hoppy with her sheer relish for bed matters. He had said to her only the night before, "I just can't keep up with you." And it was true. If she could have her way about it, they'd spent all their free time in bed.

So his mind wasn't very eased as he and Teal made their day's search, stopping in Cowell and Lurton and Pelsor and Ben Hur to make inquiries. In Witts Springs, they came across a couple of Searcy County sheriff's deputies who had been investigating a road accident, and just happened to be big fans of Hopalong Cassidy who had looked for Hoppy's coming to their towns. Hoppy told them all about Emmett Binns and what he had done, and he gave them a full description of Binns and his car, and they agreed, not only to keep an eye out for the culprit, but to contact by radio the various other sheriff's departments in the Ozarks and to send out an APB, or "all points bulletin," for the capture of Binns.

"Hell," Hoppy remarked to Teal when they were on the road again, "I didn't even know what radio was. Let alone APB. We should've done that first thing."

Late in the afternoon they came to Tilly, which was the easternmost town on Hoppy's circuit, where he was due to appear in three more weeks, and where Hoppy knew practically everyone in town. He was about to have Teal stop at Bardis Cobb's store so he could break the sad news to Bardis, when he happened to catch sight of something unusual in the meadow adjoining the cemetery: there was row after row of benches formed with planks placed across tomato crates. Hoppy's first thought was that the folks of Tilly were so eager for his arrival that they had already gone ahead and set up the outdoor theater, but then he noticed that a screen was already in place tied between two trees, and further, that a projection booth mounted on a half-ton truck bed was also already in place.

Goddamn if it wasn't the Stigler Brothers encroaching on Hoppy's territory! He was furious. All the anger that he had built up toward Emmett Binns was now directed toward Hoy and Loy Stigler, who he found right away at their camper.

"Just what in hell do you mean, anyhow?" Hoppy demanded of them.

"Why howdy, Hop," said Hoy. "You're early, aint ye? You wasn't supposed to show up in Tilly 'till next month sometime."

"I aint showing up, just yet," Hoppy said. "I mean, I aint show-ing up to show pitchers. But you fellers don't have Tilly on your route. It's mine. So what in hell are you doing here, all set up?"

"We're showing a bunch of fine John Wayne pitchers," said Loy. "We figgered that wouldn't be conflicting with your Hopalong Cass'dy pitchers, because John Wayne's westerns is of a little bit higher quality."

"The hell you say. Even if John Wayne's was the best pitchers ever made, that don't give ye no call to move in here and start taking folks' money that they're saving up for me!"

Both Hoy and Loy were hanging their heads and looking awful sheepish, and if they'd been dogs—which they practically were— they'd've been drooping their tails 'twixt their legs. "Well, gee, Hop," Hoy said, "business has been kind of slow down in Pope County, so we figgered we'd just try a little of this corner of your territory. You wouldn't of known we was here if you hadn't stumbled across us just now. What are you doing here, anyhow?"

"I'm trying to locate a certain preacher name of Emmett Binns, who absconded with every last reel of film I had to my name."

Hoy and Loy both gasped. "That bastard!" Hoy said. "We've had trouble with him everywhere we've went, but I never thought he'd stoop to stealing pitcher shows."

Loy said, "It's one thing to spew a load of preachments about the sinfulness of pitcher shows. But it's sure a horse of a different feather to actually rob ye of your pitchers."

Hoppy realized that if he couldn't find Binns and retrieve his pitchers, it didn't matter one jot whether the Stigler Brothers set up in his towns or not. "I'm up the old Shit Creek," Hoppy said, "and the paddle is busted."

Hoy and Loy went on commiserating with Hoppy for quite a spell. As showmen themselves, they could easily appreciate what a tragedy it was to have all your pitchers stolen. They were so sincere and earnest and eloquent in their sympathy that Hoppy forgot completely that they were a pair of unscrupulous pitchmen who had muscled their way into his territory.

At length Hoppy remembered the request he had made of Cap Thomson, and he thought to try it here. "You boys wouldn't happen to have some extry shows that you could be persuaded to loan me the borry of or even sell me?"

Hoy and Loy exchanged looks. Hoy said, "We don't have nothing but what we're showing, half a dozen good John Wayne cowboy pitchers and a Lone Ranger serial. But how much was you willing to pay to rent or buy a pitcher?"

"How much are you willing to ask me to pay?" Hoppy said.

Hoy said to Loy, "Have we got anything we could let him have?"

Loy said, "Let me look. We sure aint gonna let him have a John Wayne, though." Loy climbed up into his projection booth. He was gone a while. Then he stuck his head out the door and said, "Hoy, come up here a minute." And Hoy too climbed up into the projection booth.

Hoppy walked to where Teal Buffum was waiting in the car. "I've got a hunch," he told Teal, "that those fellers might be fixing to let me have a pitcher. This oughtn't to take much longer."

Finally Hoy stepped down from their booth and Loy handed down to him a whole stack of film reels, maybe a dozen cans.

"Wow!" said Hoppy. "How many pitchers is that?"

"Just one," said Loy. "Which is the main reason we don't want it. It's too long for any of our customers. But they's lots of other reasons we can't use it. So we'll let you have it, all eleven reels, for a hundrit dollars cash money plus other considerations."

"We got it by mistake, sort of," Hoy explained. "We sure didn't order it."

"What in hell is it?" Hoppy asked.

Loy handed him a reel, which had the title printed on it: "A Midsummer Night's Dream."

"Never heared of it," Hoppy said. "Who's in it?" He was hoping it wasn't some singing cowboy. He really couldn't abide singing cowboys, but the title sounded like it probably had songs in it.

"It's got James Cagney and Mickey Rooney and Dick Powell and a whole bunch of big names," Hoy said. "Lots of pretty gals too."

"Just how long is it?" Hoppy asked.

"A hundrit and forty-two minutes," Hoy said.

"Jesus Christ!" Hoppy said. "Who would stay to watch a pitcher that long?"

"Maybe you could show it like a serial, in three or four nights," Loy suggested.

"Have you seen it?" Hoppy asked and they sheepishly nodded their heads. "What else is wrong with it?"

"It's kind of hard to figger out what's a-going on," Hoy said. "The plot is kind of complicated, and the way folks talk is kind of odd."

"Is it a cowboy pitcher or not?" Hoppy asked.

"I believe they was a hoss in it," Hoy said. He turned to his brother. "Loy, wasn't they a hoss in it?"

"Yeah," Loy said, "they was definitely a hoss in it. A big black hoss."

"Aint they no shooting in it?" Hoppy asked.

The Brothers conferred and reached the conclusion that not a single shot was fired.

Hoppy needed a moment to take a look into his wallet and count his money. He just barely had enough. Then he asked, "What's the other considerations?"

"The other considerations is that you let us have Tilly and also Mt. Judea."

"Looks like you've already got Tilly," Hoppy said. "But I be damned if I'll ever let you have Mount Judy. You fellers stay out of Newton County. It belongs to me."

"Take it or leave it," Hoy said.

Teal Buffum got out of his car and ambled over. "Hoppy, it's getting pretty late," he said. "We'd best be heading on back."

Hoppy glowered at the Brothers Stigler. "This is a terrible bargain," he said. "Mount Judy is one of my favorite towns." It really was. He had friends in every corner of it. And it was the next town coming up on his route, and he was eager to show it to Sharline. He wished he had her here with him, for her advice. He wished he could show her this "Midsummer Night's Dream" and get her opinion before he laid out a hundred dollars for it and gave up Mount Judy. "Goddamn it all to hell," he said, and handed over his hundred dollars and took possession of a pitcher show that he didn't know nothing about.

Chapter fourteen

I t was mass dark when they got back and Teal dropped him off at Topper. Sharline was nowhere to be seen. Hoppy reckoned she might've already gone out looking for her fairy friends, and he waited a while for her to come back. He went ahead and stacked the eleven reels of his new pitcher show into the racks on Topper's wall, and then he loaded the first reel into the projector and turned the projector so it would face the white screen painted on the wall, and he refocused the lens. He was going to show a preview of it this very night, even if it was late and the show lasted for nearly two and a half hours. He was hoping with all his might that it would be a really good pitcher show even if it didn't have any shooting in it, and he wanted to share his first viewing of it with Sharline. But then he remembered where he'd left her that morning, so he walked over to the Faught place, across the road from Faught's store, and there she was, sitting in Faught's porch swing with Arlis beside her, the two of them just real cozy and Arlis talking up a blue streak as usual.

"You two aint gone to bed yet?" Hoppy said, making a joke, but neither of them knew what to say to that. "Well, I reckon we're back in business, sort of. Leastways, I got me a pitcher show. Just one, but it's a long one. Maybe too long. Sharline, hon, I was hoping you'd watch it with me tonight to see if it's worth watching or not."

Sharline stood up and stretched as if she'd been sitting in that porch swing ever since supper time. Her stretching sure did nice things for her figure, and Arlis noticed it too. "Okay," she said and walked down from the store porch. She asked Hoppy, "Can Arlis come too?"

Hoppy didn't like the idea of giving a free preview to someone who would be a paying customer. That wasn't the only thing he didn't like the idea of, but he realized he was indebted to Arlis for all his help and the driving the day before. He spoke to Arlis: "I don't reckon any of your posse had any luck today."

"Not a hide nor a hair of Binns," Arlis said solemnly. "It seems maybe he's just up and left the country."

"Well, come on and see this pitcher show with us, if you'd care to."

"I'd be obliged and pleasured," Arlis said.

So the three of them went to Topper, and Arlis helped Hoppy move the noisy delco out into the yard. There was hardly any of the Chism's Dew left, maybe just a pint or so, but Hoppy poured drinks for the three of them. Then Arlis took the spare chair while Sharline sat on the bed, and Hoppy started up the machine.

After the usual backward counting of numbers on the screen down to nothing, a drawing came on, that looked like some kind of gal sprite a-swimming toward you with stars over her head, and also big letters spelling "OVERTURE," and the music started. That was all, just real fancy music with that word OVERTURE over that drawing of the gal sprite staying on the screen. Hoppy hadn't heard the word before and didn't know what it meant, but he couldn't understand why the word just stayed there on the screen while the music went on and on. He glanced at Sharline and then at Arlis to see if they might be as puzzled as he was. But they both just had smiles on their faces like they were actually listening to the music and enjoying it.

If the music had finally stopped, Hoppy wouldn't have been so bothered, but the music just went on and on and on, getting faster, and Hoppy began to suspect that that's all there was to it, and the

Stigler Brothers had stuck him with eleven reels of nothing but fancy music. He puzzled over any possible clue in the word OVERTURE, and thought of other words that had TURE in them, like pasture and feature and nature and picture and future and culture. That music sure was cultured. But he thought also of vulture. And as the minutes went by with nothing but that word up there and the music going on and on, like a hundrit fiddles playing at once as fast as they could, he thought of TORTURE. And he turned the projector off.

"I've been played a trick on," he declared. "This aint even a pitcher show."

"Why'd you stop?" Sharline wanted to know. "That's so pretty. My stars! I never heared such pretty music. Don't you think, Arlis?"

"You bet," Arlis said. "Hoppy, if it aint too much trouble, let's us just listen to the rest of it."

So reluctantly Hoppy turned the projector back on, and he sat beside Sharline on the bed and tried to be patient. The music slowed down for a little while but then it speeded up again. "Do you see anything?" he demanded of the other two. "I don't see nothing but that pitcher of that swimming lady with the pointy ears, and that confounded word, OVERTURE."

"I see little fairies dancing in a dream, running and flying through the forest," Sharline said. "I see a bride at a wedding getting herself kissed before walking back up the church aisle. I see a thousand notes of music."

"Ten thousand notes," said Arlis, "all coming together to make one tremendous splendor of sound like a mountain, like a mountain announcing its spring-like flowers a-blooming out in yellow all yelling out in yellow all bunched and mighty!"

"Oh my, oh my," sighed Sharline.

"Huh?" said Hoppy. "I must be blind. I don't see nothing but that lady and that word stuck there."

But finally the music up and died. Hoppy let out a big sigh himself. The black screen had white letters on it: "Warner Brothers have the honor to present a Max Reinhardt production."

And then the big letters of the title: "A MIDSUMMER NIGHT'S DREAM by William Shakespeare."

"I've heared tell of him," Arlis said. "He wrote a whole bunch of stories."

"Not as many as Clarence Mulford, I bet," Hoppy said.

"Mulford's was all about Hopalong Cassidy," Arlis declared. "This gent's stories was long ago and far away, in Old England."

The screen declared that the music was done by a feller named Felix Mendelsohn, so at least Hoppy knew who he could blame for that Overture.

When the cast of characters came on the screen their names didn't look like Old England at all. There was a Theseus and a Hippolyta and a Philostrate. There was stuff about "Lysander, who is in love with Hermia," and "Demetrius, who is in love with Hermia," and "Hermia, who is in love with Lysander," and "Helena, who is in love with Demetrius." Hoppy decided that all of that romance ought to please the womenfolk in the audience but he doubted the kids would take to it.

It was going to be a big cast. There would be a bunch of working folks, a carpenter named Quince and a bellows-mender named Flute—Hoppy never realized a feller could earn a living just from fixing up busted bellers—and a tinker named Stout, Snug a joiner, Starveling a tailor and Bottom, a weaver. Hoppy had thought of himself as a kind of weaver, a weaver of films through the projector, so he looked forward to seeing if this Bottom had any resemblance to himself.

Sharline began clapping her hands when the screen also announced that there would be a King and Queen of Fairies, as well as fairies named Puck, Peaseblossom, Cobweb, Moth and Mustardseed. If the screen really did show those fairies and not just more music, Hoppy could have a chance to see if they were accurate representations of the critters that Sharline had been meeting in the woods.

Next came on the screen a "PROCLAMATION," some long and tedious written thing about the Duke of Athens getting married to the Queen of the Amazons, and Hoppy realized that Sharline would have a lot of reading-aloud to do for the folks in the audience who couldn't read.

Then finally there was real pitchers: a line-up of fancy-dressed fellers a-tooting their trumpets, which put Hoppy's bugle to shame and said, it seemed, *With pomp, with triumph, and with reveling.* There is this huge hall in a palace filled with hundreds of people, and this king and queen in their best outfits of armor marching in solemn procession while the trumpets blow. Hoppy knew from their outfits that the people in this pitcher show had never been west of the Atlantic Ocean, let alone the Mississippi, so this couldn't possibly have nothing to do with cowboys. But everything was so grand and large and important that Hoppy was impressed with the sheer spectacle of it all. Then the King or Duke or whoever he is starts speaking, sweet-talking his lady, and pretty soon every other word is "thou" or "thee" or "thy" and he sounds more like the Bible than the way real folks talk.

Hoppy figured out that the main thing in this story was that the Duke is a-fixing to get hitched to the Amazon Queen, but she isn't too happy with the idee, so the Duke is planning all these merriments to put her in the mood. Then there is some commotion because one of the lords wants his daughter Hermia to marry a certain feller but she has in mind to marry a different feller, which is against the law, to go against your daddy's wishes, punishable by death. Well, the Duke tells her she has a third choice: she can stay a virgin all her life and become a nun, and he gives her a few days to think it over and decide which of those three choices she wants. The feller that she is supposed to marry has already fooled around with a friend of hers named Helena and took her virginity, and this Helena is crazy in love with him. But Hermia is in love with a different feller, named Lysander, who is in love with her, and next time they're alone they talk about the hopeless situation. Lysander says that "The course of true love never did run smooth," and Hoppy thought that any fool knew that to be the truth. The couple decides to meet the next night in the woods and then elope!

Then the working folk, who look like the ordinary folks you'd see anywhere, have a meeting, and this carpenter named Quince is the leader who is going to tell each of 'em what part they will play in a little skit they plan to put on for the entertainment of the Duke and his bride. The play is called "The Most Lamentable Comedy and

Most Cruel Death of Pyramus and Thisbe." Bottom the Weaver doesn't look anything like Hoppy. He is this Hollywood gangster Cagney that Hoppy had seen a time or two in other pitcher shows, but here he is a clumsy, bumbling idjit who has in mind to play all the parts, and they have to hold him back. Quince tells 'em all to memorize their parts and they'll meet in the woods the next night to rehearse.

Then the scene changes from the town to the woods at night, and those woods look just like what you'd see right here in the Ozarks, beneath a sliver of a moon. A kid wakes up buried in a pile of leaves, and Hoppy recognized Mickey Rooney, about the same age as Sammy McKim, who played young Kit Carson in "The Painted Stallion." He's got a pair of horn stubs growing out of his head, and just in case you think this is real, which it aint, along comes a donkey with one big horn growing out of his head. "A unicorn," said Arlis Faught, a smart feller. Suddenly all the wisps of fog in the woods change into figures, and those figures are women in practically nothing, just garments that look like Sharline's chiffon, and they commence running and dancing in unison. Hundreds of them, up and around some kind of ramp, and back down again and then all over.

Sharline squealed with joy. "My fairies!" she said. Hoppy peered closely at the fairy dance, wondering if these really were the same sort of critter that Sharline had been meeting in the dark woods of a night. Then we see the Queen of the Fairies, the most gorgeous woman Hoppy has ever laid eyes on, a tall blonde, and she has this little kid, not her own, but "a lovely boy stolen from an Indian king." The kid doesn't look like an injun to Hoppy, with his head in a fancy turban. Anyhow, along comes this big feller all in black atop a mighty black horse which must've been the horse the Stigler Brothers had told him about. But just in case you think he's real, just as the young fairy named Puck or the unicorn has horns, he has antlers growing out of his head. And he growls, "Ill met by moonlight, proud Titania!" and he and his queen get in a terrible tussle because he wants that injun prince hisself. All the fairies run and hide in the bushes.

This Fairy King, name of Oberon, calls out of hiding Puck, played by little Micky Rooney, and commands him to run and fetch a certain plant called love-in-idleness which, "The juice of it on sleeping eyelids laid will make or man or woman madly dote upon the next live creature it sees." Hoppy had heard tell of such potions tried here in the Ozarks, although he'd never known of one that actually worked. The Oberon feller plans to use it on the Fairy Queen, whose name is Titania, so he can get that injun boy.

Just when you think you're watching a whole different pitcher show that has completely forgot the folks who were in the first part, here comes that young couple from the first part, Demetrius and Helena, and Demetrius is trying to get away from her because, as he keeps telling her, he doesn't love her. Oberon feels sorry for her so he decides to have Puck put the love-in-idleness juice on Demetrius's eyes and he sends Puck off to find Demetrius and do that, but by mistake Puck finds Lysander, who has come into the woods with his ladylove Hermia and they have gone to sleep there. So of course when he wakes up and sees Helena first thing, he falls madly in love with Helena, but she thinks he's just kidding and runs off.

By and by those working guys come into the woods to start rehearsing their little play. Puck comes along and watches them, and is bothered because they're rehearsing their play right smack in the patch of woods that belongs to the Fairy Queen, so Puck decides to play a trick on them by giving Bottom the head of a donkey, or jackass, just in case you think this is real, which it aint. All the other working guys run away in fright. When we lay eyes on sleeping Titania the Fairy Queen again, who has had that love juice put in her eyes, we know that when she wakes up she'll see that dumb donkey and dote on him.

All of these folks sleeping in the woods—Titania and Hermia and Lysander and Demetrius—has made Hoppy nod a bit himself, and once when his head drooped he looked down and saw that Sharline had gone sound asleep. His first notion was to nudge her awake, but she slept so deeply he got up and turned off the projector and lit the coal oil lamp. Arlis blinked his eyes and looked up at Hoppy to see what was up, and said, "Prithee, wherefore ceaseth thou?" and Hoppy inclined his head toward sleeping Sharline.

"I reckon she got bored with the show, and conked out," Hoppy observed.

"Nay, 'twas but the favor of the several sleepers who hath inspired her into slumber," said Arlis, and Hoppy figured he had been inspired into talking like the folks in the show.

"Maybe we ought to call it a night," Hoppy suggested, "and watch the rest of it tomorrow night."

But mayhap the sounds of their voices woke her. She came awake, and her eyes fell on Arlis, and her whole face lit up, and she held out her arms to him. "Awakest thou, faire lady," said Arlis, but he didn't grab her or nothing. Hoppy wondered if she really was under some kind of spell, because nobody had sprinkled no pansy-juice in her eyes.

"What angel wakes me from my flowery bed?" said Sharline. And hark! if ole Arlis didn't commence singing:

"The finch, the sparrow, and the lark,
The plain-song cuckoo gray,
Whose note full many a man doth mark,
And dares not answer nay."

Sharline said, "I pray thee, gentle mortal, sing again: Mine ear is much enamour'd of thy note; So is mine eye enthralled to thy shape…"

"I hate to interrupt you lovebirds," Hoppy said, "but it's near on to midnight and we'd better wait until tomorrow to watch the rest of the pitcher show."

But the lovebirds wouldn't hear of it, and both Arlis and Sharline protested so mightily in such fancy language that Hoppy was compelled to start the projector up again. He noted there were only three reels of film left.

Well, it seemed that there Fairy Queen has fallen head over heels for that jackass, or that weaver Bottom with the head of a jackass, and she gets her fairy servants to lead him off to her bower, or woodsy bedstead, where there's no telling what they do for the rest of the night. It turns out that Oberon is happy with his queen's infatuation, but he's unhappy that Puck has squirted the love-juice into Lysander's eyes by mistake, so he makes him correct that mistake by doing Demetrius, who sure-enough wakes later and falls for Helena. And then both of the men are fighting over Helena, and poor Hermia is bothered because her Lysander has told her he hates her, and poor Hoppy is bothered because he has got confused about all four of these lovers and who loves who.

Hermia and Helena are fighting, and Demetrius and Lysander are fighting, and Hoppy is wishing they all four had six-shooters so they could settle their arguments the way they ought to be settled in a good cowboy movie.

Puck sure is right when he says, "Lord, what fools these mortals be!" But finally he puts them all to sleep again, and puts some kind of antidote in Lysander's eyes so he will love Hermia again.

Oberon, who appears to be in charge of everything and has the little injun prince for his own at last, takes away the spell that Titania is in, and has Puck turn the jackass' head back into Bottom's.

Sharline spoke simultaneously with Titania, "What visions have I seen! Methought I was enamour'd of an ass."

All the fairies disappear and the night is over. The next day the Duke Theseus and his hunting party come across the lovers all asleep and wakes them. Lysander tries to explain everything to Hermia's daddy, who is furious, but after Demetrius explains he is really in love with Helena, the Duke decides that the lovers can all be married at the same time as himself and that Amazon Queen. And everything looks like it's going to be such happily-ever-after that Demetrius says "It seems to me that yet we sleep, we dream."

That ought to have put an end on it, but those working folk still have to perform their little play for the wedding ceremony, which turns out to be the funniest part of the whole show, although it's downright ridiculous the way those actors make fools of themselves trying to do the story of Pyramus and Thisbe. Arlis and Sharline were laughing their heads off, so Hoppy joined in too, and they had a lot of fun.

Sharline was real pleased because Oberon and Titania and all their fairies come back to bless the married couples as they head off for bed. And just in case any of us in the audience have wondered if the whole pitcher show is but a dream we've had, Mickey Rooney

the Puck puts in one last speech: "If we shadows have offended, think
but this, and all is mended: that you have but slumbered here while
these visions did appear; and this weak and idle theme, no more
yielding but a dream!"

Pretty soon a word came on the screen that just said "FINIS."
Hoppy wasn't sure what that meant. He knew a feller named Fenness
up in Carroll County but it was spelled different. The word disappeared and was replaced by "Exit Music," and Hoppy was pretty sure
what "exit" meant. Sure enough, here come ole Felix again with his
thousand fiddles and all. Apparently they was in a hurry to get out
compared with how long it took to get in, so that Exit Music didn't
last nearly as long as the Overture did.

When Felix was done and the screen went blank, Arlis said,
"Forsooth! Mine eyes ne'r beheld such enchantment, but now I am
disenchanted back into my ordinary self."

"Yeah," said Sharline, "it's real hard to be real again." But
Hoppy was glad that she was real again, because she stopped gazing
so adoringly at Arlis and laid her eyes on Hoppy again. "What did
you think, Landon?" she asked him.

"Well, I got to allow as how it's the downright prettiest pitcher
show I ever seen, as far as the pitchers are concerned, I mean, the
camera was out of this world."

"Incomparable cinematography," said Arlis, and at least he
wasn't talking Shakespeare any more.

Chapter fifteen

Bright and early the next morning, despite getting less than a good night's sleep (although Sharline was dead to the world before Hoppy got his pants off), Sharline put on her overalls and her sunbonnet and told Hoppy to make his own breakfast because she had to get on over to the Faught place. He asked her what in hell for, and she said she'd told Arlis she would come and help him hoe weeds out of his garden patch. "The thing I miss most," she said, "being on the road and roaming from town to town, is my own little garden patch. I'm real keen on planting seeds and watching things come up, and taking gentle care of them till they're growed and can be et." She and Arlis had to tend his garden early in the morning before it got too hot. So Hoppy made his own breakfast for a change, just some leftover biscuits with jam on them, and half a pot of coffee. He was of a mind to go off by himself fishing, for a change. Although he was feeling kind of jealous, let alone suspicious, that Sharline wanted to spend so much time with Arlis, he was also a bit relieved to be free from her, a thing he'd noticed on the trip with Teal Buffum the day before: after being in her constant company all the time ever since she'd first come into his life as Carl, it was good, or at least different, to have a little time to himself. The trouble was, being up on the mountain, the town didn't have a fishing creek running through it. The nearest spot, back down the road a ways, was the headwaters of the Little Buffalo River, hardly more than a trickle. But it was the same stream that ran through his home country of Stay More farther along down the valleys, and just the thought of that made him want to go there, fishing or not. He got his fishing pole and set out on foot, although it would be a mile or two to hike.

He hadn't gone as far as Faught's store when he thought that he wished he'd been able to lock up Topper, to protect his one and only pitcher show in its eleven reels. It was a shame to have to lock up anything, but once the horse is stolen you've got to find a way to keep the barn door latched. Maybe Faught's store carried locks for sale, although he doubted it, because he'd never heard of anybody having a lock on anything, and anyhow Arlis Faught hadn't opened up his store yet because he was busy elsewhere. So Hoppy just walked on past the store, turned at the road and headed west past the Faught place, where he caught sight of his truelove and her boyfriend out yonder in his garden patch, a-chopping away at the weeds. He waved, but they didn't see him. Arlis seemed to be talking a blue streak, as usual, and Hoppy hoped it was in plain English. Hoppy thought back to the way Arlis, and Sharline too, had been talking during the latter part of the pitcher show the night before. They sure had seemed to enjoy the show, but Hoppy wouldn't allow himself to take their appreciation of the show as a prediction of what other people would think. Sharline obviously enjoyed the show because it had fairies in it, and Arlis liked it because he was just naturally a bit more high class than most folks. Hoppy himself wasn't particularly high class, and he sure didn't believe in fairies, let alone unicorns and love-juice made from pansies for squirting in folks' eyes, but he had pretty much been grateful for the show: it had been uplifting and had dazzled his eyes, and it sure was a stimulating contrast to the kind of pitcher show he had been showing for years. He wasn't too sure but what he didn't even appreciate the absence of six-shooters and rustlers and thundering horses. He hadn't exactly learned anything from it, but for that matter you never learn anything from a cowboy show either. He hadn't cared too much for all that fairy-dancing, all those thin-clad women a-swaying and a-swinging and a-prancing in the moonlight, which was just sort of a performing or acting-out of ole Felix's fancy notes of music. But thinking back on the pitcher show as a whole, it was pretty comical and a lot of fun to watch. Would his audiences think so?

A logging trail led from the main road to a pretty spot where the Little Buffalo River began as just a spring coming out of the side of the mountain, and collected in a pool for a while before tumbling on down the mountainside. The hole of water looked like it might have some fish in it, but after half an hour of casting he knew it didn't. So he figured as long as he was here he might as well take a quick dip, and he stripped his clothes off and jumped in. The water being spring-fed was a bit cold for this time of year. He would have to remember to tell Sharline about this spot, in case she wanted a bath.

After he was out of the water, as he had no towel to dry off he moved on up the slope a ways to a slab of rock where the sun would dry him, slowly but nicely. There he reclined for a while and thought about how this little stream of water would run on for a number of miles and then join up with Swains Creek at Stay More. Thinking of Stay More, he realized that they'd have to make a trip there pretty soon to get some more Chism's Dew. He didn't mind. It wouldn't be too hard to revisit his old haunts, even the old Stapleton place that had belonged to his grandfather and still contained what few belongings Hoppy had in this world that weren't inside of Topper.

Hoppy heard a car engine stop not far away, and in a little bit he saw a couple coming down through the woods. They came right on down to the water before Hoppy recognized them and realized they must have in mind to rench off the sweat they'd worked up chopping weeds in the garden patch. The feller was talking as he always did (he probably talked in his sleep too), but Hoppy was too far away to hear what he was saying. He probably wasn't needing to do a lot of persuading, because before you could say Jack Robinson the girl had peeled off her overalls and her underthings and had jumped in the pool, squealing at the coldness of the water, and then the feller had jumped right in after her. And pretty soon they were splashing each other and laughing and having such a time as never you did see. Hoppy realized that his jealousy wasn't because of the situation itself but because not so long ago he had tried to get Carl to take a bath in the creek with him, and he could still hear "Carl's" words: "I'm sorry, I just caint. I'm just too shy, I reckon. Maybe when I get to know ye better, I could." She must've got to know Arlis a whole lot better in a awful short time.

Hoppy was tempted to holler something just to let them know that they were being watched. But he held his tongue. And pretty soon they commenced behaving in a way that would have kept him from giving himself away. It's one thing just to go skinny-dipping together when you hardly know each other, but it sure is a different story to start fooling around in a dead-earnest fashion. Just what was she thinking, anyhow? Maybe the problem was, she wasn't thinking nothing at all, she was pure-and-simple overcome with lust, red in the comb. And maybe Arlis was so all het up that he wasn't even stopping to think that he was betraying his good friend Hoppy, who had brought him entertainments for three years now. *Well, I've shore brought him a fine entertainment this time around*, Hoppy said to himself, and he wasn't talking about "A Midsummer Night's Dream." Come to think of it, that pitcher show had been somewhat on the raunchy side, at least by suggestion, depending on how you looked at it, and maybe that had incited both of 'em into this wantonness.

They were having a real problem making a good connection in the water, even though she'd climbed him and had her legs wrapped around his hips. They were both groaning more from frustration than from pleasure. So finally they climbed out of the water and into a bed of leaves on the bank. Hoppy caught sight of Arlis' pecker, which may have been the main reason they hadn't been able to connect: it was a sockdolager, worthy of a studhorse, and as he mounted her and tried to put it into her, Hoppy was reminded of his reel called "Assortment," the way all the men in those pitcher shows had equipment that was oversize and made you feel that you didn't have nothing to write home about. Thinking of his wicked pitcher show as he watched this couple and listened to his truelove a-crying out as the feller finally poked it into her made Hoppy realize not just how inferior his tool was but how inferior pitcher shows were to the real thing: it was mightily more stimulating to see it actually happening than watching "Assortment," and Hoppy was abashed to discover, once the insertion had been accomplished and the vigorous movements swole up on both sides, that his own equipment was a-swelling considerable. The main advantage of the real thing over the pitcher show was not just because it was in three dimensions and full color and with the fragrance of the morning woods but because you are occupying the same piece of earth as the actors, you could almost join them, or pretend you were joining them or taking their place or whatever.

All his life Hoppy had hated himself for one thing or another, but never as much as he now hated himself for watching so keenly and breathlessly. He was having so much fun that he began to suspect, in remembrance of last night's pitcher show, that this was all just a dream. It wasn't a midsummer night's dream, but it sure was midsummer, and the whole idea of his truelove fucking the daylights out of this country storekeeper was so dreamlike it couldn't possibly be real. As he watched—and it just went on and on and on, like those actors in "Assortment" who could hold off coming forever—he kept expecting to wake up at any moment, but he never did. He remembered how watching the "Assortment" had affected that bastard preacher Emmett Binns and had made him so horny he was ready to pay Sharline for gratification. But Hoppy was hornier now than that preacher or anybody had ever been, and he began to give serious thought to the idea of joining the couple and taking over after Arlis was spent…if ever he was, because he never seemed to stop or slow and both of them were moaning and groaning and Sharline had already gone into one of her squealing spells at least twice and was building up to the third one. Hoppy couldn't help himself; he grabbed aholt of his pecker and commenced pumping it. If the fairies had been right in telling Sharline to tell him that his problem was he lived inside his penis, then he was really setting up home inside his penis right now, giving it all the attention that he could spare from the intense attention he was giving to the noisily coupling couple. "Oh Lord God, I'm a-going!" Arlis said at long last.

"Don't go!" Sharline said. "*Come!*" And with that she let out a howl of ecstasy that they must have heard back in town.

And Hoppy came too. But he choked back whatever expression of fulfillment he might have been tempted to utter. Then in shame he rolled over and buried his face in the leaves and just remained like that for a long time, until finally, when he looked up again, the couple had gone. He decided that the hatred he felt for himself was overmatched by that he felt for Arlis and for Sharline.

So when it came time that night for the pitcher show, he was not in a good mood, and the turn-out wasn't enough to help his mood. Compared with the crowds they'd been getting at the camp meeting it was piddling. Hoppy wondered if word had got around so fast that he wasn't going to be showing cowboy movies. One feller with his family came up to Hoppy and asked him, "Is this some kind of childern's pitcher show you're a-showing tonight?" Hoppy assured him it was mainly for grownups but kids would probably enjoy it too. And sure enough most of the paying audience was just kids: of maybe a hundred, at least sixty weren't old enough to vote. Hoppy didn't ask Sharline how many tickets she'd sold. He wasn't speaking to her. He wasn't in any kind of mood for asking her nothing. When it came time for them to do their juggling acts, his mind and his heart weren't in it, and he kept dropping his balls. In the one act where they tossed balls to each other, keeping eight or nine in the air at once, he overthrew her badly and she couldn't catch anything, so he just quit and let her do her chiffon fascinator act, which the audience appreciated, although he didn't much care for the way she swung her hips and wiggled her bottom and swayed her whole shapely body. He noticed Arlis sitting in the front row clapping harder than anybody. And when they switched over from juggling to magic, Hoppy wasn't any good at all. His hypnotism failed to entrance anyone, his levitation act caused Sharline to fall, and his disappearing act got rid of only half of her. He was glad when it was dark enough to start the pitcher show, but real sorry that they wouldn't be starting with the first episode of "The Painted Stallion."

Before the show started, Sharline stood in front of the audience and made a little speech. "I reckon most of you folks has heard," she began, "that the pitcher shows we was fixing to show ye got stole from us, so we've had to make a replacement. You may have noticed that Landon "Hoppy" Boyd aint wearing his Hopalong Cassidy hat tonight, and I aint wearing mine, which is just like his. Because we can't show you any Hopalong Cassidy pitcher shows. But we've got a real clever and sightly show called "A Midsummer Night's Dream" that's prettier than any dream you ever had! You'll just love it to pieces!"

She sat down next to Arlis, who had been saving her a seat, and Hoppy started up the projector, and that dadblasted "OVERTURE" showed up on the screen and that lavish music started. After just a few minutes of it the audience started getting restless, and the kids started talking amongst themselves, so noisy you could hardly hear the music if you wanted to, but hardly nobody wanted to. The Overture wasn't half over when some kids started throwing rocks at the screen, trying to hit that drawing of the fairy lady swimming toward you. Hoppy was using the duck tarp painted white with alabastine for a screen, since his regular screen had burnt at the camp meeting fire and he hadn't replaced it yet. The duck tarp was pretty sturdy, but if enough sharp rocks was thrown at it there would sure to be holes. Hoppy wished there was some way to make the projector run faster so that Overture would be over.

When the pitcher show finally started and the written proclamation came on the screen, Sharline stood up again to read it out for the benefit of the unlettered. When the Duke was making his speech to the Amazon queen, the first folks to walk out walked out. They didn't even bother stopping to ask Hoppy for a refund. But before long, about when that business of Hermia's daddy wanting to kill her if she wouldn't marry Demetrius got started, a group of teenagers came up to Hoppy and one of them said, "Give us our money back. We don't keer to try to figger out what in heck is a-going on." Hoppy gave each of them their money back. When the fairy dancing started, a farmer and his wife and their five children got refunds too. The folks who did stay because there wasn't anything in this world better to do spent most of their time talking and not paying much attention to the show. An occasional teenager threw a rock at the screen…or an egg. Several of them booed. The shrunken audience seemed to have only two members who were really watching the show: Sharline and Arlis. The show wasn't half over before Hoppy's worst fears were confirmed: there just wasn't any market for this kind of show.

Finally Hoppy just let a reel run out and leave the screen blank but illuminated, and he walked out there and stood in the glare of that light and faced what was left of his audience. He wasn't accustomed at all to public speaking, but he managed a few words. "Folks, I'm real sorry. I've made a bad mistake, getting aholt of this pitcher show, which just aint what you expected and what you paid for. If you'll line up, I'll give ye all your money back. Thanks for coming, and I hope one of these days soon to have some good old Hopalong Cassidy pitchers to show ye again."

But nobody got up to leave, and nobody, of the maybe fifty that was left, got in line to get their money back. Hoppy waited, wondering if perhaps they wanted to have another gathering of tale-telling like the other night. Arlis, who had suggested the tale-telling, stood up and began to speak, but he wasn't suggesting any oral stories. "They's obviously some clods and half-wits who don't have the sense to know a great pitcher show when they see one, but I recognize all of you good folks who are still here as the smartest folks in this town. And you want to see the rest of it, don't ye?"

There were cries of "You bet!" and "Let's do it!" and "Yessiree-bob!" and "Darn tootin!"

Arlis said to Hoppy, "The next reel, please." Hoppy didn't like the tone of Arlis' voice, as if he was telling Hoppy what to do, but Hoppy was glad to do it, and he resumed showing the pitcher show. A few folks went to sleep when all that sleeping started in the pitcher show, but they woke up and watched the rest of it. There weren't any more rocks or eggs thrown at the screen. And when Puck made his final speech and "FINIS" came on, everybody clapped. Hoppy clapped himself, not in appreciation of the show but of the faithful audience.

Hoppy calculated that the paid admissions plus what Sharline had made from popcorn and candy came to almost one-tenth of the cost of the film, which wasn't bad for the first night. Nine more showings and the film would be paid for.

So his mood wasn't too terrible at bedtime but he had to remind himself what had put him in a bad mood in the first place. When Sharline climbed into bed with him and tried to get frisky or at least feisty, he rolled over and turned his back to her.

"Hey, hon, what's troubling you?" she asked.

"Haven't you had enough?" he grumbled.

"I never have enough," she declared.

"I believe it," he said. He climbed over her and got out of the lower bunk and then climbed into the upper bunk. "Why don't ye go play with your fairies?" he suggested.

And maybe she did. Because later, when he couldn't sleep, he heard her go out.

Chapter sixteen

She hadn't come back when he woke with the sun well up into the sky. He reckoned that if her fairy friends hadn't put her up for the night, then Arlis had. Or they had gone somewhere for the night, because Hoppy knew that Arlis lived with his mother the postmistress of the town, and if he was shacking up with Sharline he wouldn't want his mother to know it. Hoppy had to wonder if he honestly did give a damn where the—what had Binns called her? slut? yeah, where the slut had spent the night. But the truth was, he really did care. And it hurt. Into his morning coffee he poured the last of the Chism's Dew, just a jigger or two, not enough to kill the pain, but enough to keep the whole real world from being all black and white like the pitcher shows.

It was nigh on to noon before she showed up again. She was wearing her nicest dress, that he'd bought her at Clarksville and was meant for special occasions. She was also wearing a pair of fancy shoes that he hadn't bought her. She was carrying under her arm a stack of something…a sheaf of thick papers or something. She handed one of them to Hoppy, and he held it at arm's length and read the big printed letters on it:

HIGH CLASS PICTURE SHOW COMING TO YOUR TOWN!

Lavish Hollywood Production of
"A Midsummer Night's Dream"
with all-star cast
Performances at _____, Ark.
Week of _____

EVERYBODY YOUNG AND OLD WELCOME!
The iron tongue of midnight hath told twelve.
Lovers, to bed; 'tis almost fairy time.
—Wm. Shakspear

"Where'd you get this?" he asked her.

"Did you know this town's got a feller who does print jobs?" she said. "Matt Spotwood, right over yonder on the main road. It's a law office, but he's got a printing press in the back room, and he did this poster for us. Three hundred of them!"

"*Us?*" said Hoppy. "Who's 'us'?"

"Why, you and me, silly! Arlis helped out with what to put on it, but it's mostly mine." She stepped back and frowned at him, as if she was expecting him to praise her, or thank her, and he wasn't doing it.

"How much did Matt Spotwood charge ye for all these?" Hoppy asked.

"Just a little, not as much as he'd usually get, on account of he admires this pitcher show too and wants to see it again and again! And of course we'll have to let him and his family in free."

Hoppy had never used posters or any other form of advertisements in all the years he'd been showing pitchers. To make it work, you'd really have to get to the town a week or so early to put up the posters. But he had to have a high regard for this here poster: it was neatly printed, with big black letters in fancy type on a stock of thick cream-colored poster-paper. It bothered him that maybe the reason Sharline and Arlis had done it was because they were feeling guilty about their adultery—well, at least their fornication.

"I was fixing to move on," Hoppy declared. "I've done already shown the show to this town. I might as well get on up the road to the next town." He hoped she got the significance of his saying "I" instead of "we," because he certainly wasn't thinking of taking her with him.

"But Arlis thinks you could show the pitcher show here for another night or maybe even two or three. He's already gone out and put up these posters hither and yon all over creation, telling that the show will be *here* the rest of this week.

"Taking over, is he?" Hoppy said. "He didn't even stop to think to ask me if I wanted him doing that?"

"He just wants to help," she said. "He just has some good ideas for making the pitcher show a success. Wait till you hear some of his other idees. He thinks we ought to sell sody pop, and tonight he'll bring a tub of pop bottles in ice from his store."

"Ice? Where in hell does he find ice?"

"Not hell, where it would be too hot!" she laughed. "The mail truck brings these big blocks of ice that he keeps in his sody pop cooler."

"You know a lot about Arlis, what with all the time you've spent with him. Did you spend the night with him last night?"

"I did not." Her face didn't give away anything.

"Well, you weren't *here*."

"You weren't being nice to me. You climbed into the top bunk."

"So where did you go?"

"Did ye know," she asked, "that all them fairies in the pitcher show look nearly just like *my* fairies? They're bigger, and most of 'em look like females when fairies aint neither gals nor boys, and them shimmies they wear are not the same fabric, they're more like the thin stuff my fascinators are made of, but they move pretty much the same way, that dancing and all. I think whoever made that pitcher show must've seen some of our Ozark fairies."

"Not if I aint never seen 'em myself," Hoppy remarked. "Not if they really aint no such of a thing to begin with, except in your peculiar imagination. Binns was right when he said you don't live in this world, you just live in your imagination."

"I should have taken you with me," she said. "To meet the fairies. Tonight after the show I'll take you with me."

"I aint too certain I'll still be around tonight."

"*What?* How come? Where are you going?"

"Well, for one thing, I'd better find another town where I can put up these posters you've had made."

"But won't you show at least one more show here in this town? After Arlis has done put up so many posters already…"

"Maybe not. Maybe I'd best hit the road directly."

"I caint just up and leave like that!" she said.

"Who's asking you to leave?"

She stared at him. He almost felt a little sorry for her, the stricken look on her face. Real soft she asked, "You're not taking me with you?"

"You're not my woman no more," he said.

"I never was *your* woman, and I never will be until I've become Mrs. Landon Boyd, if that ever happens."

"Don't worry. It won't."

"I figured not," she said and gave him back the cold look he was giving her. "But just kindly tell me, what has got into you? Why have you turned off so harsh?"

"You and Arlis carrying on."

"'Carrying on?' Now what does that mean?"

"Fucking, for one thing."

"That's a ugly word. What makes you think we're carrying on and fucking?"

"I seen you," he said.

"*Where?*"

"When you and Arlis was working in his garden patch yesterday morning, I took a notion to go fishing at that place where the Little Buffalo begins, right out west of town yonder. I didn't catch any fish but by and by I caught a good look at you and Arlis jumping nekkid into that hole of water and then fucking like a pair of wildcats, except it takes wildcats just a minute or two to finish, and you and Arlis went on and on and on!"

It was the longest speech he'd ever made, and she just looked at him open-mouthed for nearly as long as it took a pair of wildcats to finish, and then she let out a big sigh and said, "My oh my." And then she commenced shaking her head. "So I guess you think he ruint me?" she asked.

"Naw, I had done already ruint you, but he done a pretty good job of doing ye better than I ever done." He added, "Or ever could do!"

"So now you know why I had to go out last night, for the whole night. Not to be with him, no, but to talk to my fairy friends about what I had done and whether I had spiled the whole notion of *you and me*. And do you know what they said to me?"

"Yeah, they said, 'Sharline, you just fuck anybody you care to, anytime you want.'"

"No, they never. They didn't give me permission to do that, to make it with him or with you or nobody. They just explained to me why I'd done it with him. You know, you were the first and only one, for me. They said that I was so thrilled to pieces to find out how good it was with you, how I was enjoying myself so much with you especially after you learnt to quit living inside your penis, how it was all so wonderful that I couldn't hardly believe it, couldn't hardly stand it, it was so fine, and I begun to doubt that there was another soul on this earth who could make me feel as good as you did. So just out of curiosity I had to find out if there was another feller who could make me feel like that."

"And sure enough, it turns out that ole Arlis with his huge pecker could even make you come *three* times!"

"They also said that numbers don't count, that it's not the repetition that matters, and it's sure not the size that matters. All that matters is that you have to feel like you and the one you're with are just one. That's it. It don't even matter how mighty you come, all that matters is that you become a part of the one you're with, and they a part of you." Sharline had begun to weep. She wasn't sobbing or nothing, but the tears were a-streaming down her cheeks. "And I never felt that way with him, not the way I do with you."

Hoppy was touched, not because of her tears but because of what the fairies had told her, assuming that they really had told her that, and although he found it nearly impossible to believe in fairies he found it even harder to believe that she could have made up that stuff all by herself. Still, even though he was ready and willing to believe, he was terrible mad at her. "But goddammit, Sharline," he tried to ask calmly, "didn't you give a thought to how it might make me feel?"

"I had no idee you'd ever know."

"And I don't reckon you'd ever intended to tell me. Wasn't you thinking of me at all when you done it?"

"I was only thinking of how I loved ye so much better."

"How can you say that when he made ye come *three* times with that big tallywhacker of his?"

"Like my fairy friends said—"

"Fuck your fairy friends!" Hoppy said, feeling really bitter, and then found himself inwardly laughing at what he'd just said, as if he were suggesting that she get her sexual satisfaction from the fairies, who didn't even possess any tallywhackers, to hear her tell it. It was all he could do to keep from laughing out loud. But just as he was able to keep the guffaws of laughter bottled up silently within himself, he was also able to keep his bawls of crying gagged too. "Get in the truck," he said to her. She misunderstood him and started to climb up the steps into Topper's rear end. "Up front," he said, and folded up and latched the steps to the back end. Then he got behind the wheel and started off.

She looked at him with panic. "Where are we going?" she asked. "I caint just up and leave. I'd have to say goodbye."

"You can wave goodbye," he said, just as they were passing Faught's store. "But we aint leaving town. Just going out for a little recreation."

They didn't even see Arlis, nor he them. Hoppy drove on, a little over a mile, to where the road turned off to reach the source of the Little Buffalo. He drove as far as Topper could go, and then stopped, and got out.

Sharline was smiling. "I think I know what you're up to," she said.

He led her down to the hole of water. "I reckon we could stand a dip," he remarked, and took off his clothes. His tallywhacker was already at full attention, stiffer than he'd ever known it to be, and he wondered at himself, that he was hankering after her so much despite her transgression. Or was it because of her transgression? There's no understanding the human heart, let alone the human tallywhacker.

Sharline was looking around for a good place to hang her fancy dress. She stepped out of her fancy shoes, which Arlis must have given her, and then took off her underthings. She wasn't doing it as fast as she had when she'd been with Arlis, as if she wasn't so eager. "That water is awful cold," she said, as if she'd know, and she didn't just jump right in like she'd done before. She stuck her toe in and squealed, and then very slowly walked down into the water, holding herself and shivering. It seemed as if her whole way of doing it was different: before, she had just plunged right in, without a thought or regard for the consequences. And she didn't want Hoppy to splash her, and she wasn't splashing him. She wanted him to hold her and try to warm her up.

And when he led her out of the water and tried to take her to the spot where she and Arlis had fucked, where the leaves and moss and twigs and fronds were all stirred up and mashed, she protested, "Couldn't we do it somewheres else?"

"No, it's got to be right here," he said, and pushed her down to the ground, and got himself between her legs and tried to get into her.

"Aren't you going to kiss me?" she asked. "You might've noticed he never did even kiss me."

Hoppy thought back and realized that she was right. So he gave her a good kiss. The kissing seemed to loosen her up some. She reached her fingers down to help guide him in.

"Don't ye think mine's nearly as noble as his'n?" he asked.

"Yes, but don't live inside it," she warned, reminding him again.

He was an old hand at that now, trying not to think of his tallywhacker regardless of how wonderful it felt. So he did manage to hold off at least past the point where he would hate himself. He had hoped to be able to step so far outside himself that not only would he be able to last as long as Arlis had but also that he would be able to view himself with her as if he were watching them in a pitcher show or better yet as he had watched her with Arlis. That did help. As long as he could pretend that he was outside himself watching himself he could hold out indefinitely, and keep on pounding away just as Arlis had done.

"What are you thinking about?" she wanted to know, as if she could read his mind and see that he was thinking about being outside himself watching them do it.

"I don't recollect you and Arlis doing any talking while you was fucking," he said.

"Because we weren't one," she said.

He realized he wasn't one, neither. That is, that he was so far outside himself that he couldn't possibly be her too, or be one with her. It was complicated. But he gave it a try: as he went on thrusting into her he tried letting himself feel that he and Sharline were just one animal, a beast with two backs, and the snug hot place where they were joined together was all of a piece, like a heart beating. A heart doesn't beat because there's two separate things working together; it's all just one big muscle beating and throbbing and pulsing and pounding. Yes, he could almost see what she meant by that idea of being one with him. "Are you one with me?" he asked, panting.

"Oh, I'm nothing but one with you!" she said, panting too. And then she came, although not with the racket she'd made with Arlis, no, not a howl of ecstasy but just a little strangled cry. Maybe she'd be louder the second time around, if he could hold out for that. But he was so busy watching and listening to her come and comparing it with the way she had come with Arlis that he forgot to avoid thinking of his penis, and when he thought of it again he realized it was part of her, and he began to pant harder and groan. Her hips were lifting his off the ground again and again as he began to shake. He could not utter any clear words but he made plenty of noise, lots more than she had made. It was the first time she had ever come before he did. But he hated himself because he could only make her come once, and after he came his darned tallywhacker went soft on him. They lay snuggled together for a while, too long maybe, because it gave him a chance to think about all the differences between the way it had happened with Arlis and the way it had happened with him. Finally he had to ask her, "How come you just jumped right into the water when you came down here with him? How come you just couldn't seem to wait?"

"Hon," she said, "you'll recollect that me and him had been working hard in his garden and we were both all hot and sweaty, and it's easy to jump into cold water when you're covered with sweat."

He let it go. They returned to Topper and drove back toward town. Hoppy noticed something and wondered why he hadn't noticed it on the way out of town: the posters for the pitcher show had been put up everywhere—on every store, on most of the houses, and on barns, smokehouses, corncribs, even outhouses. After they'd parked Topper back at the place they'd come from, only then did it occur to them that they hadn't had any dinner. Sharline started in to fix a dinner for him, but he told her he'd make do with a can of Vienna sausages and some crackers. While they were having their lunch she asked if she could have just a drop of Chism's Dew, and he had to point out that he'd poured the last of it into his breakfast coffee. "I've been thinking," he said, "that the first town I'll post them posters in might as well be Stay More, and while I'm there I can get me another jug or two."

"You keep saying 'I,'" she pointed out. "Not 'we' or 'us.'"

"Did I?" he said. "Well, I wasn't thinking."

After their light lunch, Sharline said she wanted to take a little nap. It was too hot inside of Topper, so she took a blanket to lie on under a big shady maple tree off to one side of the field. Hoppy discovered that he was out of tobacco, so he couldn't roll himself a cigarette. He moseyed over to the store to buy another poke of Bugler. Actually there were two other general mercantile stores in town besides Faught's, but he chose Faught's. That's where most of the loafers were gathered on the porch out of the hot sun, whittling and chewing and telling their dirty stories to each other. He sat with them a while, taking out his Barlow and shaving a stick of cedar. Arlis wasn't there, he must've been inside the store. After a while, Hoppy said, "I need the makings of a smoke," and went inside the store.

"Howdy, Hop," Arlis said.

Hoppy tried to say, "Howdy, Arlis," but there must've been a frog in his throat. He did manage to croak out that he needed a poke of Bugler and some papers, and he paid for them and then rolled himself a cigarette right there on the spot and lit it and exchanged glances with Arlis. Arlis had a real neat new haircut, and of course Hoppy didn't have to ask him who his barber was.

"Thanks for all them posters you helped Sharline get made," Hoppy said.

"Glad to help," Arlis said. He gestured toward the road out front. "You may have noticed, I've done put a few of 'em up."

"Yeah, they're all over town. And Sharline says you're fixing to bring a tub of sody pop for her to sell at the show tonight."

"That's right. Would you care for a sample?" He led Hoppy over to the pop cooler and opened it. There were two fifty-pound blocks of ice inside. Arlis fished out of the water an ice-cold Grapette, opened it at the opener on the side of the cooler, and handed it to Hoppy. "On the house," he said. Then he produced a contraption with a hand crank unlike any gizmo that Hoppy had ever seen. "This here makes snow cones," Arlis said. "Have you ever had a snow cone?" When Hoppy shook his head, Arlis proceeded to make him one, taking an ice pick and hacking off part of one of the blocks of ice and putting it in the contraption and grinding it up and putting the tiny bits of ice rounded off into a paper cone. Arlis asked, "What's your preference? Raspberry, strawberry, or grape?" Hoppy allowed as how since he was drinking a Grapette sody pop he might as well stick with the same flavor. So Arlis poured some syrup over the snow cone, and Hoppy commenced eating it, which, on a hot day like this, was a real treat. "Now I tell ye," Arlis went on, "I think Sharline could stand to sell a right smart of these snow cones along with the popcorn and candy and sody pop."

"You're being awful good to us," Hoppy said. "The posters. The sody pop. The snow cones. No telling what you'll come up with next."

"Well, I've got a few other ideas for you'uns to consider."

"How come you're doing all this for us?"

"You and Sharline are my two favoritest folks in all the earth," Arlis declared. He let that sink in, and then he said, "You could do a little favor for me, if you aint too busy tomorrow. I'm fixing to drive out into the back country to put up more of these posters for your show, to let folks know that you'll be showing that pitcher for the rest of the week. Do you think you could just watch the store for me while I'm gone? You wouldn't have to do much, just make change whenever a customer wants to buy something. Pump gas if need be."

"I reckon I could handle it," Hoppy allowed.

"Thank ye kindly. And would you have any real big objection if Sharline rode along with me?"

"What would you need her for?" Hoppy asked.

Chapter seventeen

Well, it had to be opined that those posters Arlis and Sharline were putting up (maybe she held the tacks while he hammered them, or something), way out in the furthest backwoods of the country just might fill the seats for the next pitcher show. Hoppy had no experience whatever as a storekeeper but he got the hang of it pretty quick. It wasn't all that complicated, just taking folks' money and making change from the change drawer. He had a little trouble locating some items—sewing needles and baking powders and certain medicinal remedies—and he sometimes had to tell the customer that he was just minding the store while Arlis was out, but sometimes the customer knew the location of whatever it was they wanted. There wasn't all that much business. In fact, Hoppy was idle enough to have nothing to think about other than the possible danger of letting Sharline ride off with Arlis to God knows where or what. But he had said to her as she was leaving, "Be good," and she had winked at him and said, "Oh, I surely will be." And he had to trust her. He couldn't just go on through life, or however long he planned to keep her, being suspicious and keeping a close watch over her.

Minding the store was easy and almost fun, and Hoppy decided that if he and Sharline ever had to give up showing pitchers and go to work for a living, he might do worse than to find himself a little store somewheres. One big advantage of owning a store is that you get wholesale prices on everything you need. Yes, if Hoppy decided to run a store somewhere and Sharline could get work as a teacher or a barber or a sign painter, they could probably do a right fair job of supporting themselves.

That afternoon while he was minding the store, a young farmer and his wife and kids stopped their team and wagon and came in and asked if this was the place where the pitcher show was going to be shown. Hoppy told them that sure enough, the pitcher show would be shown right out yonder in that meader behind the store. "Has it done already started?" asked the feller, whose name was Goodfeller. Why, no, Hoppy said, it wouldn't start until dark. "How can ye see it in the dark?" puckish Goodfeller wanted to know. Hoppy had a tough time explaining the idea of pitcher shows, how they have to be shown in the dark, and Goodfeller never did seem to get it acceptable. But later Hoppy saw that they'd parked their wagon near Topper and were just waiting patiently for it to get dark. Hoppy figured that Sharline would have to hand-letter some extra words on all the posters so they would say something like "Commencing at dark."

That night he took pains to see how the Goodfeller family was taking in the show, all open-mouthed and flabbergasted. He told Sharline to give each of them a snow cone on the house. She was doing a brisk business with the snow cones; in fact, she used up all of Arlis' ice, and he'd just have to wait until the mail truck came the next morning to replenish his supply.

Except for the Goodfeller family and several others, "A Midsummer Night's Dream" seemed to be a disappointment to many members of the audience, and was not what any of them had expected, with only one horse and no six-shooters. But there was plenty of comedy for those who weren't interested in all the romance, and nearly everybody who stayed long enough to see the whole thing laughed their heads off over all of the Pyramus and Thisbe stuff.

There was a lot of problems with smoke and bugs, both on account of the absence of any breeze. The wind died down and hardly stirred for the duration of the show, and all the men and boys who puffed cigarettes left the air full of clouds of smoke that dulled the projection but contributed to the magic of all the fairy scenes. The smoke wasn't thick enough to drive away the bugs—even the lightning bugs swarmed in unusual numbers, and the moths who were attracted to the light from the projector were flitting all over the place. As far as presentation was concerned, it was hardly fit to be seen. And quite a few folks left after enduring an hour or an hour and a half of the show, but not many of them asked for a refund. When the show was over, Goodfeller asked Hoppy if it would be okay if they just spent the night at their wagon parked alongside Hoppy's because it was too far and dark to head back. Hoppy told them to make themselves at home, and then he asked Goodfeller what he'd thought of the show.

"Hit were a marvel beyond compare," Goodfeller said. "After a time, some of my childern went to sleep but Polly and me never blinked. I didn't keer too much for that critter Puck, who was a-squealing all that jibber-jabber, but Polly said he put her in mind of *me!*"

The Goodfeller family camped out in their wagon, and after his wife and kids were settled down, Goodfeller came over to Topper carrying a stoneware demijohn and asked, "Could I interest ye in a little drap of swamp root?" Sharline was showing Arlis how the projector worked, and Arlis was helping her rewind the last reel. Goodfeller's hooch wasn't nearly the equal of Chism's Dew, but Hoppy was all out of the latter so he was glad to share the demijohn with Goodfeller, but he didn't bother to summon Sharline and Arlis to come and help drink the stuff. They didn't need any intoxication. It turned out that Goodfeller was from the vicinity of Spunkwater, halfway between here and Stay More, and he even knew some of the folks of Stay More, and had actually sampled some Chism's Dew on occasion, so they had something to chew the rag about while they imbibed. The liquor had a real kick to it, and Hoppy was almost tempted after a while to offer to show Goodfeller his private "Assortment," but he didn't want Arlis to see it. Arlis didn't need it. And besides it was already getting into the wee hours of the night, and even Hoppy himself, who rarely felt sleepy, had drooping eyelids. So after going through the ritual formalities of saying goodnight to Goodfeller—he had to invite Goodfeller to spend the night and then to decline his counter-invitation to come go home with him to his—he managed to send him off.

Hoppy climbed up into Topper and there was Sharline and Arlis lying together on the lower bunk. They were fully clothed and they were sound asleep and didn't even look like they'd been doing anything naughty, but they each had an arm thrown over the other. Hoppy just stood and studied them for a while. He wondered at himself that he felt no urge to kick Arlis' butt out of there. Maybe it was Goodfeller's booze which had mellowed him, but he felt no animosity whatsoever toward neither Arlis nor Sharline. He liked them both. If he felt any animosity, it was towards himself, for his many failures and shortcomings in general and his particular failure right now not to feel any resentment of this situation. If Arlis and Sharline had become a pair of lovebirds, maybe Hoppy deserved it. He was such a shithead that he had it coming to him. He watched them for a time, then he stepped down from Topper to smoke one more cigarette before bedtime, and also to take a piss. He noticed then that Goodfeller had left his demijohn behind. Hoppy hefted it and discovered it still had plenty in it, so he helped himself to a few more swallers. Several more swallers, in fact. Then he climbed back up into Topper, and kept on climbing, climbing up into the upper bunk, and if the ceiling hadn't been in the way he could have kept on climbing right up into the sky.

When he woke up, it was late morning, and he was alone. The lovebirds had flew the roost. Hoppy had a terrible hangover. He usually never had hangovers, but possibly that was just a tribute to the superiority of Chism's Dew. The only cure was dog hair, so he had a few more swallers from Goodfeller's jug. He noticed that the Goodfellers' wagon was gone, and Goodfeller hadn't bothered to take his jug with him, so maybe he'd meant it as a gift, a way of saying, "Let this keep you company until you get a chance to come on up home and get you some Chism's."

Hoppy was working on the hair of the third dog when a vision drifted into his view. A pretty lady, not real young but not too old neither, not any older than Hoppy, came walking up to him and said "Hello, sir." She had a thick book in her hand. She had long wavy blonde hair that was done nice, and a real nice summer dress with flowers printed on it, and he fell for her like a ton of bricks at first sight. He was too surprised to say anything, partly surprised because of how swell she looked but also because she'd said "Hello" instead of "Howdy" or "Good morning" or even "How are things stacking up?" And she'd called him "sir," which nobody had called him since Carl used to call him that in every other breath. Then the pretty lady said, "I hope I'm not disturbing you. My name is Helen Milsap, and I teach school here. Seventh and eighth grades. I've been in the audience of your show twice already, and I expect to watch it again as many times as you keep showing it in this town. I just adore it." She held up the book she was carrying and opened it at a bookmark. "Did you know that 'A Midsummer Night's Dream' is all printed out in this book, *The Collected Works of William Shakespeare*? I've read it more than once. Of course your picture show doesn't contain all the words, there simply isn't room for them, but it has most of the more important ones. Do you mind if I sit down?"

He was slow understanding her question, and then he said, "Yeah, sure, help yourself, have a seat. Or two." He realized he wasn't making too much sense. She sat down, and he realized he was holding in his hand a tumbler of the nearly colorless liquid that came out of the demijohn. He held it up to her and asked, "Would ye care to jine me in a drap or two?"

The lovely lady sniffed. "Whiskey? I wouldn't care for any, this time of day, thank you just the same." She folded her hands in her lap as if to prevent them from accepting a glass. Then she looked around her, and at the open door of Topper, and asked, "Where is your...your assistant, Miss Whitlow?"

"Damned if I know," Hoppy said. "That gal has a mind of her own."

"Would you like for me to tell you where she is?"

"How come you to ask me if you already knew?"

"Just to see if you keep track of her comings and her goings."

"Some of her comings I know about, but her goings are a

mystery." Hoppy watched the lady's face to see if she got the double meaning, but there was only the faintest trace of a smile on the edges of her mouth.

"Is she just your employee, or is she also your sweetie?"

"She's more sour than sweet lately."

"Because of my Arlis."

"*Your* Arlis?"

"Yes." Pretty Helen crossed her fingers and held them up for his view. "We were just like that...until you came to town. Now he ignores me completely."

Hoppy didn't know what to say. It struck him as mighty peculiar, that ole Arlis would have a lady friend as good-looking, smart and nice as this here Helen, yet still be a-hankering after Sharline, who was sure cute and all but just not in the same class with this lady. "I'm sorry," he said.

"Why should *you* be sorry?" she asked. "It's not your fault... unless you drove her into his arms. Have you been mean to her? Have you failed to satisfy her?" The woman blushed, and stammered, "I mean...that is...I don't mean—"

"Yeah, I know what you mean. Naw, I thought she was fairly happy and satisfied with me. But it's kind of a long story, and are you sure you don't want a little bit of this moonshine to soften things up for ye?"

So the lady relented and allowed him to pour her a glass from Goodfeller's demijohn. The first sip nearly knocked her out, but the second sip went down easier, and by the third sip she was telling him what a nice feller he was, how he was so much better-looking than Arlis that she couldn't understand why a sensible gal like Sharline would've wanted Arlis in the first place. After a while she asked him if he'd had dinner yet and he said heck, he hadn't even had breakfast yet, so she jumped up and stirred around and lit the kerosene stove and made what she called an "omelet," which was a whole lot of eggs and cheese and onions, big enough for both of them to eat, and it was sure mighty fine. They washed it down with more of the Goodfeller. And then spent a couple of hours talking, or rather she did most of the talking and he just listened and kept making sure the moon went on shining into their glasses. Finally as he was pouring the fifth or sixth he said, "You was going to tell me what went with Sharline and Arlis."

"Who cares?" she said and gave him doe's eyes of adoration. And then she reached across the table and took his hand in one of hers. "Oh, I 'spect they're just over at Arlis' store. He has to run the store, you know. But there's a couple of side rooms, you know." She winked at him.

"Yeah, yesterday I had to watch the store for him while he and Sharline drove all over the country putting up those posters for the show."

"So you know about the side rooms? The one with the stacks of feed bags and flour sacks in it? That's where I lost my cherry." Helen got red as a cherry and covered her face, and said, "Oh, will you listen to me! Honey, you'd better not pour me any more of that stuff!"

But a minute later she shoved her glass out for a refill. Hoppy was tempted to tell her that for her own good she had better go easy on the stuff. But he couldn't tell her that. He hated himself for not being able to make her stop. He hated himself for various thoughts that were popping into his mind and were immune to his conscience because of Goodfeller's beverage. When, eventually, he said, "Would you care to see my humble abode?" she was on her feet at once, unsteady and staggering, but on her feet, and he had just a little trouble helping her up the steps of Topper. They both held onto their glasses of booze. He gave her a guided tour of the furnishings and equipment in his one-room house.

"Two bunks?" she said. "Do you sleep separately?"

"Some of the time," he said. He was tempted to tell her that last night he had occupied the top bunk while her boyfriend had shared the lower bunk with his girlfriend, but he had at least enough sense left not to try to explain that. He didn't have enough sense to keep him from reaching under the lower bunk and pulling out the blanket that was wrapped around his special reel. He removed the blanket from the reel and handed it to her.

She read the label. "'Assortment.' What is this?"

"It's a secret pitcher show," he said. "It's fifteen minutes or so of real people without their clothes on doing all sorts of wicked things."

"Really?" she said, and held the reel close to her eyes as if she could see some of it. "What kind of wicked things?"

"Sexual," he said. "Like you never dreamt."

She giggled. "You don't know what-all I've dreamt." And then she pressed the reel and herself against his chest and whispered, "When it gets dark, sometime, will you show this to me?"

"It don't have to be dark," he said. "I can show it right here and now on that wall."

"You can? Oh, goody!" She clapped her hands.

So he fired up the delco and turned the projector to face the alabastine rectangle on the wall, and refocused it, and threaded the reel into it, and started it up. They sat side by side in the same place where her boyfriend and his girlfriend had spent the night. It was kind of hot inside Topper, but who cared? He wondered what might happen if Sharline came back, but who cared? He pretended that he had never seen the Assortment before, and was watching it for the first time through Helen's eyes, and he was shocked but captivated and amazed and tickled to pieces. Not to mention horny. He had to stop pretending that he was her, because she couldn't have between her legs what was bursting his fly. She had something there, though, because without even thinking about it she put her hand on it and commencing rubbing it. The pitcher show came to the part about the German shepherd and she gasped and then cried, "How awful!" and then she observed, "But she looks like she's enjoying it."

"I don't know about her," he said, "but that ole doggy is having the time of his life."

They both laughed. Pretty soon the pitcher show was showing the part where a feller slips his pecker into a gal's rear end. "Ouch!" said Helen. "You can't tell me that doesn't hurt." Hoppy didn't try to tell her that it didn't hurt, because he didn't know. He could imagine that many of the things in the Assortment which he had never tried were difficult but they all seemed to cause pleasure for both parties concerned…or, in the case of one scene where there were three fellers and a gal, all four parties concerned. In that one, the gal took turns putting the peckers of two fellers on both sides of her into her mouth, one at a time, whilst another feller was doing her in the ordinary way. Hoppy never had much cared for the scenes with multiple partners; he figured it was something to be enjoyed just between two, not three or four. Helen commenced squirming around in her seat, and said, "My stars and body! You're right, I never *dreamt* that a gal would take it into her mouth like that! Isn't that unbelievable? Well for crying out loud!" For as long as the scene lasted, until the gal made all three of the men come, Helen kept on uttering expressions of astonishment. "Well blow me down!" and "As I live and breathe!" and "Can you feature that!" After another scene in which two gals were pleasuring each other with their mouths down below, the reel came to an end, without any Exit Music or Finis or nothing. It was a silent pitcher show. Helen seemed disappointed. "Is that all?" she asked. She tossed off the rest of her glass in a couple of swallows, and Hoppy was obliged to fetch the demijohn. "I surely do wonder," she declared, "what it would feel like to have a feller's thing betwixt my lips."

He asked her, "Didn't ole Arlis ever get ye to do that for him?"

"Never. Does Sharline do that for you?"

"I aint never asked her."

"Well, then," she said, and commenced fumbling to unbutton the fly of his overalls, "we can cheat on them in a way they haven't cheated on us."

As she began, Hoppy became considerably worried on account of what enjoyment it was giving him. He was afraid that he might want it done again sometime. It really was the best thing that ever happened to his body.

The only thing wrong with it was that it made it impossible for him not to live inside his penis while she was trying to get it down her throat. He knew he was going to come in an instant but there was no way to stop it.

Yet there was a way to stop it, and it happened. The door of Topper flew open, and there was Sharline and Arlis. Helen got up off her knees and tried to stand, but staggered against the projector with a crash. Fortunately the projector was bolted to the floor, or else she would have toppled it. There was no telling what harm she'd done to it. And no telling what harm they'd done to their bonds with their sweethearts.

Chapter eighteen

H elen!" cried Arlis. "Just what in tarnation do you think you're a-doing?"

"I don't know if there's a name to it, but it sure is fun," Helen said. "Hoppy, sugar, has it got a name to it?"

"Not that I ever heared tell of," Hoppy said. "It's a silent pitcher show. No captions."

"Ila Fay Woodrum says it's called sucky-suck," Sharline said. "She did it once on Preacher Binns. It give her a tummy ache for a week afterwards. But Landon, *who* on earth is this woman?"

"This here woman, when she's sober," said Arlis, "is Miss Helen Agnes Milsap, Teacher of the Year for Newton County. But she's plainly six sheets to the wind. Helen, what have you been drinking?"

"I don't know if there's a name to it, but it sure is fun," said Helen. "Hoppy, sweetums, has it got a name to it?"

"Not that I ever heared tell of," Hoppy said, "other than baldface swamp root. I reckon you could call it love-in-idleness, whatever that means."

"How long has this been a-going on?" Sharline wanted to know.

"We just got started," Helen said, "but you interrupted before we finished."

"I *mean*," Sharline said, "how long have you two'uns known each other?"

"Three hours?" said Hoppy. "Maybe four?"

"You never did that for me!" Arlis said to Helen, pouting. "And besides, it's against the law, I bet."

"Nobody ever told me about sucky-suck," Helen said. "I might've lived my whole life without knowing about it, except for dear Hoppy's secret pitcher show."

"*Secret pitcher show?*" said Arlis.

"Landon, don't you dare tell me that you showed *that* to her!" Sharline said, with her hands on her hips and fire in her eyes. Hoppy tried to remain poker-faced. "Did you?" Sharline demanded. "Did you show her the 'Assortment?'"

"Maybe," said Hoppy.

"And it sure was fun," said Helen. "More fun than a barrel of monkeys. Arlis, you wouldn't believe all the things that folks can do with each other!"

Ole Arlis was studying the inside of Topper and remembering how it was possible to watch a pitcher show on the wall. "Let's see it," Arlis said. "Rewind it and show it to me." Hoppy pondered whether to show it to him. Probably ole Arlis didn't know nothing but the missionary position and had never done nothing else. But Hoppy remembered what had happened the last time he'd shown "Assortment" to another feller, who was Preacher Binns, who had been turned into a sex fiend by it.

"Helen, honey," Hoppy said, "do you want ole Arlis to see it?"

"Who cares, my darling?" she said. "I wish they both would just go away." Hoppy did too. He wanted to finish with Helen the unfinished business. An idee occurred to him: he could show "Assortment" to Arlis and while Arlis was watching it, maybe with Sharline, Hoppy and Helen could get up front into Topper's cab and finish what they'd been doing before they were so rudely interrupted. So Hoppy went ahead and rewound the reel of "Assortment" and threaded it into the projector. He restarted the delco and flicked on the switch to start the projector. But the projector wouldn't come on. He reflicked the switch, without luck. It must have got something knocked loose when Helen crashed into it. He tested the exciting lamp, and he tested several connection wires, and he tested the path of the film through the various sprockets, but something was sure fritzed or haywire or bunged up. He spent a long time messing with the machine. By and by Helen came and draped herself across his back and said, "What's the problem, honeybunch?"

"This goddamn projector is on the blink," Hoppy said.

"Did I hurt it when I bumped into it?" she asked.

"Maybe you did. You sure give it a good whack."

Hoppy spent several more minutes fiddling with the machine and then he realized he would just have to take it apart to fix it. The trouble was, he wasn't sober enough to take it apart and fix it properly, let alone put it back together, and there was no telling how long it would take even if he was sober. Sharline offered to make a pot of coffee. Arlis told her, "Sweetheart, don't forget what we came here for in the first place." And then, while Hoppy was trying to concentrate on the inner workings of his projector, gabby Arlis went on a-talking, telling as how he'd been thinking, and him and Sharline had talked about it considerable, and he'd done already told his Maw the post-mistress who owned the store that he was fixing to give it up, that is, he wanted to quit, and maybe see some of the world while it was still there. He hadn't never seen much of the world. He'd never been to a bigger town than Clarksville. He had met up with some folks who'd been all the way out to California, looking for work during the Depression, and had stayed out there for quite a while until home-sickness brought them back. You never dreamt of any such Paradise as California was said to be, why, folks out there even had orange trees and lemons right in their front yard! And jobs! Why, there was no end to all the high-paying jobs of work to be found all over the place. Most of the Ozark folks heading for California had to travel in old beat-up trucks loaded to the ground with all their worldly goods, but Arlis, he had him a pretty good Chevy roadster, as you know, and he could get out to California pretty quick and easy, and also he had a bit of money saved up, enough for him and Sharline to live on until he found a good job....

Hoppy was just a little surprised that this notion didn't seem to bother him at all. If he hadn't been so crazy about sweet Helen, he might have actually got bothered by Arlis' announcement of his plan. But as far as he was concerned right here and now, Arlis was welcome to take her to California or to the moon as far as he was concerned. He didn't say this, though. In fact he didn't say nothing.

"Landon?" said Sharline. "Say something."

"Helen?" said Arlis. "Say something."

Hoppy was having several thoughts. He was thinking about how to get himself alone with Helen as soon as possible. Then, on a more far-seeing level, he was thinking about taking over the store after Arlis and Sharline had gone to California. He could settle down here in this town with Helen and give up the precarious business of trying to show pitcher shows.

"I'm all confused and uncertain," Sharline said. "Tell you'uns the truth, I aint so wild about giving up Hoppy and Topper and the road and pitcher shows and all."

Arlis said, "And of course I realize how this just shocks the daylights out of poor Helen, who has been planning to spend her life with me."

"Who's shocked?" said Helen. "What daylights? Good riddance to bad rubbish, if you ask me."

Nobody said anything after that, for a long little time. Eventually Sharline grabbed Hoppy by his elbow and gave it a shake. "Landon!" she said. "Say something."

"What do you want me to say?" Hoppy asked.

"Don't you *care*?" Sharline asked. "Don't it make you mad?"

Helen said, "Darling Hoppy and I can look after ourselves, thank you."

There was something a mite familiar about all this, Hoppy suspected. He was still feeling kind of frustrated, from that unfinished sucky-suck, and he was not thinking straight on account of having drunk so much of the love-in-idleness. Hoppy abruptly had an awareness of some parallels between the four of them and the four lovers in "A Midsummer Night's Dream." It also hit him belatedly that the other girl in that pitcher show was named Helena, and the one here was named Helen. This was such an odd coincidence that he began to wonder if all of this wasn't just a dream. It sure was midsummer, although nightfall was still a ways off.

"O me!" cried Sharline. "What news, my love? Am not I Sharline? Are not you Landon? Aint I just as fair-looking as when you first fell for me? O why are you giving me up? Ye gods forbid!"

Although Hoppy recognized all of this as words that Hermia had spoken to Lysander, more or less, he was still touched that Sharline was saying every word not as if she was just quoting ole Mr. Shakspear but as if she meant it. So he answered her somewhat in kind: "Sorry, kiddo, but you turn my stomach, and I've just got feelings for Helen."

"O me!" cried Sharline again and thrust her face up close to Helen's as if to bite off her nose. "You juggler! You canker-blossom! You thief of love! What, have you come by night and stolen my love's heart from him?"

Helen got right into the spirit of the squabble, although she was too tipsy to remember all the words. "What, will you tear impatient answers from my gentle tongue? Fie, fie, you counterfeit! You *puppet*, you!"

"'Puppet,' huh?" Sharline said. "Are you talking about you being taller than me? Why, you painted maypole, I'm still tall enough to reach your eyes and scratch them out!"

Helen blanched and drew back, shielding her face with her arm. The two gals went on having their catfight, partly right out of Mr. Shakspear, partly out of their own feelings, in their own words. During the showing of that pitcher show, Hoppy had noticed how the audience had been more caught up by the fight between Hermia and Helena than any other part of the show. It was the only part of the show that seemed to have the excitement of a good gunfight in a Hopalong Cassidy pitcher show. It was almost as if Sharline and Helen had their six-shooters blazing away at each other.

Maybe they knew it too. "Why, get you gone!" Sharline said to Helen. "What's stopping you?"

And Helen answered as Helena, "A foolish heart that I leave here behind."

And Sharline, "What! With Landon?"

And Helen, "With Arlis."

And then both gals burst out laughing and fell into each other's arms, and just held each other tight while they went on laughing. Hoppy and Arlis didn't know what to make of it, but Hoppy poured a glass of the love-in-idleness for Arlis, and said to him, "Just be sure you're looking at Helen when you drink it." Hoppy felt the effects of the booze were wearing off on him. Maybe he would have that pot of coffee after all, and see if he couldn't get the projector to working.

Sharline brewed up a pot of coffee for Hoppy and Helen, but Arlis preferred to stick with the mountain whiskey, and, as he'd been asked, he kept his eyes on Helen while he drank it, which sure enough made him decide that his former girlfriend wasn't so former after all. He developed such a hankering for her that he was no longer interested in watching the secret pitcher show. But clever Sharline said to Hoppy, "Let me see if I caint find out what's wrong with the projector," and she proceeded to look it over. Hoppy was glad to let her do it, because she was the only hundred-percent sober person there and also because she'd been looking after that projector ever since the days when she'd been Carl. To get away from Arlis' grabby hands, Helen kept Sharline company while Sharline messed with the machine, and Hoppy continued to marvel at how the two gals had gone so fast from being a pair of fighting hellcats to being the best of chums.

Wouldn't you just know that Sharline would fix the projector? And with a wad of chewing gum! It turned out there was a loose solder on the underside of the transformer, and that piece of gum did the trick! "Assortment" didn't have any titles or beginning as such, it just started right up, with a feller humping a gal on the fender of his auto in broad daylight, and they got a good look before Sharline stopped the projector, saying, "Nobody needs to watch this right now." She took "Assortment" out of the machine and loaded the one leftover reel, the final reel, of "The Painted Stallion," all that remained of their collection after Binns had stolen the rest. Hoppy asked her why she was doing that.

"Just for old time's sake," she said.

Hoppy thought it was nostalgic but bothersome to see that old familiar shot of the beautiful white woman dressed as an Indian chief atop a paint horse atop a mountain crag shooting an arrow. He was angry all over again at Emmett Binns. He felt that he'd had a calling to take "The Painted Stallion" into the backwoods and brighten the lives of folks with it. But now he couldn't do it any more. He tried to explain to Arlis and Helen the significance of this fragment of the serial. Then he noticed that there was no sound coming from the film. Of course not, because the loudspeaker was still on top of Topper, and he hadn't needed it to show the silent "Assortment" to Helen. He climbed the ladder on Topper's side and brought the speaker down and inside, but there still wasn't any sound coming from it. "Have you turned on the amplifier?" he asked Sharline. And she flicked a switch, and then some other switches, but the sound wasn't coming through. Hoppy took over, and inspected all the complicated parts of the projector that were responsible for capturing the film's soundtrack: the parts of the amplifier, the spring suspensions, the photo-electric cell, the sound gate, the sound sprockets, et cetera. He confessed he couldn't find the trouble. Sharline took over, looking for another spot needing chewing gum, but she couldn't find one. Something serious was wrong with the sound system.

The quartet talked about it and realized that they wouldn't be able to show "A Midsummer Night's Dream" without any sound. As far as Hoppy was concerned, they could do without ole Felix's music, but they couldn't do without all of the spoken words, which, after all, was what Shakspear was all about.

Helen fetched her copy of the feller's *Collected Works* and opened it to the play on which the pitcher show was based. "I've got an idea," she said. "It might not work but it's better than nothing."

So they spent the rest of the afternoon and early evening, running the silent "Midsummer Night's Dream" through the projector, shining it on the interior wall, while they tried to match the words of the play to the words that would be spoken on the screen. Arlis took the part of Theseus, and Helen was Hippolyta. The quartet of lovers was as it had been, Hoppy as Lysander, Arlis as Demetrius, Sharline as Hermia, and Helen as Helena. Hoppy was also Oberon, and Sharline was Titania. Sharline as "Carl" was Puck. The "mechanicals" or laborers were done by Arlis as both Peter Quince and Snug the joiner, Hoppy as both Bottom and Snout the tinker, Helen as Flute the bellows-mender and Sharline as Robin Starveling. It was a lot of parts, and the first run-through was considerably confused. They all had difficulty knowing which words to leave out, because the pitcher show had cut so much of the play's words to save time.

But by the time that twilight fell, they were confident they could do it. Arlis' mother had brought over some supper for them to eat, and some kids had brought over from the store the tub full of ice and soda pop for the concessions. Helen helped out at the concession stand, making snow cones and popping the popcorn. Two large flatbed trucks with folks sitting all along three sides delivered a big chunk of audience for the show. There was going to be a sizeable crowd, thanks to the posters Arlis had put up. Arlis offered to handle the ticket-selling, so that the gals could concentrate on the concessions and Hoppy could do his juggling acts. He was managing to keep six balls in the air at once, one more than he'd ever been able to do before. The crowd sensed that he was doing something impossible and they gave him a big round of applause throughout. But when Sharline did her juggling with the chiffon fascinators, it brought the crowd to their feet with applause. In their magic acts, he levitated Sharline higher than ever before and made her disappear twice as much.

When it was dark enough to start the projector, Helen said, "I know just about all of these folks, so let me make the announcement." And she went to stand in front of the screen and told everybody that unfortunately the sound system on the motion picture projector had become inoperable, and therefore they were going to substitute the voices of actual people here present for the voices on the screen, as best as they were able. If this offended anyone or disappointed anyone, the management stood ready to offer refunds to one and all. "Let us begin," she said and waved her hand like a conductor, and Hoppy started the projector then ran as fast as his limp would allow to join Helen, Arlis, and Sharline as they stood below the screen sharing the Shakespeare book.

It all went fairly well, and the good audience often clapped their hands in a way they might not have done at pitcher shows without live voices. Hoppy almost missed ole Felix's music. But at one point during a silence between voices, somewhere a whippoorwill called out, beautiful as music, and later an owl hooted, and the grass and trees came alive with crickets and katydids and cicadas and all manner of peeping and piping frog, and croaking ones too. When the first scene of fairies appeared, the smoke from the cigarettes of all the smoking men and boys merged with the wispy fogs on the screen that merged with the fairies, and all of it merged with the world beyond and around the screen.

Some child in the audience was the first to notice, and stood up and cried "Oh, look!" and everyone looked and there were actual little fairy-critters a-dancing out of the woods and around the screen, and across it, so that you couldn't hardly tell the difference between the fairies on the screen and the real ones, except some were flat and some were round and deep.

"My fairies!" Sharline cried.

On the screen Oberon was saying "Ill met by moonlight, proud Titania," but he was just mouthing the words, and Hoppy, who was supposed to supply his voice, was too busy watching Sharline's fairies, and of course Sharline, who was supposed to supply the voice for Titania making all those speeches, was thrilled to pieces to see her fairies. So all of those grand words between Oberon and Titania were neglected. Hoppy ran as fast as his limp would allow to turn the projector off so they could all just watch the real fairies dancing and cavorting. *Real fairies?* He said to himself. But he stopped the projector. The fairies, however, if they had ever been there in the first place, had fled into the woods. Sharline had fled with them. Hoppy restarted the projector and rejoined Arlis and Helen. Helen whispered, "I'll just have to take her parts," and she read the rest of Titania's speech about "our moonlight revels." And then there was a long scene between Demetrius and Helena, so they didn't miss Sharline for a while, and by the time she was needed again to speak for Hermia, she had come back, saying "Oh, 'scuse me please. I just had to go and talk to them."

From there on, everything went okay. Hoppy enjoyed being Bottom, or Cagney's voice, in the scene between Bottom and Titania when Bottom has been changed into a jackass. And in the scene where he wakes up and discovers he's not a jackass any more, and reaches up over his head to see if his long ears are still there, Hoppy couldn't help reaching up over his own head to feel for his missing ears, and the audience laughed.

Very few of the audience had left early, although it was close to midnight before the pitcher show was over. Hoppy wondered if it might not be such a bad idee to just keep things the way they were, and try to persuade Arlis and Helen to go on the road with them, to show their silent version of "A Midsummer Night's Dream" at other towns. But he knew he'd better try to get the sound system fixed. He had a notion that there might be a short-circuit in the rectifier, and he could check that out first thing tomorrow.

After the last of the satisfied audience had drifted away, the quartet lingered for a nightcap from the demijohn. Sharline took a crayon and wrote on the side of the demijohn, LOVE-IN-IDLENESS, with three big Xs below it. "This is powerful stuff," she said. And then she said, "You *did* see them, didn't you? My fairies? They were really there, weren't they?" And she looked at Hoppy, and at Helen, and at Arlis, and each of them nodded their heads.

They were interrupted by the screech of a car's brakes, and a vehicle stopping as close to Topper as it could get. The driver jumped out. It was Teal Buffum. "Folks!" he exclaimed. "We just caught sight of that there preacher feller, Emmett Binns! He's a-heading north on the Alum Cove road!"

Chapter nineteen

So now Arlis runs to get his roadster, and when he comes back, they all try to get into it, with the rumble seat open, but Arlis says that only him and Hoppy can go, the girls will have to stay behind, because the extra weight might slow them down. Now as soon as Hoppy is in, Arlis lets out the clutch and roars off in pursuit of the villain in black. Never mind that Arlis' roadster is also black, like all other vehicles except Topper. There are three or four cars ahead of them, other members of the posse, and all of them churning up a huge cloud of dust that nearly smothers the folks walking home from the show, or riding their mules, or sitting in their slow wagons. These folks gesture onward with their arms or shout "Go get 'im!" as the roadster zips past them. Arlis speculates that Binns might have been avoiding the main roads, thus he must have whizzed through town in the middle of the night, probably coming up from the Parker Ridge road and intending to reach Jasper or points beyond by the back roads. The Alum Cove road is mostly just one rough lane, but there are stretches along it that will hold two vehicles abreast, and on these Arlis passes, one by one, the other members of the posse, until the roadster is the lead vehicle, with nobody else kicking dust in their face until, after a few miles, they come within sight of the trail of dust raised by what can only be the culprit's car, and, eventually, after more miles, they catch sight of its tail-lights. Those tail-lights begin to diminish. "He's speeding up on us," Arlis says. "He knows he's being follered." That's practically an admission of Binns' guilt, if there was ever any doubt in the first place that he is guilty. They chase him for a long time, up steep winding trails and down into hollers and across the vales. Hoppy has to admire Arlis' driving, which is reckless enough to keep up with the car ahead but steady enough not to plunge them off into a ravine.

Hoppy tries to imagine this midsummer midnight chase as if it's being filmed into a pitcher show. He even conjectures, aloud to Arlis, that some day they'll be making pitcher shows that have a lot of cars chasing each other instead of just cowboys on their horses chasing each other, which might be exciting but also is kind of backward, as if it belongs to the previous century. "I do believe you're right," Arlis says. "But it would be a sight more fun to watch this chase on the screen than to be in it."

Steadily they close in on the car ahead, somewhere past the hamlet of Mineral Spring, and Hoppy begins to wonder what they will do if they can catch him. Will Arlis attempt to force him off the road? Get ahead of him and block his path? Ram him from the rear? But Arlis can't catch him. They pursue him all the way to Spunkwater, a nice little town that would have been on Hoppy's route except for two reasons, one, it is just a little too little, and two, it is too close to Stay More, down the mountain a few miles. At Spunkwater, the road forks, the main road continuing on northward all the way to Parthenon and thence to Jasper. Hoppy is surprised to see that Binns turns west into the other fork, the Stay More road, which also goes eventually to Parthenon and Jasper, although nobody uses it for that purpose. Could Stay More be Binns' destination? Of all the towns in the Ozarks, Stay More is one of the most isolated, hardest to get to, hardest to get out of, and thus a good place for hiding, if you're trying to escape from anyone or anything. Hoppy wonders if that might be Binns' intention, to hide out in Stay More. But he feels an unusual jubilation to be going in the direction of home. It's a very steep and very rugged trail down the mountain, and they are so close to Binns that they can see his silhouette against his headlights, frantically clutching the steering wheel to keep the car on the terrible twisting trail.

"Right down yonder," says Hoppy, "is a place where the road divides for a stretch, I mean, there's the old road that goes one way, up high, and the newer road that goes another way, lower down, and is a kind of shortcut. They both meet up again farther along. Maybe if he takes the high road, you could take the low road and cut him off."

"Good idee!" Arlis says. "But how come you to know so much about this road?"

"Stay More is my hometown," Hoppy declares, with no little bit of pride in his voice.

Sure enough, Binns takes the high road. Here comes the part of the pitcher show that will have folks on the edge of their seats, Hoppy is thinking. Arlis mashes the gas pedal and whips down into the low road and zooms along it. It's a straighter stretch, and they reach the spot where it meets up again with the high road well ahead of Binns, and Arlis brings the roadster to a stop blocking the high road. Arlis jumps out of the roadster, saying, "I hope he don't ram me!"

"I hope he aint armed," Hoppy puts in.

Arlis opens the rumble seat and fishes around among his tools and brings out a tire iron, which he gives to Hoppy, and takes a jack handle for himself. So they are both armed in a sense.

They wait. It sure is taking a while. Finally the car comes along and screeches to a halt just short of the roadster, with the horn blaring. The driver jumps out, and Arlis and Hoppy both raise their irons to bash him with. But it's not Binns. It's Teal Buffum. Teal raises his hands. "Don't hit me, boys!" he pleads.

"Have we just been a-chasing you?" Arlis asks him.

Teal is puzzled. "Why, no, I thought I was a-follerin *you*. You passed me way back down the road."

Hoppy explains to Teal about the high road and low road and how Binns had taken the high road.

"But where in hell is he?" Arlis wants to know. "I don't see how Teal could have come along this high road without bumping into him."

They get back into the two vehicles and drive slowly back across both the high road and low road. They search the road itself carefully for any sign of Binns' tire tracks, but the dust is so dry there is no imprint of any tracks, not even their own. Binns has disappeared into thin air, almost as if a giant eagle has plucked him and his car off the earth. But eagles don't fly at night. One by one the other members of the posse arrive, and they have to explain to each one of them the weird situation of the high and low roads and Binns' strange disappearance. There is a lot of head scratching. The members of the posse walk along both the high and the low road, kicking at the dust with their shoes, looking this way and that. Hoppy hasn't felt so frustrated since he and Helen got interrupted. He says to Arlis, "This sure aint going to make a good pitcher show."

There is nothing to be done. One by one the members of the posse head for home. Hoppy thinks that since they're so close to Stay More, he might just ask Arlis to drive on down there, just for a look around, and if it weren't the wee hours of the morning they could stop by Luther Chism's place and pick up a jug or two of Chism's Dew. He could sure use a slug right now to take the edge off his aggravation. But he doesn't want to keep Arlis out any longer, and it's a long way back home.

So they too follow the other members of the posse in retreat. One more reason for disappointment: to be so close to Stay More without being able to see it again. The trip back is much slower, more leisurely, and Arlis talks even more than he usually does. He conjectures possibilities: when Binns discovered that they weren't following him into the high road, he might have stopped, turned around and headed back the other way and found a place to turn off before the other posse cars came up behind him. No, Hoppy says, there wouldn't have been any place on the high road where he could have turned around; that narrow high road runs across the edge of a bluff. Well, Arlis speculates, is it possible that Binns could have reached the place where the high and low roads meet up again before they got there, and have gone on? No, Hoppy says, not unless he was going seventy miles an hour, which would be impossible on that risky trail.

By and by, Arlis begins to talk, in a roundabout sort of way, about him and Sharline, and how he had been so taken with her, how she charmed him out of his skin, how she was so much more spirited than Helen, and how much he'd lost his head in a way that he now regretted. He had no idee that her and Hoppy were so special to each other. He hopes that Hoppy doesn't hold against him his rashness and wrongdoing. Arlis rambles on in that vein practically all the way home, until finally Hoppy puts a hand on his shoulder and says, "Feller, I might've blown a gasket if you'd've taken her out to California. But you didn't. So let's us just forget it." Having said these pacifying words, he realizes that what he has said and the way he has said it is exactly like Hopalong Cassidy does in every one of his pitcher shows, when someone has to apologize to him for something.

The dawn is coming up when Arlis drops him off at Topper. "Just one little question," Arlis says. "How was it? With Helen, I mean. What you'uns were doing."

Hoppy says, "I reckon it might've been a right smart more satisfying if she'd've finished."

Hoppy doesn't want to wake Sharline, so he decides to climb into the top bunk. He grabs hold of the bunk post and swings himself up…and nearly lands right on top of Helen. His landing misses her but jostles the bed and wakes her. "Oops, pardon me," he says, and slips down and into the bunk with Sharline. He is plumb wore out and desperate for a little shut-eye, but the thought of Helen sleeping right up above keeps him awake for a while. Before he can numb his mind to let him sleep, Sharline wakes up. She is glad to see him. He tries to explain to her what has happened, the problem with the high road and low road, but it is all so complicated and ridiculous that the effort to explain it exhausts him into deep slumber.

The heat of midday wakes him. The gals have fixed him a fine meal, bigger than breakfast but smaller than dinner, sort of halfway in between, with a ham omelet and his first mushmelon of the season. He washes up a bit, combs his hair and sits down to try to explain more clearly to Sharline and Helen just what happened in the pursuit of Binns. The gals have as much trouble as the posse did in understanding what could have happened. "Maybe my fairies got him," Sharline says, and that might be just as good a explanation as we are likely to hear.

Now it is time to take down the screen, fold it up, and leave town. Arlis comes over to help. Hoppy, not just being polite, says, "You and Helen better just go with us and we'll read ole Mr. Shakspear out loud in every town just like we done last night."

Sharline says, "I'd sure like to have you'uns do that, but I fixed the sound on the projector, Landon. While you was sleeping, I got in there and messed around with it, and I flicked a tube in the amplifier and it all started working again!"

"Well, bless your heart, hon," Hoppy says, and then he says to Helen and Arlis, "but you'uns come go with us anyhow, and we'll have a lot of fun."

"That's kind of ye, Hop," Arlis said, "but I reckon we might just head for California."

So they say their goodbyes. Sharline and Arlis is looking at each other kind of moony-eyed, as if they wish they could sneak off and do it just one more time, but Helen and Hoppy are just looking at each other polite-like.

"Are you going on to Mt. Judy from here?" Arlis asks him.

"Naw, I had to give up Mt. Judy to the fellers who sold me that pitcher show. I aint sure where we're going, maybe Piercetown or Hasty. But first I want to run up home to Stay More to take care of some things."

"Maybe you'll find Binns after all," Arlis suggests.

"That would sure be hunky-dory," Hoppy says.

Him and Arlis shake hands, and the two gals give each other a big hug, then Arlis and Sharline give each other a hug that isn't too little, and Hoppy and Helen give each other a polite hug, and they all say, "Take care," and "See you" and stuff like that. There's an old superstition in the Ozarks that you must never watch anyone go all the way out of sight, so Arlis and Helen turn away at the last moment.

On the same road as last night, going to Alum Cove and Mineral Spring, Hoppy can't help but notice that Sharline is crying. Not noisily, but she has to get out her hankie and dab at her cheeks. He doesn't ask her what's the matter, because he thinks he knows. "You really did care for him, didn't you?"

"Arlis? No. I mean, yeah, he was a nice feller, but I never wanted to go to California with him. Helen did, and she is a great lady, and he nearly broke her heart, and I'm sad for her."

"Don't be sad. They'll go to California together, and live happy ever after."

Sharline sniffled. "We all misbehaved."

"But you had a time, didn't ye?"

"Yeah, I guess I had a time."

It is getting on towards late afternoon when they reach Spunkwater and turn off down the mountain toward Stay More. Hoppy feels shivers running up his spine at the thought of seeing Stay More again and showing it to Sharline. He knows there isn't an awful lot left to the town, compared with what it once had been, and he doesn't know what Sharline will think of it. Probably it's not all that different from her own home town, and it will be just one more wide place in the road to her. But he likes to try to look at things through other people's eyes, just as he tried to watch "Assortment" through Helen's eyes, and tried to watch last night's car chase as if it were a pitcher show, and he is eager to see Stay More through Sharline's eyes. There's even a possibility, if she likes it enough, that he'll decide to set up his show there and see if the home folks care for "A Midsummer Night's Dream."

He is having a terrible time easing Topper down the mountain, not just with the roughness of the road surface itself, which hasn't known a road grader for months and months, seems like, and is full of chuckholes and run-offs, but also the trail whips back and forth in hairpins all over creation, and sheer drop-offs scare him.

Halfway down the mountain they come to the place where the road temporarily divides, where they'd lost Binns the night before, and Hoppy decides to take the high road to point it out to Sharline. He is quickly reminded of why the lower road was necessary to replace the higher road: the old road runs right along the edge of a cliff that worries the daylights out of him, and he can just barely manage to creep Topper along it. "This is the way that Binns took when he disappeared," Hoppy explains to her.

A thought occurs to him at the same instant that it does to her, but she is first to spot the car. "Stop!" she says. And when Topper is completely still, she points. "Lookee down yonder!" she says, and he has to scoot across the seat to see where she is pointing. There, down below, a black car sits on the tree tops of a grove of pines which have cushioned the car's plummet, but the car has crushed many of the tree branches. They can't see the interior of the car from this height, so they can't tell if there is anyone in it, dead or alive.

"That's his car, sure enough," Hoppy observes, and then he resumes steering Topper very carefully across the old high road until it meets the lower road and there is a place farther along where he can park Topper without blocking the road. Then from Topper's cluttered interior he fetches his coil of rope, and says to Sharline, "Looks like we'll have to do some hiking. Would you rather wait here, and let me do it?"

"Are you kidding?" she says, and she goes with him, first removing her pretty shoes that Arlis had given her and putting on her old shoes.

They walk on down the road toward Stay More for a good ways until they find a place where they can climb down into the ravine and hike to the grove of pines holding the car aloft. There would ordinarily be a stream of water tumbling through the ravine, but the drought has dried it up, and they have little trouble climbing over boulders to reach the base of the grove of pines. Inside the grove they crane their necks to stare upward but can just barely detect the silhouette of the car against the sky. The first tree limb is maybe twenty feet up. From that limb it would be easy to reach all the other limbs, on up to the car. But among all the things that Hoppy Boyd hates himself for is his fear of heights. The thought of trying to climb those tall pines and reach that car, maybe sixty feet up, scares him something awful.

"Let me go," Sharline says, reading his mind. "When I was just a young'un, I used to climb trees all the time."

"But I'm worried the car could come loose and fall down on you," he says.

"That's just a chance," she says. "Just one more chance in a life full of chances. Throw the rope up there over that limb."

"What if he's in the car, and still alive?" Hoppy wonders.

"That's just another durn chance," she says. "Throw the rope."

So Hoppy throws the coil of rope over the first limb, and brings the other end down so that Sharline can grab aholt of it and climb up, hand over hand, her feet braced against the tree, to reach the first limb. Hoppy is amazed at her nimbleness, and believes that she really has had a lot of experience climbing trees.

She climbs to another limb, and another, and soon she is out of sight. He can only wait. He waits, commencing to get real nervous. Finally, he calls, "Sharline? Are you all right?"

"I'm nearly there!" she calls back. He waits some more. Then she says, "I've caught hold of the door handle!" He waits, holding his breath. She calls, "There's nobody in it!" He waits, just a bit relieved to know that Binns isn't up there. But what has happened to him? Then he hears Sharline holler, "Glory hallelujah! The back seat is full of reels of film!" He continues to wait, feeling elated to be in possession again of "The Painted Stallion" et cetera. "Wait!" she calls, "There's something else! A tote, a big hold-all satchel sort of thing. I'm opening it!" Now she begins to recite the contents of the bag: two men's shirts, a pair of trousers, three neckties, three pairs of socks and underpants, a comb, shaving mug and razor, toothbrush, a Bible, and a pack of rubbers. "Wait!" she calls. "There's money!" Then there is a silence for several long moments. "Lots of money!" she calls. "Hundreds! I declare before goodness, maybe there's thousands!" And, finally, she calls, "I'm a-coming down to get the rope." Sharline returns to the first limb where the rope is draped, coils it up, and says, "I'm going to attach the tote to one end of this rope so's I can let all the reels and stuff down to you." Then she reclimbs the tree limbs, nimble as a monkey, and soon is lowering the satchel attached to one end of the rope, all the way down to where Hoppy is waiting for it. It's a big bag, but she can't get everything into one lowering of it, so he takes out all the reels and a smaller bag holding scads of bills, twenties and fifties and hundreds, and then Sharline pulls the empty bag back up and reloads it. Three trips are necessary to get all of the stuff down to the ground. And three trips to transport as much as they can carry to Topper.

The sky is red as blazes above the mountains west of Stay More. Since all this story is only in black and white, Hoppy is truly puzzled at the intensity of the red, until he realizes that it is a spectacular sunset for them to ride off into.

Nearing his hometown, which is golden beneath that fabulous red sky, his ladylove lifts the bugle and puts it to her lips and blows. *From far yonder down the road here they come again, folks, Hoppy and Sharline, the happy moving showmen of moving pitchers to show you a bunch of good'uns.*

F I N I S

Chapter twenty

This will all be Exit Music. You'll be right to see "FINIS" writ on the screen right over that red sunset, with our hero and heroine riding Topper off into the distance until they'll not be nothing but a disappearing speck. A sunset is an ending, the end of a day, the end of a story, and the reason why cowboys ride off into the sunset is so they can move from the here-and-now into the there-and-whenever.

All of this will be whenever. All of this, from here on out, just might could happen, but it might not. We will just have to see. You know, the big difference between the pitcher show and so-called Grim Reality is that the show has to stop somewheres but life just goes on and on and on. Which is good and bad. Even though we know in our heart that Hopalong Cassidy will come back tomorrow night and the night after in more shows without end, once he has rid Topper off into that sunset at the end of tonight's show, that's all there is. It's over. We might as well go home. The screen is all black, black as death, and will stay that way for all the whole sad length of the here-and-now. It hurts, don't it? But we're still alive, and we will have to get a good night's sleep tonight and get up and go to work tomorrow, and we will just take for granted that we'll keep on keeping on. If we was forced to choose, none of us would swap our bare-fact existence for the wonder and the delight of the pitcher show. But the secret of the pitcher show, which Hoppy will come to understand all by and by, is that she has a life of her own that goes on and on after the screen goes black. We can't see her but she's still out there and will endure everlastingly. We will even, from time to time, catch glimpses of her in the fabulous theater of our mind, which is the best theater, after all, where there are never any endings.

So we will be able to project in that theater that our story of Landon "Hoppy" Boyd and Miss Sharline Whitlow will be never-ceasing, ongoing, and for the most part happily-ever-after. Who knows, we might could even make a whole new pitcher show out of what will happen to them during the two weeks they will spend in Stay More. There will certainly be other pitcher shows about Stay More along the line, and in fact one of them, name of *When Angels Rest,* will have a part of it set at the old Stapleton place, which Long Jack will have bequeathed in its rundown and abandoned condition to his grandson Hoppy, who will be staying there with Sharline during those two weeks. Some years later, during the latter part of the Second World War, a platoon of soldiers on maneuvers will use the old deserted house for their bivouac. And what they do there would make an interesting part of a different pitcher show. But of course Hoppy will have no idea that it will be put to that use eventually when he and Sharline will finally abandon it and move on into Jasper, the county seat.

There will be problems from the moment of their arrival in Stay More, the moment that they discover the blowing of the bugle will have had no effect. Nobody will come a-running, not even kids, let alone womenfolk. Hoppy will have attempted to explain to Sharline just how exceptional this town of Stay More actually is, that it has had a reputation for being not only very hard to get to, practical impossible for some, but once you do manage to get to it, you discover that it is mighty peculiar, distinctly different from all other towns, what some might call eccentric. Things have happened in Stay More that never happened anywhere else. People have lived in Stay More who were not like anyone anywhere else. Hoppy will have given her one good example, his own grandfather, Long Jack Stapleton, but he will also have told her of the legends about Jacob Ingledew, the founder of the town, who eventually became governor of the whole state of Arkansas. Hoppy will have tried to tell Sharline why he has avoided his hometown, how hard it is to live in the shadow of his grandfather, the legendary Long Jack Stapleton.

"It's such a pretty town," Sharline will remark. "It's a sight prettier than any of the others."

He will have pointed out to her, after they will have hit what might be called Main Street, the old hotel, the doctor's office, the stone ruin of the Swains Creek Bank and Trust Company, the big general store and the small general store, and all the homes. He will have attempted to see each of these through Sharline's eyes, as if he's never seen them before, and it sure is a pretty town.

Hoppy will spot Doc Swain sitting on the porch of his house and clinic, and will pull over.

"You folks celebrating your wedding? What's all that bugling about?" Doc will ask. And then he will ask of Hoppy, "Say, aint you Long Jack's grandchild?" Hoppy will know he's only a-bantering, because Doc Swain has known him well since the moment he delivered him from his mother's womb. "'Roaming Pitcher Shows,' eh?" And he will say, "We aint never had none of them in this here town."

"Where is everbody?" Hoppy will ask.

Doc will chuckle. "Well, there aint that many to begin with. Town's got mighty tiny since you lived here, Landon. Some of 'em's over yonder on Latha's store porch. Some of 'em's gone to a play-party up at Duckworth's. I reckon most of 'em's just a-settin at home in their favorite chair a-wondering if that bugle means the end of the world."

They will visit with Doc Swain in the gloaming, as the first lightning bugs come out, and Hoppy's eye will be drawn to Latha's store porch, where, in just two more years, another pitcher show, called *Lightning Bug,* will be played out and seen and felt and heard.

They will learn from Doc Swain the last of the part of this here pitcher show, *The Pitcher Shower,* which will involve a certain preacher called Brother Emmett Binns, who will have spent the cool night lying in the woods on a rock which will have retained the day's warmth, and then will have somehow managed the next morning to drag his broken leg to the road, where eventually a farmer passing in his wagon, a feller named Goodfeller from up over to Spunkwater, will pick him up and bring him to Doc Swain, who will put a plaster cast upon his broken leg and will return him to Goodfeller, who will put him back into the wagon and transport him God knows where. Doc's services will not have been paid for, and he will not be happy about that.

No one will ever see Emmett Binns again. Not in this pitcher show, leastways, nor in any other. Heroes may reappear again and again but if you need you a real good mean villain, he has to be a fresh one. You can't use the same villain twice.

Since they will have come into possession of all the pitcher shows which Binns had stolen, Hoppy and Sharline will decide to set up a theater in the broad meadow which runs along Swains Creek across the road from the old Ingledew place. All the posters that Matt Spottwood had printed for them referred only to "A Midsummer Night's Dream" and will therefore be useless for the showing of the westerns, including "The Painted Stallion" serial. So they will attempt to advertise their show by word of mouth, but all the mouths they talk with will tell them of various activities going on which would conflict with the showing of pitcher shows: there will be a square dance planned for one night, a coon hunt planned for the next night, a box supper planned for the next, a quilting bee for the next, and a major shivaree in the works for the next, which is a traditional teasing harassment (from the French *charivari*) of a newly married couple on their wedding night.

What about the following week? Well, the town will be planning a kind of Centennial celebration; one hundred years ago Jacob Ingledew and his brother Noah arrived here to start a town, to begin the town's one hundred years of solitude. Hoppy and Sharline, who will not have been comfortable at the old Stapleton place, with its remoteness in the woods east of Stay More, its mildew and infestation by rodents, will decide to move on, first paying a visit to Luther

Chism to purchase not one but five demijohns of his remarkable moonshine, at least a year's supply, practically.

But one night and one night only before they will leave town, perhaps inspired by the taste and other qualities of Chism's Dew, Hoppy will hang his screen between two trees, fire up the delco, and show the second chapter and that chapter only of "The Painted Stallion," just to see if it might actually produce some much-needed rainfall for this drought-stricken town. And sure enough, it will rain. Hard. All the alabastine will be washed off the screen, and it will have to be repainted. Hoppy will not have made any bets with anyone on the chance of the rainfall, because he will not have needed the money. Although he will never bother to count exactly how much of Binns' riches they will have come into possession of, it's more than he'll ever need, and he will have no qualms in relieving Binns of it, because, as he will have said to Sharline, "Far's I'm concerned, it was all ill-gotten to begin with."

Most people will not even realize that Hoppy's showing of that episode of the serial is accountable for the blessèd rainfall. It will have been one more of Hoppy's random acts of kindness, in the wake of many such throughout the Ozarks. And he will want to get on out there to all the other little lost towns all over the hills and dales of the country. But before leaving Stay More, he will check his mail box at the post office, something he will have managed to do not more than semiannually, and there amidst a stack of junk mail he'll find the catalog for a St. Louis distributor of pitcher shows, with tantalizing descriptions of all the latest releases, including new Hopalong Cassidy shows being offered at bargain prices.

They will head northward to the next town, Parthenon, a very pleasant place where the Newton County Academy, a kind of rustic finishing school, is still in operation (and where the makings of a pitcher show called *Butterfly Weed* will have transpired some years before, starring Doc Swain). Hoppy will ask the storekeeper if he thinks there might be any audience for some good Hopalong Cassidy pitcher shows. The storekeeper will point out that Parthenon is so close to the county seat, Jasper, just six miles up the road, that anyone who wants to see a pitcher show would go there to watch it in the air-conditioned comfort of the Buffalo Theater.

Mountain-locked Jasper is the smallest of all of the state's seventy-five county seats, but it is big enough to have an actual square with a courthouse in the center and buildings along all four sides, including a hardware store where, Sharline will suggest, they had better stop and see if it carries alabastine, since their gallon can is practically empty. There is also something Sharline will never have seen before: a drugstore, and she wonders aloud if they might carry anything that she could take for the stomach problem or whatever that will have been making her throw up in the mornings. And also there will be among Jasper's stores a nice variety store, not exactly a department store such as they'd visited in Clarksville but a store big enough to carry any little old thing that Hoppy might like to get her for her eighteenth birthday, which will be coming up in just another week. And finally, there will be that air-conditioned stone building called the Buffalo Theater. "Could we go?" Sharline asks. "I aint never felt what air-conditioning feels like."

"It sure is one hot day," Hoppy will allow.

Along with the alabastine, Hoppy will have purchased at the hardware store a lock for Topper's door. In a fair-sized town with lots of people coming and going, you don't want to leave any of your valuables unprotected while you go to a pitcher show.

On the front of the Buffalo Theater there will be a poster for the current attraction, Gene Autry in "Git Along, Little Dogies." "Goddamn," Hoppy will say, and will tell Sharline that he doesn't think that he will be able to sit through a singing-cowboy pitcher show, even if it is air-conditioned. He will urge Sharline just to go by herself, and he will buy her a snow cone and will tell her that he'll meet her in the lobby in an hour and a half.

He will wander around the square for a little bit. He will have always liked Jasper, which is not too big of a town but not too little either. He will kill some time among the loafers on the courthouse lawn, listening to them swap windies, and even joining in their whit-tling. After a time he'll go back to the lobby of the Buffalo, where there's a bench he can sit on to wait for Sharline. While he will be sitting there, the manager of the theater will approach him and ask, "That your rig out front?" and when Hoppy will admit that Topper belongs to him, the manager will eagerly want to know all about the career of itinerant pitcher showing. He will be full of questions, which Hoppy, with nothing better to do, will patiently and gladly answer. Hoppy will tell the feller many of his more interesting experiences, omitting the business about Emmett Binns.

After the conclusion of Hoppy's interesting narrative on the life and travels of a roaming pitcher show projectionist, the manager, who will have paid bright attention throughout, will ask, "How'd you like to swap?"

"Swap?" Hoppy will say.

"Yeah, if you'd care to let me have your rig and take over your route, I'll sell you this theater for a good price." About that time, the show will be over, and the manager will say, "Don't go away. I've got to run up and turn off the projector."

Sharline will come out, along with the few other folks who will have attended the matinee. Hoppy will tell her about the offer the manager has made.

Sharline will be thrilled. "We could cool off in there anytime it's hot," Sharline will point out. "Also we could have us a little house with a piano in it and a garden patch out back." When Hoppy will look as if he'll still be having doubts about the idea, she'll say, "And you don't have to get me a birthday present. This theater would suit me just fine."

So Landon "Hoppy" Boyd will give his truelove Sharline Whitlow the Buffalo Theater of Jasper, Arkansas for her eighteenth birthday present. That will be the day that he stops hating himself, for anything. However, he will not let that manager have his Hopalong Cassidy pitcher shows, which he will intend to show here in the Buffalo. Hoppy will also remove his other belongings from Topper, including "Assortment," but he will give the manager the can of alabastine along with one demijohn of Chism's Dew.

Hoppy will also retain possession of "A Midsummer Night's Dream," which he will show at the Buffalo on a special night once a month, although Sharline will show it alone from time to time when she will have the theater to herself. For months and months, adjusting herself to the busy life of a lively town, she will grieve over the absence of her fairies, who will have faithfully followed her from place to place but will not seem to care for urban life in Jasper. Eventually, she will decide that all of the advantages of living in a cozy, pleasant town like Jasper with a nice little white cottage easy walking distance from the Buffalo and a sure-enough piano in it and a sure-enough garden patch out back, plus the ability to watch the fairies of "A Midsummer Night's Dream" anytime she takes a notion to, will mostly make up for the disappearance of the real fairies.

She will have other things to occupy her life in their stead. Leaving Hoppy to run the matinees by himself, she will get a daytime job at the square's barbershop, the only female barber there, indeed the only female barber in Newton County, a novelty that will keep her much in demand among the male customers who will shiver beneath her touch. She will earn almost as much barbering as they will earn running the Buffalo.

Of course she will discover in due time that what will have been making her throw up in the mornings is the fact that she will be with child. She will not know, nor could scarcely guess for certain, whether Hoppy is the child's father. If anybody will ask, and few will, she will tell them that she and Hoppy have been married for some time, and, if any proof will be needed, she will have a thin gold wedding band which she will have bought at Jasper's variety store. Her swelling abdomen will not detract from her barbering business; indeed, her regular customers will look upon her pregnancy as further evidence of her femininity, and they will all take such a constant interest in it that when she will finally be rushed to the hospital in Harrison for the delivery, every last one of them, bearing flowers and other gifts, will follow her there and will hang around to accept and smoke Hoppy's cigars.

It will be hard to tell if the baby, named Stapleton Boyd but called "Stay" all his growing-up years, looks more like Hoppy than like Arlis, since the two men will have looked so much alike. But the boy's mother will always remain convinced that Hoppy is the father, and the boy's father will be so proud that he will, with the help of a generous libation of Chism's Dew, offer a proposal of marriage to the boy's mother, which she will, of course, accept, but it will be a small and private ceremony in the cluttered office of a justice of the peace.

The boy will grow up in the double world of barbershop and movie theater, getting two distinctly different educations from each. It will always be conceivable that a pitcher show will be made out of the clever chronicle of his life, especially that part of it concerned with his favorite place for vacations, Stay More.

But one of Stay More's better citizens, John Henry "Hank" Ingledew, whose chronicles may be found in several of the Stay More pitcher shows, will come home from the Second World War and set up just across the square from the Buffalo Theater a little shop, "Ingledew's Television Service and Sales." Nobody will blame Ingledew for the fact that the Buffalo Theater will go out of business. Actually, as Hoppy himself will be the first to observe, it will not be television that will kill the pitcher show. Indeed, it will be many years before the quality of color television shows can match and replace the quality of the pitcher show. Folks will not stop coming to the Buffalo just on account of their TV sets. They will, many if not most of them, have air-conditioning in their houses. And many if not most of the new houses will be built without front porches, because whatever it is that will make people not want to sit on the porch in the cool evening and visit with each other and swap old tales will also keep them from going into Jasper to watch the pitcher shows, even though Hoppy will have long since added to his repertoire of Hopalong Cassidy pitchers a wide range of other kinds of shows. Television will commence showing re-runs of all the Hopalong Cassidy shows, and a whole new generation of kids will grow up devoted to Hopalong Cassidy who will never have been inside a motion picture theater.

So, in time, Hoppy will have to close the doors of the Buffalo Theater, which, eventually, some other folks will convert into a bakery, making all manner of tasty breads and pies and cakes and pastries and other confections.

Hoppy will consider buying a little grocery store, but those too will be rendered obsolete by the supermarkets.

The last time we will catch sight of Hoppy, and this will be only a glimpse, he and Sharline will be operating on the highway on the north edge of town a combination barbershop and video rental store, where you will be able to get yourself one of the best haircuts to be had in this whole county and, while you're at it, load up for the weekend with several of the latest VHS videos and DVDs of all the latest Hollywood pitchers.

Sometimes when business will be slow, Sharline will stand out front of the shop and blow an old bugle. If you will just slow down as you zip down the highway, you will be able to tell what that bugle is saying: something about pitcher shows and about a man and a woman.

About the Author

Donald Harington

Although he was born and raised in Little Rock, Donald Harington spent nearly all of his early summers in the Ozark mountain hamlet of Drakes Creek, his mother's hometown, where his grandparents operated the general store and post office. There, before he lost his hearing to meningitis at the age of twelve, he listened carefully to the vanishing Ozark folk language and the old tales told by storytellers.

His academic career is in art and art history and he has taught art history at a variety of colleges, including his alma mater, the University of Arkansas, Fayetteville, where he has been lecturing for nineteen years. He lives in Fayetteville with his wife Kim.

His first novel, *The Cherry Pit*, was published by Random House in 1965, and since then he has published twelve other novels, most of them set in the Ozark hamlet of his own creation, Stay More, based loosely upon Drakes Creek. He has also written books about artists.

He won the Robert Penn Warren Award in 2003, the Porter Prize in 1987, the Heasley Prize at Lyon College in 1998, was inducted into the Arkansas Writers' Hall of Fame in 1999 and that same year won the Arkansas Fiction Award of the Arkansas Library Association. He has been called "an undiscovered continent" (Fred Chappell) and "America's Greatest Unknown Novelist" (Entertainment Weekly).

The fonts used in this book are from the Garamond family

Other works by Donald Harington
available from *The* Toby Press

The Architecture of the Arkansas Ozarks

Butterfly Weed

Ekaterina

Lightning Bug

The Choiring of the Trees

The Cockroaches of Stay More

Some Other Place. The Right Place.

When Angels Rest

With

The Toby Press publishes fine writing,
available at leading bookstores everywhere. For more
information, please visit www.tobypress.com